Maggie & Abby
AND THE
SHIPWRECK TREEHOUSE

Also by Will Taylor

Maggie & Abby's Neverending Pillow Fort

Maggie & Abby AND THE SHIPWRECK TREEHOUSE

WILL TAYLOR

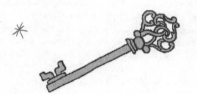

HARPER

An Imprint of HarperCollinsPublishers

ISBN 978-0-06-264434-3

Typography by Jessie Gang
19 20 21 22 23 PC/LSCH 10 9 8 7 6 5 4 3 2 1

First Edition

For Amber and Lindsey

ONE
Maggie

There's no silence in the world like the silence of two hundred super-excited summer campers who've just been told to hand over their cantaloupes.

I whipped my head around as the sea of yellow-T-shirt-wearing, cross-legged kids surrounding me broke into whispered protests.

"—can't do that!"

"Who says we have to—"

"So unfair!"

The whispers became murmurs, then a roar as the sprawling semicircle of Camp Cantaloupers—from eight-year-old first-timers right up to twelve-year-old seniors like Abby and me—started letting the white-mustached man standing on the porch of the mess hall clutching a megaphone know exactly what they thought of his announcement.

"Can you believe this?" said Abby, whapping me on the arm. I looked over and tried not to grin at her expression. Just one week before, we'd both been groomsmaids at the wedding for her dad—Alex and Tamal were married!—and Abby still had salon-quality eyebrows and waves in her dark hair from the world's most beautiful braids. Not to mention an early-summer tan, which for me always meant turning grapefruit-juice pink but for Abby meant gliding from her usual warm brown to deep brown, which only made her smile look that much brighter.

Only Abby wasn't smiling now. Right now Abby looked like someone was trying to force-feed her turtle-poop soup with a ladle.

"They absolutely cannot do this!" she said, glaring at the grown-ups up on the porch. "The cantaloupe tradition is in the literal *name of the camp*! And what about all the first-timer kids? There go their chances of ever seeing the moose!"

"You don't *have* to have a cantaloupe to see the moose, do you?"

"I've never heard of anyone seeing it without one."

"Except us."

"Right!" Abby gave me a flash of a grin. "Except us."

And that was true. Abby and I had met the famous ghost moose of Camp Cantaloupe the summer before, when we were lost in the middle of the night in a desolate patch of sub-arctic Alaskan tundra. I wasn't technically a summer camper back then, and we weren't anywhere near Orcas Island and Camp Cantaloupe, but Abby and I had still managed to summon the moose, get my uncle Joe to the hospital, and save the complete entire day. By our powers combined.

That should have made us extra cool, because seeing the ghost moose was *the* thing every Camp Cantalouper wanted to do. From what Abby had told me after her stay here last year, moose spotters were pretty much guaranteed a permanent spot in camp legend. The problem was, Abby had made me promise not to tell anyone we'd already seen it. I could see her point about not having any actual proof, and not wanting to draw too much attention to ourselves, since we were here on a totally different mission. But hey, it would have been nice to get at least a little recognition.

The crowd was getting seriously noisy now, so noisy the teenage counselors were wading in, waving their hands and shouting for us all to settle. Up on the porch, a freckly middle-aged lady wearing fluorescent-purple overalls, a peacock-pattern flowy shirt, and a rose tucked into her hair took the megaphone from the mustache man. He scowled. I could see the angry V of his eyebrows from across the field.

"Quiet! Quiet, please, young people!" Flowy Shirt Lady called into the megaphone. "Remember your better selves!"

Abby leaned in. "That's Ms. Sabine," she whispered, "the art teacher. She's kinda weird, but she's nice. I think you'll really like her."

"I'll take your word for it," I whispered back. The noise slowly died away as everyone remembered their sweater elves or whatever. A girl three down from Abby with a blond bob was aggressively shushing some younger kids in front of her. They hushed, and she folded her hands in her lap and sat up straight. I rolled my eyes back to the porch.

"Thank you, young people," Ms. Sabine said. "Now, I do understand why Director Haggis's announcement might have been, um, alarming. This is Director Haggis's first year here, and he's bringing lots of new ideas, and one of those new ideas is that maybe having cantaloupes lying around to attract the ghost moose isn't the safest thing. But I assure you he has no intention of taking your cantaloupes away forever. He understands that our camp traditions—"

The megaphone shrieked and crackled as Mr. Haggis yanked it from Ms. Sabine's hands. The crowd gasped.

"I understand that your camp traditions are in serious need of a shakeup!" Mr. Haggis hollered into the mouthpiece. His face was going red around his mustache. "And I have *every* intention of taking away your cantaloupes forever. It's ridiculous letting children keep produce lying around camp. That's how you get rats! Plus I've already tripped over three this morning! It's a wonder I can still walk!" He held up his right foot and waggled it angrily.

The crowd was silent. No one seemed to know how to react. This was like a bad dream. Abby had been mildly curious when the precamp orientation letter mentioned the old director retiring, but we had never imagined his replacement would be someone like this.

"I want a volunteer," Mr. Haggis continued, "to coordinate the cantaloupe collection. I want them all gathered up today, before bedtime! Teachers?" He looked around at all the other adults on the porch. None of them stepped forward. "I see. Counselors?" He looked out over the field, his eyes popping. I glanced behind me. All the teenagers had crossed their arms and were staring back in defiance. Director Haggis exhaled hard through his nose, right into the megaphone.

"Okay, then. *Older children?*" he shouted.

I almost laughed. Like any kids sitting here would help this guy spoil a classic camp tradition. Like any camper would be willing to—

The girl I'd seen shushing the younger kids threw her hand in the air, reaching right up for the perfect blue sky.

"Thank you!" said Director Haggis. "We have a volunteer. Come meet me after the final announcements, young lady, and we'll get you set up." Every head turned. Kids in the front were craning their necks, twisting around to see who'd volunteered to crush all their moose-meeting dreams. I'd have hidden my face in my arms if it had been me, but bob-cut girl just sat there, smiling calmly, looking smug.

"Whoa, that's Charlene Thieson," Abby whispered. "She's our age. We hung out last year. She was always helping the teachers with camp stuff and keeping little kids in line. She's okay, though." Abby frowned. "At least I thought she was."

Oof. Not the most awesome start to my very first—and very last—summer at Camp Cantaloupe. Horrible new director? Treasured traditions being scrapped? This was rough. Good thing it wouldn't really impact me, seeing as my real reason for being here wasn't cantaloupes, and it wasn't the moose, it was the Shipwreck Treehouse. Or, more specifically, the trapdoor of the Shipwreck Treehouse.

Or, super specifically, the *lock* on the trapdoor of the Shipwreck Treehouse.

When Abby had gotten back from Camp Cantaloupe the summer before, things had been kind of weird between us. But we got over that quick when things around us got *actually* weird and we found ourselves tangled in the world of linked-up, possibly magical, pillow fort networks. Basically an avalanche of utterly unbelievable amazingness happened, including the rescue mission that got us stranded in the middle of the night up in Alaska, and when it was all over Abby and I were left standing in the ruins of my pillow fort with nothing but a pair of silver sunglasses, some fresh scratches from Abby's snagglepawed cat, Samson, and a three-hundred-year-old key.

The key was an artifact from a secret room in the palace of Versailles, in France—a room only kids in the pillow fort networks could get into. The big mystery, though, was that the key didn't work on the room's only door, and none of them knew what lock it was supposed to fit. The pillow fort kids thought it was super important *because* it was so mysterious, and Miesha—NAFAFA Council Member and Queen of the United Southern Gulf-Pacific Fortresses—gave it to Abby and me to keep safe. Five minutes later we got unexpectedly cut off from the NAFAFA networks, and bam, there we were with the mysterious key: stuck.

Only right then, when everything looked like it was lost, and the magic or whatever was over and done, Abby had recognized the swirling oak leaves and shining sun carved into the handle of the key. She recognized them because the exact same markings were—according to Abby—carved on the lock of the trapdoor. The trapdoor of the Shipwreck Treehouse. Here at Camp Cantaloupe.

So now, ten months older, ten months wiser, with our first year of middle school under our belts and more expert-level planning from me than the world had ever seen, we were here too. With the key. Waiting for our chance to try it out.

"Now that the hazardous melon business is settled," barked Director Haggis, yanking my attention back to the sunny field, "I have a few more safety announcements. I took a tour of the campgrounds earlier this week, and in my opinion this whole place is one giant hazard. So, to start with, the rope swing over the lake has been taken down." Everyone groaned, and some of the teenage counselors booed. "A five-foot barrier has been erected around the fire pit, which means dangerous marshmallow roasting is out." Boos from all sides now, so loud they echoed off the trees surrounding the field.

"And, finally . . ." Director Haggis paused, letting the noise die away, and despite the sweating sunshine I felt a sudden chill prickle the back of my neck. "That pile of driftwood you call a treehouse looks like an utter death trap, so I'm declaring it off-limits until it can be professionally inspected. I repeat," he yelled, the megaphone making his voice crackle and hiss into the second shocked silence of the morning, "absolutely no campers will be allowed in, on, or anywhere near the Shipwreck Treehouse at Camp Cantaloupe this year!"

TWO
Abby

"Shh! Mags!" I said. "Not so loud." Maggie was a massive fan of hushed plotting and whispered secret plans, but the truth was she had one of those voices that carry. Especially when she got excited.

Maggie stopped midsentence. She looked theatrically up and down the lunch table at the rows of yammering kids still venting about Director Haggis and his horrible changes. It was all anyone had been talking about from the minute orientation ended, through our cabin assignments—Mags and I were sharing a bunk bed, so yay! But Charlene was in our cabin, so less yay—and now into lunch in the clamoring mess hall.

"Who's gonna hear me?" she pretend-yelled, cupping her hands around her mouth.

I threw a crouton at her, but she had a point. My friends from the summer before had waved for us to join their table, but Maggie had that look in her eye, so I'd found us a spot on our own. I knew from experience you couldn't hold Mags back when she wanted to talk plans.

"Fine," I sighed as Maggie tossed the crouton into her mouth. "But that doesn't mean you need to shout, 'We'll have to sneak out tonight!' at me."

Maggie stopped midcrunch, her eyes going wide at something over my shoulder. I swiveled around to find Charlene standing right behind me, carrying a plastic tray and wearing a big yellow sash that said SAFETY MONITOR, decorated with an aggressively shiny badge reading LITTER PATROL.

"Oh, hey, Charlene," I said. Shoot. She'd totally heard me. "We were just talking about, um, a dream Maggie had." Maggie nodded vigorously, but Charlene gave us two slow double blinks. She wasn't buying it.

"So, you're collecting all the cantaloupes," I tried. Redirect! Distract! "How's that looking?"

The kids sitting closest to us had all stopped their conversations to glare at Charlene, but she didn't seem bothered. She pursed her lips like she was deciding something, then smiled.

"It's looking great, thanks! Director Haggis is gonna

have one of the counselors drive me around in the golf cart. They're putting a rolly bin from the laundry on the back. I get to start collecting cantaloupes right after dinner!"

She sounded so proud of herself. Seriously, what was wrong with her? From what I'd seen last summer, she loved it here. She was awesome at archery, a decent swimmer, and an okay joke and ghost-story teller, and before this it had seemed like enough people liked her. Was this really how she wanted to spend her final summer? With everyone angry at her and no one making room for her to sit next to them at lunch?

"That sounds great," Maggie said loudly. "Bye."

She and Charlene locked eyes. Chance of them getting along this summer? Zero point zero. Charlene broke the stare first, gave me a very knowing smile, and walked away.

Oh, I hoped she wasn't going to be a problem.

Maggie leaned forward over the table. "So anyway," she said, "back to Operation You Can't Stop Us. We definitely *are* going to have to sneak out tonight to get to the treehouse. Let's go over the steps again."

"Do we have to? We've been going over them for months and months."

"And I don't want to mess anything up now that we're so close to putting them into action! Besides"—she peered suspiciously over at Charlene—"circumstances have shifted!"

I tsk-sighed. "Fine. *Step one: plan out steps.* Check. And I still don't know why we needed that one."

"You should always start a list with something you can cross off right away," said Maggie. "It builds momentum. *Step two: equip supply packs for all possibilities.* Check."

"*Step three: get to Camp Cantaloupe.* Check."

"*Step four: figure how to get alone time in the Shipwreck Treehouse.* Check, I guess, since we're doing that right now."

"*Step five: unlock trapdoor of treehouse with Oak Key.* Pending."

"*Step six: go through trapdoor and have the world's most spectacular adventures on the other side.*" Maggie's eyes were shining as she finished.

I looked at her. "So you're not secretly worrying we're gonna go through that door and disappear into a slug-infested dungeon or locked cellar or impossible labyrinth or something?" Worst-case scenarios were a regular feature in Maggie's made-up games, and usually part of her plans in the real world, too.

"Oh, it might. But, Abs"—Maggie grabbed my hand, apparently not caring that her arm was now in my lunch— "wherever it leads, we are gonna drop through that trapdoor into the most magical, amazing, epic summer ever! We are gonna leave this camp behind!" She rolled her eyes around the room. "And whatever we find, you and I are going to rule.

It'll be *so* epic I'll bet we blow right past steps seven and eight without even knowing it!"

"Wait, step seven? What was that one again?"

"*Step seven: uncover the origins of the First Sofa!* Solve the mystery of how the linkable pillow forts work, and all that. Remember the prophecy Ben was so obsessed with? It said whoever used the Oak Key and unlocked the door of le Petit Salon in Versailles would uncover everything. *And* start a new golden age for the global pillow fort networks. That's gonna be us."

"But we aren't unlocking that door in Versailles," I pointed out. "We're opening a different lock on the other side of the world."

"The Oak Key doesn't go to the le Petit Salon door anyway," Maggie said. "Ben's been trying for years and years. We can figure that part out later. I bet using the key in the *right* lock on the trapdoor will be the thing that counts. Ben is gonna be so annoyed we beat him to it!"

Ben was Maggie's nine-year-old nemesis from last summer. He was also the only person I'd ever met who was even more into organization and planning than she was.

"I guess, if he ever finds out," I said. "What's step eight, then? I don't remember that being a thing."

"Step eight," said Maggie, leaning in closer to whisper dramatically, "is the step that even I don't know yet. It's the mystery step. The step we'll only know about when it's already happened!"

She looked so hopeful. So excited. So ready.

So different from how I felt.

I knew Maggie couldn't care less about Camp Cantaloupe. She was here for the Shipwreck Treehouse, and the grand adventure she hoped it would send us on, and that was it. But I honestly loved this place, and with everything going on back home, I really needed the camp time just to get myself set.

Because my whole entire life was about to change.

Last year all I'd had to worry about had been starting middle school. And sure, yeah, that had been a lot. Middle school was . . . middle school. But I had Maggie, who kept us both busy going over every single tiny detail of our pillow fort adventures, making plans and drawing maps from memory of the NAFAFA Hub and all the forts. And I had my brothers and their terrible middle school advice, and my dad and his sweet boyfriend, Tamal. And, of course, Samson, the best cat in the world. So everything was going okay.

Then bam, Dad and Tamal got engaged over spring break, and things started changing fast. I mean, it was definitely exciting! I adore Tamal, and my dad was so happy it was ridiculous, and helping with all the wedding planning was fun. But then came the big family meeting where my dad announced that our house was too small to add one more person, and he and Tamal had been looking around, and they'd found a great place they could afford four blocks over, and basically they were putting our house up for sale and we'd be moving August first.

Mags and I had an emergency meeting on her roof that night. We'd been next-door neighbors all our lives, and four blocks wasn't that far, but it wasn't nothing. Mags made me promise to still come over every day, and I made her do the same, and we agreed there was at least a chance the trapdoor might reveal some way to link up our houses like the pillow forts had done last summer. But the only thing I was certain of anymore was that after Camp Cantaloupe everything was going to be different. Whether I liked it or not.

That feeling kicked into high gear just recently, because as the school year wound down, my family started packing. The twins dismantled their broken bike "art installation" on the patio; my dad donated most of his old books that had been spilling off the shelves in the living room; and one sort of traumatic May morning, we rented a truck and turfed out everything we didn't use from the garage, including the orange-plaid sofa that had given us the pillows for Fort Comfy last summer.

Mags agreed it was sad when I told her, but she didn't really get it. That sofa had been in our garage as long as I could remember. I used to hide my Halloween candy under it when I was little. And now it was gone.

Dad and Tamal were gone too, on their honeymoon while I was away at camp. They said it was perfect timing. The twins were still home, in charge of getting the house and yard ready for whoever was going to live there next. When I got back in six weeks, I'd have a few days to pack up the last of my room, help with the very final cleaning, and say goodbye to the house and all my memories, and then we'd be starting over in our new place. A whole new family.

Was I kinda happy? Yes. Was I kinda sad? Yes. Was I completely confused about what I was supposed to be feeling when everything about my life back home was changing? Oh, yeah. That was why I needed this time at camp. Maggie was excited about epic adventures, but I was excited about a good long stretch of easygoing, predictable Camp Cantaloupe before I had to face the world again. And the sooner we got this treehouse explored, the sooner that could start.

A loud clanging pulled my brain back to the mess hall. "Attention! Children, attention please!"

I looked up. Director Haggis was standing at the front of the room by the garbage cans, hitting a coffee can with a metal spoon. The hubbub died away.

"It has come to my attention that I already need to clarify one of our camp rules," Director Haggis said, eyeing the room disapprovingly. "This should go without saying, but part of maintaining a safe, secure camp experience is staying where adults can check on you twenty-four hours a day. This includes at night!" He put a lot of emphasis on that last part, and Maggie and I shared a glance. "So consider this your one and only warning: Any camper caught sneaking out of their cabin during bedtime hours will be expelled and sent home immediately. And there will be no refund!"

Gasps and chatter filled the hall. Most people had probably never even considered sneaking out, but being sent home was the very worst punishment possible.

Maggie's hand clamped on my arm. "Look," she said, pointing. "Look look look!"

I looked, and there was Charlene, standing off to the side behind Director Haggis, looking pleased with herself again.

"Whoa!" I said. "I can't believe it. She went and told the director what we said!"

Maggie gave a grim nod as Director Haggis left. "Definitely seems like it." She squeezed my arm harder and turned to me, the fire back in her eyes. "We cannot let them win, Abs. Those two are not allowed to stop us from getting to step six of our plans."

"But you heard what he said about sneaking out! Mags, I cannot get sent home. My dad would freak out and cut his honeymoon short to come home too. I can't do that to him and Tamal." *And I can't miss out on my last summer here,* I shouted in my head. *I'm not ready for what's next.*

"Hey, don't forget we're experts at sneaking around!" Maggie said. "Anyway, my mom's gone at that medical conference in France. Getting kicked out would mean she'd have to come back too, and that's almost as bad as spoiling a honeymoon. We just won't let it happen. We're in this together." She beamed. "By our powers combined, Abs!"

Oof, she would bring out that old catchphrase. But she had a point. It was too late to back out. And Maggie would never settle into life at camp until we'd tried the key at least once.

"By our powers combined, then," I said, hitching up a smile in return. "But if we get kicked out because of this, you're buying me ice cream for the rest of the summer."

"Deal," said Maggie, snagging another crouton from my plate. "But seriously, Abs, nothing bad is going to happen. I've thought of everything. We are absolutely, completely, foolproof-level ready to head through that trapdoor tonight."

THREE
Maggie

The rest of the afternoon plodded by full of orientation stuff, including a visit to the camp store, where Abby made me buy a Camp Cantaloupe journal and a stack of postcards like the ones she'd sent me almost every day the year before.

"Abs, this is pointless," I told her. "My mom's all the way in France, and you're literally right here. Who else am I gonna be writing postcards to?"

"Seriously?" she said. "Your uncle Joe, for one! He's researching up in Alaska again, right? And I'm writing to Kelly, since she's catsitting Samson, so that means you are, too. And then there's Matt and Mark, and—"

"Okay, okay, fine! I get the picture."

After dinner there was an incredibly embarrassing sing-along around the safety-barriered campfire, and a performance of the camp dance by some of the other senior kids. I was kind of annoyed they didn't ask me to join in. Not that I wanted to dance in front of everyone, but after that incident with the moose last summer, I knew every move by heart, and it would have been nice to have that acknowledged.

Back at the cabin we had the excitement of Charlene coming around in her golf cart, driven by one of the teenage counselors. We all refused to speak to her as we handed over our cantaloupes, watching as they got added to the laundry rolly bin tied to the back.

Charlene returned to the cabin a little before lights-out, smiling an extra-wide smile for reasons I was totally unable to understand, and we all finished getting ready for bed while pointedly ignoring her.

I honestly thought our cabin would never go to sleep. I lay in my bunk, twitchy with nerves, listening as one by one the other girls dropped off, until . . . finally! It was time! I tapped twice on the bed frame, Abby tapped back from overhead, and I jumped up, grabbing my supply pack.

"Where's your bag?" I breathed as Abby started for the door empty-handed.

"Oh, yeah, I forgot." She headed back to her bunk, half climbed the ladder, and began quietly rummaging around. I crossed my arms. Honestly, forgetting her supply pack?

Where was her head? Charlene was breathing softly in the bottom bunk right across from mine. One wrong move and we'd be so busted.

But soon Abby was ready, and we were slipping out of the dark cabin—two super-spy secret-agent adventurers in sneakers, pajama pants, and yellow Camp Cantaloupe T-shirts—into the cool summer night.

And the night was gorgeous: a bright half-moon hung like a lamp in the star-dusted sky, and the air coming up from the beach smelled like salt and wet rocks and pine needles.

I'd never been happier in my life. I was twelve and a half years old, on an island, with my best friend, plans, gear, backup plans, more gear, and a possibly magical key, evading the authorities on a covert operation to a forbidden treehouse. Somewhere in the trees a night bird sang a few notes, and I whistled back a reply.

Abby led the way along the tree line, avoiding the other dorm cabins and the admin building. We passed a green wooden sign marking a path that led down to the beach, where the moose had first been sighted. Fifty-plus years ago some kid had salvaged a locked piece of wood on that beach and carried it all the way up here for the treehouse. And tonight, half a century later, we were finally going to open it.

We tiptoed behind the teacher cabins—Abby would not stop flapping her hands at me and shushing every time I stepped on even a pine needle—and I realized all the grown-ups were basically camping here too. That must be weird, coming to sleepaway camp as a grown-up, settling into your room and resigning yourself to six weeks of screaming kids and camp food. I wondered if any of them liked the cucumber casserole.

We reached a bend in the path, and Abby stopped and held up a hand.

"We're almost there," she said in an impressively formal tone, which I appreciated. A whole hurricane of butterflies began swirling in my stomach. "Welcome, Maggie . . . to the Shipwreck Treehouse."

We took three steps forward. And there it was.

It was enormous, way bigger than I expected, like someone had wrapped the deck of a ship right up against the trunk of the tree. We were out of sight of the cabins and field, so I pulled out my flashlight as we tiptoed forward.

The tree's leaves and branches floated above a wide plank floor, with a wall of driftwood curving around it like a fence of twisted bones. And every inch of that driftwood was carved and painted and decorated with shells, rocks, beach glass, and braids of seaweed. Forget the deck of a ship; this thing looked like an underwater temple to some octopus sea god had wandered up out of the ocean and decided to try being a bird's nest for a while. My hurricane of butterflies fluttered straight up into my heart. The

Shipwreck Treehouse was perfect.

Something yellow flapped in the night breeze, and I lowered my flashlight to see security tape staked up all around the base and a big sign saying STAY OUT nailed to the trunk above. Someone must have climbed partway up the plank ladder to put it there, so it looked like that part at least was safe. The whole thing actually looked pretty sturdy. What was Director Haggis's problem? I bet he just didn't like the idea of kids having fun.

"Where's the trapdoor?" I whispered to Abby, who'd been politely hanging back and letting me take it all in. It felt right to whisper. An entire school year had come and gone, and I'd spent most of it thinking about this . . . moment . . . right . . . here. I patted my pocket. The key was safe.

Abby raised her own flashlight. "There," she whispered, pointing to the underside of the treehouse.

"Wait. For real?" I stared. "That?"

"Yeah. Why? What's wrong?"

"Well . . ." I waved a hand upward. "It's . . . a door."

And it was. All this time I'd been picturing a traditional trapdoor: a wood panel with a hinge on one side and a padlock holding it in place. The padlock was there, all right, but it was attached to a real door. A *door* door, like the one in my bedroom, with a handle and everything, set into a dark frame in the floor of the treehouse, just off the trunk.

The only unusual things were the metal bands running

sideways across the wood and the fancy design on the pad-lock linking the door and the frame. Abby had called it old-timey, and she was right. I couldn't make out the details from down here, but I didn't have to. I knew what I was look-ing at: the sun-carved lock.

"You never told me it was a regular door," I said to Abby. "Not in any of our planning meetings."

"Didn't I? Oh, sorry." Abby looked over, and a smile spread across her face. "Anyway, we're here! I'm guessing you have a speech prepared?"

"Ha! Funny!" She was joking, but I actually did have a speech prepared. Just a short one, for after we got through step seven: go through the trapdoor.

"What's the best way up there?" I whispered. The ladder in the trunk led up and over the side through a gap in the driftwood wall, but our target wasn't so easy to get to.

Abby pointed her flashlight at a knot below one of the lowest branches. "Start with one foot there," she said, "and I'll talk you through it."

With Abby directing, I worked my way up the tree until I was perched on a branch just beside and below the door. Bending my neck at an angle gave me a good look at the lock. It was weathered and dirty, but the oak-and-sun pattern showed through the grime. I pulled the key from my pocket and held it up. Oh, my confiscated cantaloupe, Abby had been completely right. It was a perfect match.

A wave of nervous expectation sloshed through my limbs as I got a good solid grip on the branch, making sure I was clear of where the door would swing down. This was really happening! "Here we go," I said. "You ready?"

"Ready," said Abby, giving her whole body a shake, making her supply backpack wiggle. "Do it!"

I took a deep, slow breath and let it out silently, then pushed the key into the lock.

It fit.

Instantly I flashed back to my visit to le Petit Salon the summer before. The Oak Key had fit that door too, but I hadn't been able to turn it, and the door stayed closed. There was no way that could happen this time. Not here. Not now.

I held my breath. I turned the key. It slid neatly to the side, and the lock opened with a satisfying click, swinging gently from the frame.

Abby gave a cheer.

I waited for five thudding heartbeats, but there was no boom of magic, no sparks, no sizzling explosion. I turned the handle and pulled. The door above me stayed solidly shut.

"Why isn't it opening?" asked Abby, pointing her flashlight.

"Maybe it's stuck. You know, from being old and getting rained on all the time?" I jerked the handle back and forth, tugging hard. Nothing. I might as well have been trying to tear off one of the branches.

"I don't get it." I bopped the door with my fist, getting a sprinkle of dust in the face. "It's unlocked, and those hinges mean it should open this way. . . ."

There was a rasping sound right by my ear, and I looked over in time to see the key slide out of the lock and tumble to the dark earth below.

"On it!" Abby said, leaping forward with her flashlight. She retrieved the key and tucked it safely into her pocket. "Hey, idea," she said, directing the light back at me. "I'm going up in the treehouse. Maybe I can kick it open from above."

"Aw, why do you get to do that?" I said.

"Because you got to use the key," said Abby brightly, already heading for the ladder. I lost sight of her as she climbed, but a few moments later there were footsteps creaking above my head.

"Stay clear," Abby called. There was a wham, then another wham, and more dust sprinkled down. "Oh, come on," I heard her say. And the next kick did it. The trapdoor of the Shipwreck Treehouse burst open.

Disappointment crashed over me. I could see Abby through the opening, her dark shape clear against the leaves of the tree. There was a telescope pointing out toward the ocean behind her. She put her hands on her knees and looked down.

"Wild!" she said. "Are you seeing what I'm seeing?"

"Just you," I said sadly.

"Really?" said Abby. "'Cause I'm not seeing you, Mags."

"What?" Hope seared through my chest.

"There's nothing but darkness from this side. Here, try shining your flashlight up at me."

I fumbled for the flashlight and shone it right through the open door. It hit Abby full in the face. I could see every detail of her skin and hair and perfect eyebrows. Only she wasn't squinting. It was like she couldn't see the light at all.

"Any time," Abby said.

"Um, I'm already doing it."

"You are?"

"Yup, flashlight to the face."

"Whoa."

Whoa was right.

"Wait there," I called. "I'm coming!" I was not about to let Abby go through that door first. I got to use the key, she got to kick the door open; we were back to my turn. I grabbed a branch and started pulling myself up.

"Hey, what are you doing?" asked Abby. I heard footsteps. "Are you seriously climbing? Just go back down and use the ladder, Mags."

I kicked off the branch and grabbed the treehouse wall with both hands. "No way. I'm almost there. I just need to get over this—" A dull creak cut me off, then a crack, and the wood in my left hand snapped, coming away completely. I swung free, my legs flailing fifteen feet above the ground.

"Mags!" Abby yelled. I dropped the broken wood and scrabbled at air until my fingers caught something solid. Then Abby was there, half over the treehouse wall and tugging on my hands, my arms, my supply pack, my shoes, until I was up and over the side and safe.

"Whew!" I panted, sprawling out on my back. For some reason I felt like laughing. "Well . . . I finally . . . made it . . . to the treehouse."

"Don't you scare me like that," Abby said, looming over me. "That was the most—"

But before she could finish, there was a toothaching squeal, a sickening snap . . . and with a heave, the whole octopus-temple treehouse broke free from the trunk.

There was not one single thing I could do as it all went down in perfect . . . slow . . . motion. As the planks lurched and disappeared beneath us. As the falling floor twisted, giving me a glimpse of the darkness filling the open trapdoor. As Abby staggered, fell, and vanished with a terrified gasp into that darkness. As I choked out a scream in the cool summer night.

As the Shipwreck Treehouse came crashing down.

And I came crashing down with it.

FOUR
Maggie

"Miss Hetzger, I need you to tell me."

I swished my tongue around my lower lip. It had stopped bleeding, but the metallic taste was still there. I shifted in the hard plastic chair in front of the director's desk and winced. That was going to be a nasty bruise on my hip.

"Tell you what?" I asked, playing for time. My story-spinning skills felt sluggish and slow.

"I need you to tell me exactly what you thought you were doing in that treehouse." Director Haggis leaned over his desk. "Apart from proving my point that it should be condemned."

Ugh. I thought back. After the floor lurched, and Abby disappeared down the open trapdoor, and the treehouse and I plummeted to the ground in a heap, there had been thirty seconds of hollow, ringing silence. Then the shouting had started: counselors, grown-ups, Director Haggis. Their shock over the collapse of the treehouse had turned to alarm when they found me under it, and suddenly there were more grown-ups, and the camp nurse, and people waving their hands and yelling into their cell phones.

But while they were all doing that, I wiggled my toes and elbows and legs and discovered I was mostly okay. I managed to tell the nurse so, and once he'd confirmed I only had a cut lip, a bunch of bad bruises, a twisted ankle, and a few splinters, everything changed. Suddenly I wasn't the poor child who needed rescuing but the seriously-in-trouble camper being marched to the office for questioning.

Which was why Director Haggis was sitting across from me, his white hair and mustache gleaming in the fluorescent lamplight, waiting for an explanation.

"I just wanted to see inside it," I said finally. "I heard all about that treehouse before I came here." Okay, good, that was good. The most important thing was not to mention Abby. As far as I'd been able to tell, they had no idea she'd been out there with me.

"But you heard my announcement, didn't you, that the treehouse was unsafe and strictly off-limits this year?"

"Yeah."

"And you saw the sign and the caution tape all around it?"

I nodded.

"But you decided to explore it anyway."

I shrugged. Director Haggis's eyebrows locked together in one disapproving line.

"I expect campers to follow the rules, Miss Hetzger," he said. "Especially rules that are there to keep them safe. But before we get to your punishment for sneaking out of bed . . ." He leaned to one side and pulled something bulky off the floor. "I'd also like you to explain this." My supply pack hit the desk between us, the zipper hanging open. I could see my compass, first-aid kit, and backup rope poking through.

Oof.

I touched my wrist to my lip as through checking for blood, stalling. What could I say? How could I explain away a backpack of survival gear?

"It seems to me," said Director Haggis, "that this is the backpack of someone not planning on returning to their cabin after a quick tour of the Shipwreck Treehouse. This seems to be the backpack of someone planning on . . . running away."

"No! Not running away," I said. "I mean, it's an island, isn't it? How far could I get?" Director Haggis blinked, like that was a weird point to make. "I wasn't running off, I was just going to hide . . . in the treehouse . . . for a bit."

"But why? After one day? I see from your records this is

your first year with us. Were you feeling homesick already? Are the other campers bullying you?"

"No! I'm not homesick, and no one's bullying me. I was..." *Come on, Maggie!* "I was ... trying to see the moose!"

Ah. There it was. The perfect cover story. The tension in my chest eased.

"Trying to see ... the what?" said Director Haggis carefully.

"The moose. The ghost moose. Some of the other campers were talking about it, and how it rescues lost campers, and it sounded really cool. And since this is my last year, and my only chance to see it, I thought we could try and find it, you know, the old-fashioned way."

There was a silence while I mentally patted myself on the back for the top-rate recovery, and Director Haggis looked at me.

"*We?*" he said quietly. "Are you saying you weren't the only camper who snuck out of bed tonight?"

Oh, double oof.

Think, Maggie, think!

I'd have to fall back on a partial truth.

"Um, yeah," I said. "My best friend Abby—Abby Hernandez—she wanted to see the moose, too, so we ... made a bet! Just for fun. We thought if we split up and both got lost in the woods, it would have to choose one of us to rescue first, and that person would win."

Director Haggis put his head in his hands. "You and your friend snuck out of your cabin so you could deliberately get lost in the woods, in the dark, in order to see a moose," he said, speaking to the desk. "On the first night of camp."

"Not *a* moose," I said. "THE moose. The ghost moose of Camp Cantaloupe."

"There's no such thing," said Director Haggis. "If you were eight-year-old campers, I might understand, but for two seniors to go out in search of an absurd campfire legend—"

"It's not absurd," I said, bristling. The ghost moose was real! I'd already seen it! If only I could tell him exactly how wrong he was.

Not that he was going to believe *that* story right then.

"Listen to me very carefully, Miss Hetzger," said Director Haggis, raising his head. "There is no ghost moose of Camp Cantaloupe. There never was, has been, or will be. It's nothing but a ridiculous kids' story, and pretending to believe in it will *not* excuse your behavior." I had to literally bite my tongue to keep from correcting him. "Now I want you to tell me clearly and honestly: where is your friend?"

"She went . . . the other way." I waved a hand vaguely toward the far side of camp. "My plan was to camp out in the treehouse so I'd have a better view, but she decided to head to where the woods were the thickest."

"Of course she did. And did she have a similar backpack of supplies?"

I nodded. Director Haggis looked slightly relieved.

"Well, that's something," he said. "It's a temperate night, and so as long as she doesn't fall down or trip over any tree roots, she shouldn't be in any real danger. We'll get the staff out looking for her right away. Do you know where exactly she went?"

"No, we were both keeping our plans secret."

Director Haggis shook his head again and reached for the phone on his desk. "What on earth were you two thinking? Did you really believe you'd find the thing? Maybe ride into camp during morning roll call tomorrow? Were you picturing some impressive grand entrance that would earn you a spot in Camp Cantaloupe history?"

I twisted my face in a noncommittal reply and winced as my lip throbbed.

"And instead here you are, injured and in very deep trouble, after causing the collapse of a historic treehouse. And your friend is out in the woods somewhere, waiting for an imaginary moose and forcing me to wake up the whole staff to go find her. Now, I want you to *think* about the impact of your choices and actions tonight, Miss Hetzger."

He gave me a look I felt right down to my toes, then dialed the phone and started filling the remaining adults in on the situation. I sat there, pretending to think about my actions, relishing the chance to finally go over what had actually happened in the treehouse.

Abby had vanished through the trapdoor—that much was clear. I'd seen it happen, and she and her backpack weren't in the driftwood pile when they found me. So the big question was: where was she now? Was she in another treehouse somewhere? Or in a locked safe in a secret bank vault? Or an underwater volcanic library? Or even back in the pillow fort networks?

I thought and thought. Outside the window the moon had disappeared. A little clock shaped like a woodchuck on Director Haggis's desk said 1:45 a.m. My brain got foggier and foggier as the minutes ticked by, but I couldn't come up with any way to follow Abby. Not with the Oak Key gone and the trapdoor shattered in the wreckage. What I really needed was more to go on, more possibilities for where that trapdoor could have led. Hmm. There was no chance of going back to the scene of the accident to look for clues from the door itself; they wouldn't let me within a hundred miles of the Shipwreck Treehouse now.

But the Oak Key had opened the lock. And the Oak Key had come from le Petit Salon, the heart of the global pillow fort networks. Okay. That was somewhere I could begin. . . .

★ ★ ★

It was after two by the time the director finally hung up the phone for good. And despite my need for sleep and my various injuries, I felt good. I had something like a plan. All I needed was a few hours safely on my own tomorrow to put it into action. That is, if I wasn't expelled from camp first.

Director Haggis set the handset back into place, heaving one of those big sighs grown-ups do when they want you to know how inconvenient you're making things for them. "Well," he said, "half the staff are heading out to look for your friend. Obviously they're not happy, but keeping our campers safe is our top priority. If she's not back by morning, we'll have to notify the island police. And let's not even discuss what will happen if they can't find her and we have to call in the sheriff or even search and rescue.

"As for you, Miss Hetzger, I've decided not to send you home immediately, but only because we may need your assistance in the search for Miss Hernandez. Instead, I'm assigning you a place in our new buddy system."

"Um, thanks," I said. "And a place in your what-now?"

"Our buddy system," Director Haggis said. "It's a program I've instituted, pairing first-timers with more experienced campers. I never dreamed any seniors would be childish enough to need one, but after tonight I think we can both agree that isn't the case. So I've chosen one of the most dedicated, well-behaved, and responsible campers here to look after you. You'll eat meals with your buddy, walk to and from every class and lesson with your buddy, and so on. The two of you will be joined at the hip until I see you can be counted on to navigate your time at camp more appropriately."

I gaped at him. "What? But . . . who is it?" I stammered, really not wanting to know the answer.

"Someone far too mature to believe in silly things like ghost mooses, for one thing," Director Haggis said. "The ideal person to keep you from getting into any more trouble. Your buddy will be Charlene Thieson."

FIVE
Maggie

I was still in a state of shock when our cabin counselor arrived to walk me back to the cabin. She left me at the door, grumbling as she headed out to help with the search for Abby. I sidled over to my bunk as stealthily as my throbbing ankle would allow. There were five hours left before wake-up call, so hopefully I could grab enough sleep to get my head to stop spinning.

One of my cabinmates turned in her sleep as I passed. Another was snoring. Charlene was sleeping with one arm straight up over her head under her pillow, and the other out to the side, like she was telling on me using semaphore code or making up some responsible new dance move. Ugh. Starting tomorrow I'd be stuck with her. How on earth was I supposed to rescue Abby with Charlene tagging along every second of the day? That was definitely going to require a solution.

I dropped my supply pack on the floor—it had been a near thing, but Director Haggis had decided not to confiscate it— plopped down on the edge of my bunk, and stared into the gloom.

I'd been planning for this day for ten whole months. I'd worked out every single obstacle, every pitfall, everything that could possibly go wrong, but I'd never in my wildest of wild planning dreams imagined that our attempt on the tree-house could end with me walking back into this cabin alone.

But it had happened, and here I was. On the wrong side of the trapdoor. Stuck at camp. With no Abby.

I got to my feet, pulling off my sweatshirt, and something shiny on the wall of the top bunk caught my eye. I was half-way up the ladder when I realized it was taped-up pictures. Abby sure hadn't wasted time settling in. I ran a finger over them in the faint light: Samson curled up with Creepy Frog, his very favorite of Abby's old stuffed animals; Abby and me at Alex and Tamal's wedding, all dressed up and squeezed into a group hug with the beaming, adorable grooms; Abby racing bikes with Matt and Mark, her handsome older twin brothers; and—best one—me and Abby looking completely embarrassed about having our photo taken on the first day of middle school.

I slid back down the ladder, got under my blanket, and looked up at the dusty slats of the bunk above me. That was where Abby should be, right there. Where was she instead? What awesome, possibly dangerous adventures was she having? And how on earth was I going to get her back?

Well, somehow, I'd have to. Partly because my best friend needed me, partly because otherwise I'd be stuck alone at camp with Charlene Thieson all summer, and partly because of the warning Director Haggis had given me as he sent me out of his office.

"Oh, and I should tell you, Miss Hetzger," he'd said. "If Miss Hernandez hasn't been found by the end of breakfast, I won't just be alerting the local police, I'll also be calling her parents."

Clearly, that was not an option. I wasn't about to let Director Haggis ruin Alex and Tamal's honeymoon by scaring them with the news about Abby. They'd come right home, and the truth was there was nothing they or any other grown-up could do to find her.

Only I could do that.

But I did need help, and that was where the plan I'd cobbled together in Director Haggis's office came in. I wasn't going to get any answers from the wreckage of the trapdoor, but I might get some leads about the key that had opened it from the people who knew it best: the kids on the Council of the North American Founding and Allied Forts Alliance, also known as NAFAFA.

The pillow fort kids were the ones who had taught Abby and me how every link between every fort in the whole worldwide network relied on a scrap of fabric from the First Sofa in le Petit Salon to work—the same room the Oak Key came from. Bits of the First Sofa were few and far between on the west coast, but somehow at least one piece had made it out here in a patchwork quilt, and that quilt found its way into the odds-and-ends bin in the Camp Cantaloupe arts and crafts cabin. And last summer Abby had made me a scarf using pieces from that bin, and that was how our whole pillow fort adventure had started.

So, new plan.

Step one: come up with a name for the plan. Operation Patchwork? Check.

Step two: search the arts and crafts cabin for scraps of that quilt. Pending.

Step three: build a pair of pillow forts and link them up, forming a mini-network, then go back and forth between the forts until I get the attention of NAFAFA. Pending.

Step four: hope my friends in the Hub can help me figure out where the trapdoor might lead.

Of course there was no way I could get that done, rescue Abby, and be back by the end of breakfast. Not with my ankle throbbing, and grown-ups and teenagers swarming all over the grounds. I could scope out the arts and crafts cabin during class tomorrow, but the best time for fort building would be tomorrow night, which would mean sneaking out again. Which would mean no sleep. Which meant I'd better do some marathon snoozing here while I could.

Worries jostled like dinosaurs inside my brain, but I did my best to ignore them as sleep pulled me under. My best friend in the whole world was lost and probably in a world of trouble. She needed me, and to be honest I needed her, and there was nothing on Orcas Island—or off it—that could stop me from going to her rescue.

SIX
Abby

So the first thing I remember thinking was *Maggie, Maggie, why are you climbing over the side? Why do you have to be like that? There's a perfectly good ladder I just used. Seriously, it's right there.*

The second thing was *What was that cracking noise?*

The third thing was *Maggie, watch out!*

After that there was the falling, and the darkness, and the SLAM as my backpack hit solid ground with me splayed on top of it.

And there I was, in total darkness, with my head spinning. I tried to raise my hands. Huh. There were smooth wooden panels pressing down barely an inch from my face. Apparently I was in some sort of long crate. Or box. Or . . . coffin.

It was like one of Maggie's stories come to life. Last

summer she was always worried that every new pillow fort we discovered would lead to a creepy abandoned classroom or booby-trapped space station or something. Figures the one time she turned out to be right, she wasn't here to see it. Not that I wanted her to be here. No way would we both fit in this . . . whatever it was, and I'd have to spend all my energy keeping her calm and then we'd never escape.

Man, I hoped she was safe, though. The treehouse definitely felt like it was collapsing, and Maggie was barely clinging to the railing. . . .

Okay, obviously my job was to focus on getting out of here. I twisted to my left, trying to at least get on my side so I wouldn't be stuck like a flipped-over turtle anymore. My hand cracked against something cold and hard. Ouch. Nope. Not working.

I tried twisting to the right, keeping my hands in. Better. Much easier. Maybe just . . . a little . . . more . . .

Victory! I was half curled on my side!

Only now what? I reached out again, and my hands found squishy fabric running alongside me. Did coffins have padded edges? I ran my fingers back over the wood panels. There had to be something. Some sort of lid, or latch, or— got it. There was a definite seam right at the edge where the main panel met another one.

I wedged my fingers into the crack and shoved. For five awful seconds, nothing happened, then—yay! Movement!

The panel gave a creak, and a blaze of light stabbed me hard in the eyes.

I kicked, pushing even harder, and felt something slide out of my pocket. It hit the floor and bounced, sending out a pair of sharp, metallic plinks. The Oak Key! I scrabbled with one hand, found it down by my knees, and pocketed it again. No way was I losing that key. It might be my only way back to camp and Maggie.

If there even was a way back.

No thinking about that, Abby. Back to pushing. I squinted into the light, gritted my teeth at more awful creaking from the panel—right by my ear, thank you very much—and pushed, pushed, pushed until finally the gap opened just wide enough for me to heave a whole arm through, propping it open.

I wiggled the fingers on my liberated hand. The stabby light was hot on my skin, and the air trickling through the gap smelled like ocean. Hmm. So the panel led somewhere outside. Maybe it was another summer camp! Was there a secret global network of linked-up summer camps? I was about to find out. Hopefully they didn't all serve cucumber casserole.

By a completely embarrassing combination of pushing, grunting, and flailing, I managed to work my shoulder through the gap, then my head, my other arm, torso, backpack, and finally legs, and yes! I was free!

I heaved up onto my knees as the panel snapped closed

behind me, and raised both hands against the glare, squinting around.

Hmm. So yes, I was technically free, but I was also completely confused.

I was kneeling on a huge stump surrounded by trees. Big trees, with silvery bark and long droopy green leaves. I didn't recognize them.

The sky overhead was blue—like *blue* blue—and between the trees I could see a beach with golden sand and scattered white shells and gentle waves rolling in. This sure wasn't Orcas Island anymore. For one thing, the sun was up. I must have linked somewhere hours away. Time zones away. Oceans...

But where?

I turned to search the panel for clues, yelped like my dad that time Matt and Mark somehow superglued themselves to the fridge, and jumped to my feet. There was nothing behind me. *Nothing.* Just more stump. There was no sign of a door, panel, tunnel entrance, or even pillow fort that could explain how I'd ended up where I was. There was just me, on a stump, in the sun.

Like I'd freaking grown there.

SEVEN
Abby

Okay. What? What what what what *whoooot?*

I spun a few more circles, but the stump wasn't giving up any clues, so I stepped down onto the springy grass and wildflowers growing around it.

Time for a status check. The trapdoor led to the coffiny thing, and the panel in the coffiny thing led here. I'd definitely gone through *some* sort of link. But judging by the vanishing act the panel had pulled after I squeezed through, this kind of link only offered a one-way trip.

And that was a problem. Unless I found another door or coffin dealy going back the way I'd come, it looked like I was trapped here. Meaning Maggie was trapped on her own at camp. Oh, doom. I had to get back pronto. I loved Maggie dearly, but she'd never make it two days at Camp Cantaloupe without me.

First things first, though. I was stranded in an unknown realm, and thanks to an entire lifetime playing along in Maggie's imaginary adventure games, I knew exactly what to do: survey my surroundings and look for water and shelter.

I picked my way through the trees, heading for the golden beach and its army of pearly shells. Ooh, so many shells! I squished right up to the waterline and stared out. Ocean, as far as I could see. Nothing but ocean.

Fine.

I rehoisted the backpack on my shoulders, put the trees on my left, and set out to explore my new home.

Turned out I was on an island. A tiny island—I walked around the whole thing in maybe twenty minutes—but a beautiful one. There were rocky tide pools full of crabs and anemones on one end, a shady lagoon by a big field of boulders on the other, and those trees crowning the whole thing like a hat. I even found fresh water bubbling up between some rocks at the edge of the boulder field. Hey, at least I could check dying of thirst off the list of problems on my desert island escapade.

The funny thing was the island couldn't always have been deserted; I mean, that stump didn't cut itself, did it? But there were no other signs of past people. No empty buildings, no crumbling mosaics, no remnants of walls. Nothing.

Which also meant no way home.

My surveying did turn up one other mystery besides the stump: a kind of disturbance offshore not far past the little lagoon. A bubbling, like a boiling pot, only there was no steam or anything. It was very odd.

When I finally spotted my own footprints again, I kicked off my shoes and socks and waded into the water to cool my toes, looking out at the waves. The horizon stretched farther than I could spread my hands, one big rolling expanse of ocean, sky, and wind, so wide I could almost see the curve of the earth. It made my island feel like a little ship, sailing along on its lonesome.

With me as the only crew.

I really wasn't a fan of being alone.

But hey, cheer up, Abby. It wasn't the worst home ever. By their powers combined, the Oak Key and Shipwreck Treehouse had sent me here, and the thing to do now was try to enjoy it while I figured out how to get back to Camp Cantaloupe and rescue Maggie.

I returned to my stump in the trees, happy to see the sun had shifted enough to put it comfortably in the shade. Good. It was still the middle of the night for me, and after my adrenaline fest in the tiny wooden coffin or whatever, I was seriously considering a nap.

But actually I needed a snack first, and some company. Or the next best thing. I plopped my bag down, leaned against the stump, pulled out my camp journal, and settled in to write my best friend.

Dear Mags,

Heyyy! I hope you're doing okay after whatever happened with the treehouse! And I'm so sorry you're not here. I mean, I'm glad you're not stranded like I am, but I know you really wanted to go through the trapdoor and have an adventure, so sorry you're not. The trapdoor sent me through this sort of box-coffin thing, and then through another panel-door thingy that sent me here.

"Here" is an island somewhere in the ocean. I mean, obviously. That's where most islands are. Do you think it means something that the trapdoor went from one island to another? You'd probably have a theory about that. Anyway, the sun's up here, and it's getting hot, so I'm guessing I'm far away from Orcas.

Here's an island breakdown:

The Flappy Trees. (Where I'm sitting. The panel-door thingy sent me here, right in the middle of this super-mysterious stump. The trees are tall and flappy.)

The Beachy Beach. (Lots of this, it's pretty.)

The Little Lagoon. (Flowers and fish and birds.)

The Inexplicable Boulders. (The other half of the island is covered with rocks, just because, I guess.)

That's basically it. It's a small island, and I'm all alone. You'd be proud of me—I surveyed for food and water and shelter first and made a mental map and everything! High five! There's a place to get fresh water up by the boulders, and I think I can go fishing in the lagoon if I have to, but I hope I'm not here that long. I really like the word lagoon, by the way! Lagooooooooooon. And boulder. Bowl-derrrrr. Bowl-der-gooooon.

Anyway, I hope things aren't too bad at camp, and that you're covering for me with the counselors. Sorry you're there all by yourself to deal with that. I'll be back as soon as I can! I'll keep writing down cool or interesting things, so you won't be missing out on the adventure. I'm not sure if being stranded all alone on a desert island counts as an adventure, though.

Okay, writing that sentence out, it totally does. Either way I'll take notes. Right now I think I'm gonna take a nap. I am the sleepy.

Talk to you so soon,
Abby

It was funny how much better writing the letter made me feel. It was almost like having Maggie there to talk to.

I returned the journal to my bag and was just pulling out my sweatshirt to use as a pillow when something caught my eye. I looked around, and my nap plans went right out the window.

There to one side, half hidden by the trees, was a door. A door, in a frame, standing in the grass among the trunks. And it looked . . . familiar. It looked almost exactly like the door that had started this whole thing.

It looked like the door in the Shipwreck Treehouse.

And at its base, scratching in the grass and flowers climbing up its sides, was a chicken.

EIGHT
Abby

"Hey," I said, completely without thinking. "Hey, chicken."

It was a very fancy chicken, with a white floofy body and a sort of matching hat thing going on. It did not look up.

I got to my feet and started tiptoeing toward the door. The last thing I wanted was to scare my new friend, but as I sidled closer, then closer, then so close I could have stretched out and poked the door with my toe, the chicken didn't even acknowledge I was there.

Neither did the door, which I guess was normal door behavior. It looked really old up close. The wood was all rough and stained, and the grass and vines were climbing way up the sides. That explained why I hadn't spotted it before: from some angles, it looked like a tree trunk. I stepped in to examine it while Chicken McNewfriend went on ignoring me, pecking at bugs in the grass.

The door in the Shipwreck Treehouse had had a handle, and the elaborate sun-carved lock. No handle, and the old-fashioned padlock and chain tying it to the frame were aged and grimy, with no carvings at all. Boo. That meant it probably wasn't a match for the key stowed safely in my pocket. Wherever this door went—and it was a door, so it had to go *somewhere*—it wasn't super likely it led back to the Shipwreck Treehouse.

"Can you tell me where this goes?" I asked my new friend. "Any chance it goes someplace useful?"

The chicken looked up, burped, and went back to the grass for more bugs. Which was fair, to be honest. I was asking a lot of someone I'd just met.

Well, there was nothing for it—I'd just have to pick the lock and find out for myself. My attempts at picking the lock on the Shipwreck Treehouse the summer before hadn't been even a tiny bit successful, but what other choice did I have? Although I guess it made sense to at least *try* using the Oak Key first, just in case.

"Are you sticking around while I do this?" I said to the chicken as I dug in my pocket for the key. "If we're gonna be hanging out, you should have a name." I paused and considered. "I'm gonna call you . . . Wallace."

"Do not be ridiculous, child," said a voice from right behind me. "Her name is Ariadne."

I shrieked at the top of my lungs, spun around, tripped, and landed on my butt in the grass.

A woman was standing over me. She was old, with a round, wrinkly olive face, silver hair piled around her shoulders, and dark eyes. And she was wearing, well, an *outfit*: black slacks, a flowy white blouse, silver chandelier earrings, and a gold-and-green silk neck scarf. She was also carrying two baskets. The one on her left arm was full of what were clearly Cheerios. The one in her right hand was empty.

I blinked up at her. Where on earth had this old lady come from? Had she been hiding the whole time I was exploring the island? Why hadn't I seen her? Why was she carrying so much cereal?

There was a noise in the distance, and the lady looked back over her shoulder.

"Ah, here come the others." She turned to me. "You know perfectly well you're not allowed up here. But since you've decided to start the day by breaking the rules, you can spend the rest of it suffering the consequences. That means chores." She had a strong accent I couldn't place but spoke like she was used to giving orders in any language she liked. And her tone was making it clear I was in very big trouble.

"The others?" I said, getting to my feet. "Chores?" But Fashion Lady was pressing the basket of Cheerios into my arms, and then I saw them. The others were more chickens.

So many more chickens. They came bopping toward us from the rocky side of the island, all clucking and grumbling and making chickeny noises. Ariadne greeted them with a polite burp as they surged around our feet.

"Well, what are you waiting for?" Fashion Lady asked. She gestured to the basket. "Feed them."

"Oh. Okay." I tossed out a handful of Cheerios, and the chickens jumped on them like Samson on a badminton birdie.

"Scatter it about," called the lady, crossing to a tree covered with flowering vines. She started pinching off blossoms one by one and placing them carefully in the empty basket. "Don't clump it all in one place or they'll make the grass thin."

So, yeah. I fed the chickens. And the old lady picked flowers. On our magical island.

And no one explained a thing.

When all the Cheerios were gone and the chickens were dusting off the crumbs, I went over and joined my new boss, who was settled on the big stump, tying the flowers she'd gathered together in a chain.

"Chickens fed!" I said. "My name is Abby, by the way, if you were wondering." I held out a hand. "What's yours?"

Fashion Lady finished knotting two flowers together, then looked up with a face so stern it almost made the balmy, flower-scented air feel chilly. "Antonia," she said. She examined me for several long seconds, then went back to her basket.

Well, that was kind of awkward. I lowered my hand. I was happy to have company again, and there were fifty thousand questions pecking at my brain, but it didn't look like getting answers was going to be easy.

Still, I had to try.

"So, you live here?" I said conversationally.

Antonia flicked a crumpled flower out of her basket. "I do, Abby. I live in the Palace like I always have. Now will you stop this ridiculous charade?"

"Huh?" I said. Did she just say she lived in a *palace*? "Stop this what?"

"This charade! I'm sure you thought you were very clever, sneaking up here before my morning walk. I expect you gave yourself a grand tour of the island, yes? And now here you are, testing your luck with this make-believe game. You know, when I was younger, I carried trespassing children like you out to the lagoon and sent them below myself."

"Below?" I squeaked.

"Right below the waves!" said Antonia. "But since I'm not as young as I was, your punishment will be a day of chores. Hard chores."

She was on her feet before I realized she was moving. She

waved a hand, indicating I should grab my stuff, then set off at a bit of a creaky pace through the trees. I pulled on my shoes, shoved everything into my pack, and followed. What else could I do?

The well-fed chickens tagged along. Well, most of them.

"Isn't Ariadne coming?" I asked. My first friend in this place, with her odd, pretty name and floofy feather hat, was still pecking around the locked door that needed explaining.

"She always finds her own way," Antonia said without looking back. "Keep up."

Okay, something seriously, seriously weird was happening on this island. On top of all the other mysteries piling up like chickens around a Cheerio, Antonia clearly thought I knew who she was. And that for some reason I was pretending not to. What would happen when she found out she was wrong?

I trailed Antonia through the Flappy Trees, past the Little Lagoon, and around one side of the Inexplicable Boulders. I thought I'd explored the whole pile pretty well before, but I got another surprise as Antonia stepped up to a big lopsided stone, slipped neatly behind it, and disappeared. A hand slid back into view, beckoning me to follow.

Whoa. I angled in after her and found Antonia standing beside a set of stone steps leading down. Down into the island.

"How . . . ? Wha-ha?" I said. The chickens milled around our feet, settling into cool pockets of dust and dirt between the boulders around us, clearly right at home.

"After you," Antonia said, standing to one side in the cramped space.

Hmm. Going into other people's secret lairs hadn't been on my list of things to do today, but I wasn't going to find a way home on my own. And frankly, this looked like it might be pretty cool, even if there were chores involved. Feeding the chickens hadn't been too bad. What other sorts of chores could there even be on a desert island?

Maggie would have ideas. Probably involving polishing every grain of sand on the beach, or ironing out all the crinkled seaweed, or scraping the barnacles off passing krakens.

Ooh, Maggie. I could absolutely not forget to keep up my adventure notes for her.

Hoisting my backpack over my shoulders, I stepped onto the staircase—Antonia grumbling about her knees behind me—and headed underground.

NINE
Abby

The steps led down into a sort of cave amid the boulders, with a patio floor leading up to a set of carved double doors. There was a bench beside the doors, and a mat for wiping our feet. Lines of sunlight angled down from all around through the rocks, making the dust the chickens were kicking up shimmer. The air was cool and smelled like stone and the flowers in Antonia's basket. It was a nice moment.

"This is awesome," I said, smiling around. Antonia pinched her eyebrows together like she thought I was trying to be funny, tugged open one of the double doors, and waved me through.

One of the things I love most about my house back home is the clutter. Me, my dad, my brothers, Samson, none of us are super neat, and before the pre-move cleanup our house was packed with books, third-grade art projects, blankets, sports gear, and cat toys. All the sprawly mess of a close family. It was familiar and homey and perfect and I loved it.

But this place took clutter to an Olympic gold medal level.

I'd stepped into a massive room, way bigger than the cafeteria at school. It must have stretched out all the way under the rock pile. And it was *fancy*. The ceiling and what I could see of the walls were carved and decorated like a ballroom in a Disney movie. The floor at our feet was white marble. There were no windows, but wall sconce thingies and rows of chandeliers made the place so bright and shimmery, it instantly made me think of the NAFAFA Hub.

But the wildest thing was, it wasn't just one room. It was mini rooms, tons of them, all packed in together like one of those mega furniture showrooms.

Antonia and I were standing in a tiny entryway, marked out with four brass umbrella stands and more elaborate benches than was probably necessary. To our right was what looked like a sitting room, with two delicate couches drowning in velvet cushions flanking a table stacked with at least a hundred coasters surrounding a vase of dried roses.

On the left was a long, old-fashioned kitchen with a huge stove, a massive silver fridge, towers of shelves and drawers, and a lunch table–sized work island capped with black marble. It was super impressive, but I only managed to glance at it before my eyes bounced along trying to take in everything else. Just from where I was standing, I could see a hutch full of gold-lipped teacups, silver suits of armor peeking out from behind velvet-tasseled curtains, dramatic marble statues elbowing between bookshelves and ornamental screens, and a grand piano trying to look dignified under a flock of painted ceramic peacocks.

"Welcome to the Palace," said Antonia, heading for the kitchen and setting her baskets down on a clear corner of the counter. "I expect you've heard all about it. You may run around and explore while I make tea. But then chores!"

She didn't need to tell me twice. I dropped my bag on one of the benches and took off down the wide red-carpeted aisle running through the center of the Palace like a hallway. There was so much to see! Most of the mini rooms were easy to identify: bedrooms with four-poster beds, a tiny ballroom, a music room, a game room, a library. Others were more mysterious, like a room full of dusty trunks and boxes, and another that held nothing but paintings hung facing the wall, all of which turned out to be portraits of cats. And all these rooms were squished right in together, marked out with rugs, grandfather clocks, bookcases, and sometimes tapestries and banners hung from the distant ceiling.

But as I moved down the aisle, I started noticing only a few of the rooms were really clean. Most of them were dusty, and some were almost disappearing under cobwebs. It looked like Antonia needed some help in that department. I had a sinking feeling what my chores for the day would be.

Right at the far end of the Palace, I found a massive stone fireplace with a portrait hanging over it, surrounded by drooping flowers. The portrait showed a teenage girl. She had Antonia's olive skin and round face, and was wearing a strange outfit, sort of a cross between a pirate costume and a Girl Scout uniform. She actually looked pretty cool. I headed to the fireplace for a better look, but Antonia's voice came warbling down the aisle.

"Abigail?" she called. "The tea's ready in the kitchen!"

I took a last glance at the flower-draped portrait, registering the cracked varnish and old-fashioned frame, and set off, thinking. Where had all this stuff come from? There was no way Antonia had built this up on her own. No way all this had washed up on shore, like the materials for the Shipwreck Treehouse had. There was a bigger story here.

Antonia was pouring two cups of tea as I walked into the kitchen area. "We used up the last of the chicken feed today, so we need to make more," she said. "Later this afternoon you will clean and dust the entire Palace. Yes, you will!" My mouth was open in protest. "You deserve it for wandering the island without my permission. But for now, you may choose your first chicken-feed-making chore. Would you rather measure the oat flour and water or shape the mixture into small Os on the baking trays?"

I blinked. "Wait, that sounds exactly like Cheerios. You're *making* Cheerios? From scratch?"

"We are making chicken feed, Abigail," said Antonia.

"Out of oat flour?"

"Mostly. Also a hint of sugar."

"And you shape the mix into little Os and bake it?"

"Yes, the chickens prefer it that way."

"So how is that not Cheerios?"

"What is this word you keep saying?" Antonia said, pulling a bag of flour out of a cupboard with a grunt. "Are you trying to distract me? Stalling so you can avoid your chores?"

"No! I just—it sounds like we're . . . you know, never mind. Where do we start?"

Antonia slid the bag and a mixing bowl toward me, and we got to work.

"So what do you think of the Palace?" asked Antonia, once we got into a mixing and oat-flour-O-making rhythm. "I assume you've heard many stories about it. Does it meet your expectations?"

Antonia was still convinced I knew all about her, and the island, and the Palace. But how could she think that, seeing as she lived here all on her own? I'd have to play along until I could get some real answers. And hey, with Maggie for a best friend, playing along was one of the things I did best.

"It's even better than I ever imagined," I said, hoping that was the right thing to say. "The grandest palace I've ever seen."

Antonia smiled. "Oh, but it was much grander than this," she said. "Back when I was young."

"What was it like?" I asked. "Will you tell me everything? Every single detail?" Maggie would have been proud of my smooth secret-agent info-gathering skills.

"It was enormous, to start with." Antonia gazed around. "This was only the basement, where the kitchens and everyday dining room were. The Old Palace rose many, many stories above. It had turrets and towers and balconies, and it was full of life. I am just old enough to remember. On sunny days we would fly kites from the roof and take the waterslide down to the lagoon, and on rainy days we played hide-and-seek in all the hidden passageways and performed plays in the great hall.

"But then the world changed, and the grown-ups said the planes would see us as they flew overhead, and they had a meeting and decided the Old Palace would have to come down." She looked over at me. "I was just a little younger than you, I think. Imagine all the grown-ups in your life deciding to dismantle your home. Deciding to change everything you'd known, and not giving you any real say in it at all."

Whoa. I could totally imagine that.

"A few insisted on staying, my parents among them," Antonia continued, "and they decided on this compromise." She waved a hand at the compact spaces around us. "Every important Palace room was re-created in miniature, and we moved down here and went on with our lives, living according to Captain Emily's wishes as best we could. The others took the Palace apart story by story, disguised where it had been with the rocks, and left. None of them ever came back. And now, seventy-five years later, I am the last."

Wait. This happened seventy-five years ago? Antonia was *old*. And, from the sound of it, lonely. Although, really, who wouldn't be, living like this? This was way too much space for someone on their own.

"Hey, that's a lot," I said, trying to keep the conversation moving. "But what was that you just said about Captain Emily's wishes? Who's Captain Emily? What's the story there?"

Antonia put down the baking tray she was holding with a clang. Her eyebrows came together, just like Director Haggis's when he was yelling into his megaphone. "Are you being serious, Abigail?"

Shoot. Wrong thing to say.

"Yes?" I said. *Just keep playing along, Abby. There's gotta be a clue here that'll help you get home.* "Would you mind, you know, maybe, talking about that . . . some more?"

Antonia snorted. "I suppose I shouldn't be surprised. They don't teach the story properly anymore, do they? Would you like to hear it? It's been a long time since I've told it to anyone else."

"I'd love to!"

"It's a very long story," Antonia warned. "It may run into lunchtime, and you will still have to clean and dust the entire Palace afterward."

"Got it," I said.

Lunchtime? Hey, being Maggie's best friend had taught me a thing or two about stretching out a story. If I could keep Antonia talking, maybe I'd never actually have to dust at all.

"Then get your heart ready," my strange new old lady friend said, "for the tale of Captain Emily."

TEN
Abby

Long before you were born, when the 1700s were fifteen years old, there lived a pirate captain named Emily Fairchild, and she was fifteen years old, too.

She was a captain by rank and a pirate by birth. Her mother had been a pirate, and her father, and her great-aunt, the famous Argenia Grimsworth Monty Anna Bee, before that. But although she loved her family, and she loved sailing and navigating and chantey singing, she never felt right about the other parts of the pirate life. Namely stealing. From sailors. On ships.

She didn't mind collecting treasure from the captains of the ships she caught, or from the wealthy nobles who sometimes rode in them to get from one of their palaces to another, but the friendly, hardworking sailors were another matter.

Raids could involve a certain amount of pushing and shoving, and sometimes members of her crew came back with nasty bruises. She upheld the family tradition faithfully, but on long nights when she lay awake watching the moon kiss the tops of the waves, Emily secretly admitted to herself that the whole business left her feeling rather empty.

And then there was her secret. Captain Emily's heart was split. The sweeping sea sang in her soul, that was certain. But sometimes, just sometimes, she longed for a room that stayed put. A view that stayed still. A house on the land she could live in.

But Emily Fairchild was a pirate by birth and a captain by rank, and she knew it was one or the other.

One spring day, Emily and her crew set their sights on a decadent-looking confection of a ship from the French Royal Navy. But they had misjudged. The ship proved surprisingly strong, and they were outgunned in a major sea battle. The pirates barely escaped, limping away into the Atlantic. They sailed for days and weeks, and the food ran out and then the water, and everyone was miserable. Just when it seemed all hope was lost, the desperate pirates came upon an island.

It was a very small island, uninhabited, and crowned with a grove of strange and ancient-looking trees. It was also packed with treasure: a freshwater spring, shellfish blanketing the rocks along the beach, and schools of slow, delicious

fish wandering sleepily around the little lagoon. So every-
one ate and drank and was happy again, and they stayed on
the island while the pirate carpenters cut down some of the
trees and set about repairing the ship. The captain's cabin,
in particular, needed a whole new door and frame, owing to a
cannonball that had passed right by Emily's head during the
battle.

At last the ship was as good as new, and they set sail, all
waving goodbye to the hospitable little island. Captain Emily
announced she was retiring to her cabin to plan their revenge
on the French Royal Navy ship, but as she walked through the
newly installed doorway, she vanished in a blink. The horri-
fied crew dashed around, calling her name and peering under
barrels and behind coils of rope, but there was no sign of her.
Finally they spotted the captain's red-feathered hat waving
from the shore of the island behind them, and they sent out
the rowboat to get her back.

As Captain Emily climbed aboard, she told her aston-
ished crew how she'd been stepping through the doorway one
moment, then was back on the island the next, standing in the
center of a huge stump. Just as if she'd grown there.

I looked up from my oat-flour mixing, feeling a wave of
tingles run up my spine and along my scalp. That was exactly
what had happened to me!

I opened my mouth to ask for details, but Antonia was barreling on with her story.

It was the carpenters who figured it out. They put their heads together and realized that Captain Emily had been transported to the stump of the very tree they'd cut down to make her new cabin door in the first place. Somehow the tree and the stump were still connected, like they couldn't bear to be separated. And walking through the door had brought their captain in a blink from one to the other.

Obviously, it was magic.

Emily tested it again immediately. Every pirate eye grew wide as they watched her vanish midstep in the doorway, and every pirate voice cheered as the red-feathered hat appeared on the beach.

The pirates were delighted. Now they would always have access to food and fresh water, which was often a problem at sea. But the practical first mate pointed out the connection only worked one way, and they couldn't just sail around within rowboat distance of the island forever, and so a solution had to be found. While the carpenters added a second, nonmagical door so the captain could get into her cabin, Emily and the others threw a brainstorming party, and soon they had a plan to put into action.

Everyone returned to the island, where they cut down the

largest of the remaining trees. The carpenters and the cap-
tain stayed on the island to work on its trunk, while the rest of
the crew carefully dug up the stump, roots and all, floated it
out to the ship, and hauled it up on deck.

The carpenters turned the trunk into a new door in its own
sturdy frame and fixed it firmly into the earth amid the trees.
Squaring her shoulders, the feathers in her hat rippling in the
wind, Captain Emily stepped through and in a blink appeared
on the stump aboard her ship, just as if she'd grown there.

The crew broke into applause, and Emily broke into her
favorite jig. It worked! She danced through the cabin door
back to the first island stump, then through the new door in
the trees right back to the ship again. Soon all the crew joined
in, a great circle of pirates dancing and whooping in a loop
from ship to stump to door to ship. And the loop worked every
time. "It's an odd sort of magic, these inseparable trees,"
Emily commented later that night, as their celebration con-
tinued under the stars. "But one can't be picky."

Now any of the crew—with the captain's permission—
could hop from the ship to the island and back, as often as
they pleased.

"I'm sorry," I said. "But I'm getting totally lost. Will you
say that part about the doors and stumps again, please?"

Antonia frowned over her mountain of unbaked homemade not-Cheerios. "Have you never been taught even the

most basic fundamentals of our history?" she asked.

"Oh, yes, sure I have," I said quickly. *Keep playing along, Abby.* "Only I'd love to hear you tell it. You know, properly."

Antonia sighed, but she scooped a handful of flour out of my bowl and clapped her hands over the counter, blanketing the dark marble. "The trees of the island," she said theatrically, and maybe a little sarcastically, "are magical. They always lead back to their roots." She drew a stick-figure tree in the flour, then an arrow pointing to a sort of scribble.

"What's that supposed to be?" I asked.

"The stump and roots of the tree."

"Really?" I peered at it.

"Yes."

"Oh. If you say so."

Antonia sighed again.

"But you see, yes?" she said, tapping the arrow. "The tree trunk always connects back to the stump and roots, no matter where they are. That is the way the traveling works."

"Yes, good."

Antonia drew a circle in the flour under the tree. "This is the island." She drew a triangle below that. "This is the pirate ship."

"You should add a little flag or something," I said. "Maybe a skull and cross—"

"This is not fine art!" Antonia snapped. "This is flour drawing to illustrate the story!"

"Okay, okay."

"Pay attention now. The first loop was created when part of a tree was used to repair a doorway on the ship. From then on, that doorway led to that tree's stump back on the island." Antonia drew an arrow from the triangle to the circle. "They became known as the Island Door and the Island Stump. Now, in order to get back to the ship, they needed to bring a different stump aboard. Because—"

"Because the tree always leads to the stump, and never the other way around," I said, tapping the tree and squiggle pictures with my stirring spoon.

"Yes, well done," said Antonia. "So they built the Ship Door on the island, which led to the Ship Stump on the ship." She drew another arrow leading from the circle to the triangle. "Clear?"

"Island Door is on the ship, Ship Door is on the island," I said. "Door to stump, door to stump, around in a loop." I looked up and smiled. "Neat!"

"Yes, it is neat," said Antonia. "Now please get back to stirring, and I will continue with the telling."

Being able to resupply whenever they liked was an enormous advantage, one any ship's captain would dream of, but as they returned in triumph to their usual waters, Captain Emily felt her old sadness returning. She still didn't feel right about traditional piracy. If only she could limit her raids to people who could afford it, like the lords and kings and admirals who had sent out that vicious French Royal Navy ship in the first place. The trouble was, most of those people didn't sail. Those people spent their time on land, lounging around their palaces and castles, full of grand rooms and fancy furniture. . . .

And that was when the most glorious, perfect plan unfolded in her mind.

A small tree and its stump were collected from the island. The carpenters got busy making a beautiful chest from the stump, and a door in a frame from the body of the tree, and after thoroughly testing the connection and adding one important secret touch, the pirates put their plan into action. Captain Emily dressed up, and the crew dressed up, and they made a new flag and dressed the ship up and sailed to a rich port in a famous city, presenting themselves as ambassadors of a far country—which was true enough, since the hospitable island had become their home—and Captain Emily made a grand entrance and presented the exquisite chest as a gift to the king there.

Later that night on the ship, Emily put on a very different disguise made especially for creeping through palaces in the dark. She stepped through the new door—which they called the Palace Door—and found herself curled inside the chest, inside the palace. Success! She slipped out and went from room to room, sneaking trinkets and treasures and fine clothes and apple cider and good food from the kitchens. When she couldn't carry any more, she wrapped everything in a wildly expensive carpet and returned to the chest.

Her heart was pounding. This was the moment of truth. If this didn't work, she'd be stranded in the palace with her arms full of loot. She opened the chest and pushed hard on the back panel, the special secret panel made from the very same wood that had given them the Island Door to start with. The panel opened, and the carpet and treasure slipped through, and Emily followed, closing the trunk after her.

And there she was, standing on the stump on her own dear island just as if she'd grown there, surrounded by treasure. And there was the Ship Door, gleaming in the moonlight, and Emily sang her very favorite pirate chantey as she stepped triumphantly through to rejoin her crew.

The pirates held a monumental party all that night and all the following day. They drank the cider, ate the food, and sang songs celebrating the whole new way of life opening before them. No more robbing poor sailors, no more pushing and shoving, no more risking nasty bruises. Just sailing and singing and stealing beautiful treasures from overstuffed palaces. The stars blazed in the sky, then the sun, then the stars again, and they were the happiest pirate crew in all the world.

A few days later, when they had recovered from the party, Emily asked for volunteers to begin building a little palace of their own on the island, so they could store all their fine new things.

Emily also decided it was too risky having the Palace Door standing around on the deck of the ship. What if someone went through it by mistake? So she had the door moved to the hold belowdecks, and she purchased a fine-carved lock and key and locked the door tight in its frame, placing the new key on a ring at her belt.

And so the crew settled happily into their new life as palace pirates, and between the ship and the island, Emily had everything she ever wanted. The split in her heart was healed. Every few months they would dig up another tree, place another door in the hold, and plant another piece of furniture in another fine and famous palace. Their home on the hospitable little island became more and more comfortable and lavish, and the legend of the unknown ambassador with her ring of keys grew and grew among the rich and powerful. As did the legend of the Palace Pilferer. Emily had been spotted more than once in her second disguise, and her shadowy crimes and impossible escapes were becoming so legendary that a rough WANTED portrait of her hung in every town square along the coastlines of Europe.

* * *

"Hang on a second," I said, raising my spoon to interrupt. I spread my own handful of flour on the counter. "They took down another whole tree and made the trunk into a door they kept on the ship"—I drew a rectangle—"and that door led to a piece of furniture made from the tree's stump and roots." I drew a circle. "And they used that to sneak into the palaces. Only there was no way back, so they *also* gave the furniture a secret panel thingy made from the trunk of that very first tree you told me about, leading to the Ship Stump on this island. So all the furniture had stump parts so you could get there from the ship, and trunk parts so you could get back to the island, and from there back to the ship. Loop complete."

I looked down at the disaster area of lines and squiggles I'd drawn in the flour.

"Did I get that right?"

"Yes," said Antonia. "But I hope you've got more talent at dusting than you have at flour drawing. Here," she suddenly called down the kitchen, "it's not ready yet, love!"

I looked where she was yelling. Ariadne was standing on the far end of the counter, settling her feathers, watching us.

"What the . . . ?" I glanced over at the heavy double doors. They were definitely still closed. "How did she get in here?"

"I told you. She always finds her way wherever she wants to be. Come back later, dear," Antonia called, waving a hand.

Ariadne gave a grumbly cluck and sat down. "All right," said Antonia. "But you'll be waiting awhile." She turned back to our cereal project and went on with her story.

So, Captain Emily and her crew had loops to palaces all across Europe and were getting richer and happier every day. But the end was drawing near. There were only so many mature trees on the island to build furniture with, and the time came when they had used up all but one. One bright autumn morning they threw a grand party and took down the final tree, and the ship's carpenters—who were very skilled by that time—crafted its trunk into the Last Door, which Emily outfitted with the finest lock money could buy, and its roots and stump into something they had never attempted before: a beautiful sofa, wrapped in velvet of green and gold. And Emily presented it to the most famous, rich, and powerful person she could think of: the young king of France.

I almost knocked my entire bowl of chicken feed off the counter. Could she possibly mean—?

That night, while her ship waited in the harbor, Emily went through the Last Door and made her first visit to the final palace. The beautiful sofa, she discovered, had been placed in the king's own private salon, which she took as a good sign.

And when she stepped out into the palace and discovered it was opulent and lush beyond her wildest dreams, she knew that she'd been right. Almost waltzing through the shadowy halls, she gathered a spectacular, dizzying collection of loot. When she finally returned to the private salon, she shoved everything through the hidden panel in the back of the sofa, and was so pleased with her work that she indulged in a short rest, stretched out with her feet up on the luxurious green and gold velvet cushions, whistling sea chanteys.

Finally she slipped through the secret panel, stowed the treasure in their island palace, and leaped triumphantly through the Ship Door, only to find her crew in a state of severe anxiety.

The crew had received a visit from a Royal Navy harbor inspector while Emily was away. The ship had been thoroughly searched, and many awkward questions had been asked about the hold full of locked doors and the unclear origins of the ship itself.

Emily was angry, but she grew even angrier when she checked the pockets of her Palace Pilferer outfit and realized that the key to the Last Door, which had not joined the others on her ring of keys yet, was missing, and she would have to go right back to the palace to find it. The head carpenter put a hand to his mouth when he heard this, looking horrified. Under his captain's glare, he revealed that he had clicked the lock on the Last Door shut when the harbor inspector came aboard, for fear she might be discovered.

Emily put a hand to her mouth too, as what that meant hit home: with no key, her door to the final palace was sealed forever. The locksmith had promised the lock was unpickable, even by the world's best thieves, and she couldn't very well take the whole door into his shop and ask for a replacement. He would talk, and then other people would talk, and then there would be investigations.

So there was nothing to be done. Emily had had one solitary night to pillage the richest, most decadent palace she'd ever seen, and there was no chance to try again. Her heart ached thinking of all the lovely treasures she'd left behind, but one night would have to be enough.

Emily ordered the ship be made ready to sail. She was just giving the order to cast off when there was a cry from the docks. The Royal Navy harbor inspector was back, and he had reached the top of the gangplank before anyone could move. He stood, frozen, staring at Emily in her Palace Pilferer outfit, then pulled out his sword and roared.

A quick-thinking pirate managed to knock him into the sea, but the alarm had been raised, and the crew had to scramble to cut the mooring lines and get the ship underway. Emily looked back as they cleared the harbor. The entire French Royal Navy was on their tail.

And so they ran; first for days, then for weeks. They didn't dare head back to their secret island while the navy pursued them, and for all their efforts, they could not shake them. They crossed the sea, and the well-equipped navy followed. They sailed down the southern tip of the Americas and up the other side, and while the smaller navy boats were forced to turn back, the biggest and strongest of the ships still dogged them.

It was lucky for the pirates they had the island to return to for food and fresh water and a rotating vacation schedule, or they never would have made it as far as they did. The Royal Navy could not understand how their prey was able to maintain such a journey on such a modest ship, how they still had the heart to sing chanteys to the stars at night, or how they always had fresh eggs to hurl when their pursuers got too close.

Finally, in the cold waters of the North Pacific, the last two navy ships—the biggest and strongest, and by that time, the angriest—caught up with them and shot them so full of holes, the pirates began to sink.

But Captain Emily and her crew had thrown a strategy party and worked out a plan. They brought up the doors for the best palaces from the hold and one by one sent them back to the island. They got most of them through before the hold was submerged, and as the waves finally began lapping around their ankles, they all prepared to return to the island themselves, leaving behind the ship that had carried them so far.

It was only then that Captain Emily realized there was a terrible flaw in their escape: with no lock to close the Island Door, the whole sea would rush in when the ship sank. It would come pouring through forever, roaring out of the Island Stump like a volcano, sweeping away everything they'd built and them along with it. There was only one solution: someone would have to stay behind and destroy it.

So, as was a captain's duty, Emily prepared to go down with the ship. She forced her crew through the door at sword point, until only her faithful first mate stood beside her. Captain Emily looked into her friend's eyes, which were full of tears. "It's up to you now," she said. "Keep the crew safe. And look after the Palace for me. And if you ever get the chance, pay another visit to Versailles—and this time, get their full attention!"

And before the first mate could say a word, Emily shoved her ring of keys into his hands, pushed him through, and slammed the door shut. With the frigid waters of the North Pacific biting at her ribs, and the horrible creaks and dying groans of her ship tearing at her ears, Captain Emily Fairchild smashed the doorframe with a hammer, cracking it to smithereens, saving the others and dooming herself to the waves.

The crew huddled together on their island and wept. Their captain was gone, their ship was gone, and the life they'd known was over. But they were safe, and they had the hospitable little island, and they had their beautiful palace home and the looped doors they'd saved, which still led to fine palaces full of food and clothing and gold.

They mourned their captain for weeks and months, but day by day they carried on, and their lives on the island became happy and full, though they never again found the heart to return to the tumbling waves of the sea.

ELEVEN
Abby

Three completed cookie sheets of chicken feed later, Antonia and I sat down for lunch in front of the fireplace and the portrait of Captain Emily. Antonia had replaced the wilted flowers around the portrait with the fresh ones from that morning, and I'd helped her prepare big bowls of panzanella—toast and tomatoes and basil and onions all tossed together in olive oil and salt. It was delicious, but there was so much intel thundering through my brain I barely noticed it.

Because I knew everything now. Everything.

I knew how the magic in the pillow fort networks had started, and where the First Sofa came from. I knew the history of the Oak Key in my pocket, and how the locked door it went to was left to sink with Captain Emily's ship. I knew how it drifted around the cold waters of the North Pacific until a storm washed it up on Orcas Island, where it became the trapdoor of the Shipwreck Treehouse.

I knew how falling through that door had looped me to le Petit Salon, dumping me under the First Sofa, trapped up against the coffiny wooded slats by my backpack. I knew that all my flailing had cracked open the hidden panel in the First Sofa, and how that panel had looped me to the stump on this island. I knew the whole story. I knew more than Antonia, more than Ben, more than Maggie.

I knew more about all this than anyone else in the whole world.

So what the heck was I supposed to do now? It wasn't like I could just tell Antonia about NAFAFA. I'd learned last summer that most grown-ups were pretty bad at believing there's a global pillow fort network run by kids that they're not allowed in.

I chewed my panzanella in silence, listening to Ariadne's chicken noises as she poked around the floor and to Antonia's fork clanking against her bowl. I tried to make a mental note to tell my dad about panzanella when I got home—that was another fun word, panzanellllllaah—but my brain just laughed and went right on swirling like a Tilt-A-Whirl.

Dad and Tamal would probably be too busy with all the new dishes they'd discovered on their honeymoon in Mexico to need any more, anyway. Tamal was a decent cook, but he was a seriously brilliant baker, even better than my dad. I'd known for sure they were in love when my dad let Tamal make cookies in his precious kitchen and only had two mini-freakouts. Tamal even taught Matt and Mark how to make his famous cinnamon rolls, and they were planning on practicing them while the rest of us were away.

I smiled, picturing the state of the kitchen after that. Good thing half my dad's cooking gear was already packed up. The twins had better make sure they had the kitchen spotless by the time he and Tamal got home.

And they'd be home real soon if I couldn't get myself off this island and back to camp. Even with Maggie playing defense, there was obviously only so long I could be missing before someone called in the authorities, and they would be sure to contact my dad.

And the really real trouble was I was totally stranded. That locked door up on the beach wasn't an option anymore. That had to be the Ship Door from the story, and the only place it would lead now was straight to the bottom of the Pacific Ocean. And okay, that was a lot closer to Camp Cantaloupe than here, but still not anywhere I wanted to be.

Good thing Antonia had arrived before I could pick that lock and doom us all.

"Hey," I said, pulling my brain back to the wonderland I was having lunch in. "Antonia. What happened to all those doors the crew saved?" Why hadn't I thought of that right away? One of them must get me somewhere useful.

Antonia frowned over her panzanella. "Now that really is enough, Abigail," she said. "You know the answer to that. The others took them when they moved off the island. It was part of the compromise."

Shoot. Of course they took the looped doors with them. Shame I wasn't whoever Antonia thought I was. Then I might know how to get unstuck from this place.

Somewhere back in the Palace a clock chimed, then another, and another. Antonia looked up as though she was waiting for something.

Knock-knock-knock.

A loud clanging from the double doors echoed down the red carpet toward us.

"I wonder who that could be," said Antonia, looking at me very deliberately.

"Huh?" I said. What did she mean *who*? That sound couldn't have come from a person. The whole point of her story was that we were the only ones left on the island.

Antonia set her bowl aside and got stiffly to her feet.

Knock-knock-knock.

It happened again. Antonia walked away down the main aisle, her feet brushing the carpet. I stayed in my armchair, staring, my brain barely registering what was happening.

Was . . . was someone really knocking out there?

I got up, hurrying after Antonia. She threw a half glance back at me as she reached the double doors. She turned the handle. She pulled.

A woman was standing on the other side. A tall woman, maybe the same age as my dad, with a long, olive face, curly black hair pulled into a bun on top of her head, and dark eyes. She was wearing a navy blue Henley shirt and had a bucket of cleaning supplies in one hand, a mop and duster in the other. A ring of old-fashioned keys hung from her belt.

"At last," the lady said. "What took you so lo—"

Her eyes found me, and she stopped midword. I couldn't see my own face, because of course not, but it was a fair bet I looked just as sky-shatteringly shocked as she did.

There were other people wandering around here? This whole time?!

"Well," said Antonia, looking between us. "There's obviously no need for introductions." She turned to the woman. "As you see, dear, I won't need your help this afternoon. Your young friend Abigail here will be helping me clean instead."

TWELVE
Abby

Maybe I'd missed something important, but I for one thought introductions were totally necessary. Who was this lady in the doorway? Why did she look so horrified at the sight of me? And why did Antonia think we were *friends*?

The lady stepped into the Palace, dumped her cleaning supplies right on the floor, and put her hands on her hips. "What is going on here, Mama?" she demanded. And suddenly the family resemblance was obvious.

"Mama?" I rounded on Antonia. "You told me you were alone here! You said the others moved away from the island years ago!"

"No, I said the others moved *off* the island years ago," said Antonia as the new woman gaped at me. "You know perfectly well you all live *under* it."

"They . . . how can you . . . under . . . There are more people here?" I was spluttering worse than Samson that time he got into a bag of Pop Rocks.

"Mama, I insist you tell me where this girl came from!" the lady shouted, stabbing a finger at me and actually stamping her foot. She looked furious, but also more than a little scared.

"Do not take that tone, Helene," Antonia said, squaring up to her daughter. They made a serious pair. "This girl comes from the Island Underneath."

"No, she does not!"

"Of course she does!" They were face to face now. "She's one of the children, on an early visit home from school. Clearly she decided to sneak up and explore the island when she thought I wouldn't catch her, most likely on a dare." Antonia looked me up and down. "I'd guess she's Lyric and Caleb's daughter. Though it has been a long time since I've seen her."

"Mama, Lyric and Caleb's daughter is seventeen years old and studying theoretical mathematics at MIT!" Helene yelled. "She is not this young, she does not have an American accent, and she is not standing here in this room!" She turned and grabbed me by the shoulders. "You, child, how did you get here? How how how?"

"Hey!" I said, pulling myself free. Grown-ups or not, these

two were not going to treat me like a toddler. "My name is Abby, not *child*. And I got here through . . ."

I hesitated. How much should I tell them? Antonia had never asked, so she didn't know I'd gotten to the island by following in Captain Emily's footsteps. They would understand the loop just fine, but the part I couldn't explain to them was the key. Not without saying where I got it and spilling the beans on the whole pillow fort situation. Who knew how this Helene lady would react to that? Given how messy things were getting, it was probably safer keeping my facts vague.

"I got here through a door," I said. "My best friend and I opened this old door in the treehouse at our summer camp, and I fell through it. I ended up stuck under this boxy piece of furniture, and then I went through some sort of panel and was suddenly standing in the sun on that big stump." I waved a hand overhead, then looked at Antonia. I couldn't help myself. "Just like I'd grown there."

Antonia seized her daughter's arm, and the two women stood faced, united in shock.

"And . . . and where is your summer camp located?" asked Helene.

"On Orcas Island. That's on the west coast of the US, kinda near the Canadian border."

"That proves it!" Helene gasped. "Mama, if she got in through *that* door, and the other castaway got in through the wardrobe . . . One outsider finding their way here might have been an accident, but two in three days cannot be coincidence. Something has happened out in the world."

Hang on. The *other* castaway? Someone else had arrived here like me?

Antonia was looking from Helene to me and back again, her eyes as wide as Ariadne's floofy hat. It must have been a real shock to discover the person she'd just made homemade Cheerios with and allowed to wander around her home was actually a total outsider.

And speaking of Ariadne, my first island friend picked that moment to bounce into sight around the end of the counter, spot the open door, and bobble toward it, clucking happily. The three of us watched her pass. I had a sudden urge to follow on after her and leave all this chaos behind. I mean, yay for more people, but my goal was to get home, and this whole situation was starting to feel like one of Maggie's more ridiculous adventure games.

"There will have to be a meeting, dear," Antonia said, yanking me back into the moment. "Bring some of the others up tonight, and we will talk."

Helene was shaking her head. "No, this calls for more than a meeting. This will require a party."

"No!"

"Yes!"

"It cannot be that serious. Nothing has really changed."

"Everything has changed!"

"Well, I won't let it!"

My head was pinging back and forth like I was watching a badminton match.

"Mama, hush," said Helene. "I'm bringing the others up whether you like it or not. I expect you and Abby"—she showed off her pointing skills again—"to be at the lagoon in thirty minutes. We will find out what these outsiders know, determine just how they came here, and decide what to do about it, *as a group*."

She scooped up her cleaning gear, gave her mother and me a curt nod, and marched back through the door and out of sight.

Antonia stood watching the empty entryway, her eyebrows pinched together, apparently going through some feelings.

"So," I said, after one long moment became several. It looked like I was getting out of all that dusting and cleaning, which was cool, but I really needed some proper answers. "So, everyone who used to live up here, they're still around? In this Island Underneath place?"

Antonia nodded vaguely. "The ones who left built a new home there. I haven't visited since Helene moved down too, leaving the Palace behind." She paused. "And me along with it."

I didn't know quite what to say to that. Antonia gave her head a little shake and turned to face me, her eyes sharp and bright again.

"And you knew, Abigail," she said. "When you told Helene how you arrived, you knew you'd gone through the Last Door, and appeared under the sofa in Versailles, and taken the hidden panel back to the Island Stump. You must have known, after hearing Captain Emily's story from me. Why didn't you say so?"

Antonia was putting the pieces together fast. "That's . . . sort of complicated," I said.

Antonia grunted and walked back into the Palace, waving a hand for me to follow. We stopped in one of the bedrooms beside a large dresser covered in ceramic tigers.

"It's simply impossible," she said. "When Helene informed me about the other castaway, I was shocked, but it made some degree of sense. Then you arriving . . . through that door . . . there's much more going on than you're telling me. But it will have to wait." Antonia yanked open the top dresser drawer, revealing piles of silk shirts, scarves, and blouses. "Right now, we've got to find you something to wear to this party."

Twenty minutes later we were climbing back through the shady coolness of the rocks, past the dozing chickens, and off under the hot sun toward the lagoon. Antonia hadn't asked me any more questions while we got ready, but she'd also refused to answer any of mine, and I was still trying to understand exactly what sort of party we were heading to.

I mean, there were our outfits, for a start. Antonia had accessorized her already fancy ensemble with a silver sequined cape and white feather hat that made her look more than a little like Ariadne. I was wearing a fitted red velvet jacket over my Camp Cantaloupe T-shirt, a necklace made of giant pink silk roses, and an eighties-style electric green headband Antonia said had once belonged to an Italian duchess. On top of that we were both carrying the most incredible inflatable pool chairs—an old-fashioned clawfoot bathtub for Antonia, and a pink-and-gold teacup and saucer set for me.

"Hey, question," I said as we walked along. "Is this a, you know, birthday-style party we're going to, or—"

"It's a serious party," Antonia said. "You should remember from the story. Captain Emily and her crew had parties whenever they needed to make big decisions or form important plans. We in the modern crew carry on that tradition." She glanced back over her silver-sequined shoulder, her feather hat floofing wildly in the wind off the sea. "Dignity and tradition are the most important things."

"Oh," I said. "Cool."

We rounded a clump of tall bushes covered in blue and

purple flowers, and there was the Little Lagoon again.

And it was packed.

At least fifty people were floating around on inflatable chairs, rafts, pizza slices, unicorns, cactuses, dragons, even a moose. All of them had on fancy hats, fake wings, capes, bow ties, and crowns. And all of them were belting out what could only be an old-timey pirate sea chantey.

Two wooden rafts were bobbing in the middle of everything, one with a group playing instruments—whistles, a toy xylophone, a tuba—and the other with a bar setup, where two of the crew were pouring out drinks with little paper umbrellas and passing them around to all the other partiers.

It was about as different from the quiet, sleepy lagoon I'd paddled my feet in just a few hours before as it could be.

There was a cheer as Antonia and I reached the shore. Antonia raised a hand and nodded in acknowledgment, which might have looked super regal if she hadn't been wearing that hat. People were looking my way and talking excitedly to each other. I distinctly heard the phrase "Castaway Number Two!" Some of them waved, and I waved back. This was almost like walking into the Hub last summer.

"Has anyone seen my daughter?" Antonia called over the singing.

A woman in a T. rex costume cupped her hands around her mouth. "Over there!" She pointed along the curve of the shore. "Fetching Castaway Number One!"

Antonia and I looked together. Helene was walking toward us, and a man was gaping around behind her. The sunlight bounced off his balding head, white feather boa, and well-worn sweatshirt.

I squinted, my heart kicking up a beat. No. Wait. Was that—?

The man caught sight of me and stopped dead.

I yelled, and the man did the same, and I dropped my floaty and raced for his open arms. I could have cried with relief.

Castaway Number One . . . was Maggie's uncle Joe.

THIRTEEN
Maggie

My first morning wake-up call at Camp Cantaloupe came way too early. Loudspeakers shocked eveyone awake blaring military-style trumpet music, then a voice crackled in, ordering us all to *"Rise and shine and shine and rise and shine and shine and shiiiiine!"* Seriously.

There was a chorus of groans and squeaking bunk springs as the kids around me sat up, yawning. I waited for someone to ask where Abby was, but no one seemed to notice until our cabin counselor clomped in, called for our attention, and grumpily told everyone what had happened the night before.

"You tried to get lost on purpose?" Charlene said, right in front of everyone. "And you broke the Shipwreck Treehouse? What in the world were you thinking?!"

The counselor cut in before I could reply, saying I was in

enough trouble already, that Abby would be found soon, and that we all needed to get ready for roll call.

Charlene cornered me while I was tying my shoes, her Safety Monitor sash and Litter Patrol badge looming over my head.

"I can't believe you talked Abby into doing that," she hissed. "All you've done is ruin everything! And now"—she pointed at our counselor—"I'm supposed to be your *buddy* for the rest of camp! Do you have any idea how inconvenient that is for me?"

I opened my mouth.

"No, you don't know," Charlene continued. "I had plans for this summer too, you know! Big plans! Important plans! And I'll tell you one thing: if I miss out on them because I'm stuck keeping you out of trouble, I will never, ever, *ever* forgive you."

She whirled away and stood tapping her toe as the others filed out of the cabin, then headed for the field, letting me limp after her, my hip and ankle still throbbing from my fall. Ugh. This was going to be a rough, rough day.

I was so down I couldn't even bring myself to come up with a witty reply when they called "Hetzger, Maggie!" at roll call, and I just answered "Here," like everyone else. No one but Abby would understand what a bad sign that was.

It got worse when Director Haggis told all the rest of camp

what had happened, shouting into his megaphone about how "This incident entirely justifies my new safety campaign!" The stares and grumbles Charlene had gotten the day before were *nothing* compared to what I was getting now.

Breakfast in the screaming mess hall was awful, especially since Charlene, who was taking her buddy duty very seriously, sat right beside me but refused to say a word. It was almost a relief when Director Haggis summoned me to his office, telling Charlene she could stay and finish her food.

Director Haggis and I took our positions across the desk from each other, just like the night before. The little woodchuck clock read a quarter past nine. The camp director looked very tired.

"How are you?" he said. I blinked, surprised he had asked.

"Okay, I guess. My ankle feels the same. And my hip hurts. And I miss Abby."

"And we still haven't found her." Director Haggis rubbed a hand over his eyes. "We've just alerted the local police, and they're on their way to help us search the woods. We're not going overboard yet, since you've told us she set off deliberately, and with plenty of provisions, but the situation is still very serious. Are you certain you have no idea where she is? Even what direction she might have gone?"

I shook my head. And I was telling the truth. I had no idea where Abby was at all.

And . . . hey, what if she *was* in real, actual danger? What if the trapdoor had led to a long-lost nuclear submarine, and Abby was miles below the sea, fighting off giant squid attacks? Or what if it led to a secret celebrities-only ski resort on top of a mountain, but she'd fallen down as soon as she went through and was lying in a crevasse with a broken leg while big-time movie stars skied by overhead?

I felt sick. Abby might be all alone and scared, maybe even injured, and here I was feeling sorry for myself safe at camp. I had to get to the Hub tonight. Plan Patchwork had to work. I had to get her back.

"Well, it's a shame you don't have any ideas," Director Haggis continued. "I'm going to have to call Abby Hernandez's parent or guardian now, Miss Hetzger, and let them know what's happened. And since you two seem to be so close, and you know more of the—ahem—*reasoning* behind the events of last night, I've asked you here in case they need more explanation than I can provide."

Wait, what? Director Haggis wanted *me* to talk to Alex? Did he even know Alex was out of town on his honeymoon? Did he know Abby's brothers were the only ones home? Maybe he didn't. A plan began clicking together lightning fast in my brain.

"I'd like that, sir," I said, doing my best to keep the excitement out of my voice. "Do you think . . ." I had to be careful not to overdo this part. "Do you think I could talk to Abby's dad first? It could be less of a shock coming from me. From you, it would sound all official, and that might scare him."

Director Haggis considered me over his desk for a long moment, then nodded. "That will be acceptable. But I'll need to speak to him after you're done. There are legal questions to consider here, you know, and I have to look out for the wefare of the camp itself."

I nodded back, and he handed me the phone on his desk. I dialed.

The phone rang once, twice. . . . "Hullo?" said a sleepy voice. I almost grinned, and caught myself just in time. It was Matt. Or Mark, maybe. Either way, it was one of Abby's brothers, and it was the first friendly voice I'd heard since she'd disappeared.

"Good morning, Mr. Hernandez," I said, being sure to keep my tone on the edge of mournful. "This is Maggie Hetzger."

"Maggie! Hi, it's Matt!" My stomach filled with a happy sort of glow. Both the twins were awesome, but Matt was my, um, very favorite. "Why are you calling?" he asked. "Aren't you at summer camp?"

"Yes. I'm afraid I have some news, Mr. Hernandez," I said. Director Haggis was watching me closely.

"Huh? Why are you calling me that, Maggie? You know

Dad's away on his huh-nee-moooon!"

I almost snorted like Abby. "The thing is, *Mr. Hernandez*," I said, pressing on, "Abby and I made some poor decisions and decided to try and get lost in the woods last night. On purpose. It was so we could be rescued by the friendly ghost moose they always talk about here."

Matt's voice became serious. "Maggie, what? Is everything okay? Why are you acting like this?"

"Oh, no, not really. I hurt my ankle a little, but the staff are taking very good care of me," I continued, with a glance at the director. "Only I'm sorry to tell you Abby hasn't come back from the woods yet, and we can't find her."

"What?"

"She had a backpack of supplies with her," I said quickly. "And she wasn't going far. And this is an island, so she must be around somewhere. But the director thought we should let you know."

"Hey, Maggie, hey, hey, hey. I need you to tell me exactly what's going on here."

"Yes, they've got everyone out looking for her, including the local police. And you know how good Abby is at hiding when she wants to. I am one hundred percent certain she's okay. After all, she is FORT-ified with courage and planning." I put a definite emphasis on the key word there. This wasn't technically a pillow fort matter, but I could at least let Matt know it was related. Then he'd understand why I couldn't speak freely.

Matt was silent for a few seconds.

"Does this have anything to do with the pillow fort stuff from last summer?" he said finally. "Is that what this is?"

"YES," I said, nodding. "I feel the same. Abby certainly does know her way around the camp terrain after exploring it so thoroughly last year. And the staff are taking advantage of this CUSHION of time to resolve this on their own."

Director Haggis waved a hand and pointed at the phone, then himself. I nodded.

"So it's pillow forts again," said Matt. "And Abby's okay? Do you need us to do anything? Should we build some forts here?"

"No, I think everything will be fine without that, Mr. Hernandez. Director Haggis would like to speak to you now, since YOU are Abby's DAD. I'm sure she's fine and will be back soon, and we'll carry on having a wonderful time at this well-run and very safe camp."

There was a longish pause, long enough for me to become aware of the shouts and screaming from my fellow campers enjoying the start of their summer. Then Matt blew out a breath. "Okay, Maggie. Okay. You're her best friend and I know you'd never let anything happen to my sister. I completely trust you."

It took every ounce of focus in my body not to break into the world's biggest smile as I handed the phone back across the desk. My cheeks hurt from the effort.

Director Haggis spoke to Matt, who was apparently doing a decent job impersonating his dad, for only a few more minutes. There were lots of reassurances, and promises to keep in touch, and in the end it sounded like Matt was saying he was on his way, but might not make it to the island until late that night at the soonest.

I really hoped he'd worked out that he shouldn't come at all. Matt was the best, but the last thing I needed was him wandering around Camp Cantaloupe pretending to be his own father. He'd be way too, um, distracting. And with the entire rescue mission depending on me, that was the last thing I needed.

At last Director Haggis put the phone down and sat back in his chair. "Well," he said. "Thank you with your help with that. Mr. Hernandez seems like quite a calm and reasonable man, for a parent." He shook his head, his mustache fluttering. "I still can't understand why you two purposely set out to get lost. And you didn't even succeed, did you? Well, your *friend* did. You only succeeded in destroying an irreplaceable piece of camp history."

Oof. It was hard taking the blame for that all by myself.

"I'm sorry," I said. "But can't you rebuild it?"

"The Shipwreck Treehouse? Oh, no. Too many pieces were shattered in the collapse. Proving once again that it was totally unsafe to begin with. Several counselors and staff members have already requested we start building a replacement, but that takes money, which we don't have lying around. And anyway, given how distraught they all appear to be, it was the long, precious history of the thing that made it special. There's no way to replace that."

Oof times ten. That made one more thing I'd have to find a way to set right if I could.

Director Haggis looked at his watch. "You'd better head back to rejoin your cabinmates, Miss Hetzger," he said. "I have to meet the police when they get here, and you've got"—he consulted a schedule on the wall—"drama right now, then arts and crafts. Your buddy will be in class already. Would you like someone to show you the way?"

"No, thanks." I got to my feet. "I know where those classes are." I'd learned the layout of Camp Cantaloupe by heart as part of my prep work for the summer. I was in no hurry to rejoin my cabinmates or—ugh—my new buddy, but I had pillow fort kids to contact, and that meant surviving camp until arts and crafts was just the next stage of my mission.

A mission I was not going to fail.

FOURTEEN
Maggie

I found my class sitting in the grass outside the drama cabin, listening to the teacher, who was pacing back and forth. He was barefoot and had a manicured red beard, clear-framed glasses, a denim shirt tucked into denim shorts, and shadows under his eyes.

"—got some seriously major set design plans for this year," he was saying. "So I hope you're all ready to wo-*ooo*-rk." He hid the rest of his yawn behind the big stack of papers in his hands. Great, he'd probably been one of the teachers up half the night searching for Abby. He spotted me, and his frown told me I was right. "And now we're all present, break into pairs, please, and I'll come around with your scenes."

There was a surge of noise and movement as everyone jumped up, grabbing arms and screaming, fighting over who was with who. I waited for exactly no one to pick me, but Charlene found me in less than five seconds. "So, you're still here," she said. "Did Director Haggis yell at you? He seems like the kind of director who yells. Also why aren't you expelled?"

I shrugged. "Sorry, just not. And Director Haggis didn't yell. He wanted me there when he called Abby's dad." I looked around. "Are we a team, then?"

"Obviously!" Charlene said. "And what are you two staring at?" She rounded on a pair of boys who were openly eavesdropping.

"That girl is still missing?" one of them asked. I nodded. The boys shared a look. "That's bad."

"The moose should have rescued her by now."

"She must be really, *really* lost."

"Or hurt."

"Or abducted by aliens!"

"Or kidnapped by pirates!"

"Or—"

"That's enough, break it up," cut in the drama teacher. "Don't let those wild imaginations run away with you just yet. I'm sure the missing kid is fine and will turn up soon."

I wanted to burst out laughing. *Wild imaginations?* These boys weren't even scratching the surface. They had absolutely nothing on me.

The teacher handed the boys a bundle of papers, then turned to me and Charlene. "There are only two left," he said, "so I'll let you choose. Would you rather do *Orpheus and Eurydice* or *Theseus and the Minotaur*?"

I blinked. "What is this for, exactly?"

"Your senior scenes. You'll be performing them at the end of the week."

"What?"

"It's camp tradition. You hear the old Greek myths your junior year; you perform them first week your senior year. So, which one?"

I had no idea. I looked over at Charlene, but she was frowning at the two boys, who were laughing over something in their script.

"The second one, I guess," I said. If I had to do a scene, I didn't want it to be about Orpheus. I knew that story after last summer, when Uncle Joe had named his favorite whale Orpheus because they were both super-good singers. But the story ended all sad, with Orpheus losing the person he cared about most forever. And given the Abby situation, I didn't need to be acting out a story like that.

I scanned the script as the teacher walked away, shouting at us all to pick our parts and get practicing.

"Um, okay," I said, shuffling the papers. "Looks like there's one big part and three little ones. Do you want to be the main guy on a mission, or the king, the girl with the string, and the monster thingy?"

Charlene didn't reply. I looked up. She was still glowering at the boys. "Hello? Should we maybe, you know, start?" It honestly didn't matter to me—I had a rescue mission taking up most of my brain. But I couldn't fast-forward the clock, and practicing a play seemed like a decent way to fill the next forty-five minutes.

Charlene looked at me. "I don't think it would, you know," she said.

"What?"

"The ghost moose. Those boys were wrong. I don't think it will rescue Abby, and it definitely wouldn't have rescued you."

"Huh?"

"Think about it—you and Abby got lost on *purpose*. Abby did a much better job getting lost than you, but obviously the moose saw right through it, because she hasn't been rescued back yet. It would never reward someone trying to cheat. Your plan was a complete waste. And now"—the full power of her glower turned on me—"the whole summer will be messed up. You know they're gonna double down on rules and head counts and stuff, even when Abby gets found. It's seriously unfair and inconvenient."

Inconvenient? There was that word again. "Oh, I'm so-o-o

sorry," I said. "Maybe next time I see the moose, I should ask it to tell Director Haggis to relax."

Charlene's eyebrows disappeared into her bangs. "You have never seen the moose, Maggie.".

"Actually, I already did!" I hadn't meant to tell anyone that, but I couldn't help it.

"When?"

"Last summer."

"Ha! You weren't even here last summer, so how could you have seen it?"

"I can't tell you that part."

"Or, you know, you're making this up for attention. I think—"

"Hey hey hey!" The drama teacher strolled by, twirling a whistle. "Less talk, more acting over here, please!"

I glared at Charlene as I handed over her script, but with the teacher watching, we had no choice.

"You play the three little parts," she announced. "I'll be the main character on a mission. It'll be more believable that way."

It was my turn to glower, biting back a retort that would have gotten me even deeper in trouble. I had light-years more mission experience than Charlene. We weren't even in the same universe. I was on one right now! Ugh. Why did no one here know how good I was at stuff?

Although my spy senses had caught something interesting: Charlene had already bragged about having plans for the summer, but now she was hinting she had a full-blown mission. What could she possibly be up to? Was it her mission to get every other kid in camp in trouble with the teachers? To give ten lectures a day until the end of summer?

"Fine," I said. "I'm happy doing most of the work if you want to take it easy."

Charlene's mouth fell open, but the sound of tires tearing over gravel cut through our argument. The drama teacher stopped twirling his whistle. The whole class looked across the field.

Two dark blue SUVs were pulling up in the little parking strip in front of the admin building. ORCAS ISLAND POLICE was written on the sides in yellow, above an official-looking seal. The doors opened, then slammed, and four people in matching uniforms marched toward Director Haggis, who was coming down the steps to meet them.

The local police had arrived.

"Wow," the teacher said. "That's serious." He caught my eye and blinked. "I mean, it's probably no big deal!" He faked a smile. "I bet those folks are only here so the director can say they're involved. They'll probably just do a sweep through the woods near camp looking for clues. Anyway, your friend will be back safe and sound before they're done, right?" His smile was sliding into more of a grimace. For a camp teacher, he wasn't all that good at talking to kids. *"Anyway,* how about you two keep working on that scene? Your friend can join your group when she gets back!" He waved again and walked off, clutching his whistle with both hands.

Charlene flipped through her script. "He's right," Charlene said irritably. "Let's get this over with."

I stared down at the pages in my hand, pondering.

The local police being there should actually be a good thing, since they'd want to do their own search before calling for more authorities. That should buy me enough time to put my plan into action. I'd just have to make extra certain they weren't still searching when I snuck out that night.

There was a new Charlene clue to consider here, too. Her blond bangs had whipped around like a duck taking off from the lake when the teacher mentioned "a sweep through the woods near camp," and a look of genuine alarm had flashed across her face.

And now here she was, staring right through her lines, clearly thinking hard about something else. Did Charlene really have a real mission of her own, after all?

Maybe I wasn't the only one at Camp Cantaloupe keeping secrets.

FIFTEEN
Maggie

By the end of drama class, Charlene and I had managed one complete read-through of the not-very-long script, which was impressive considering we were both so distracted by our own plans and problems that we even forgot to keep fighting. We headed off to arts and crafts with the rest of the group in silence.

Abby had described the art cabin for me in her postcards the year before, but hearing about it and walking into it were two very different things.

It was, in one word, dramatic. There were faded posters overlapping each other on every bit of wall; metal shelves collapsing under paint cans and stacks of butcher paper; jar after jar of googly eyes, brads, rainbow glitter, and fuzz-bristled paintbrushes; colonies of lopsided easels, stools, and drying racks; and—best of all—two dingy sofas and a spray-painted loveseat shoved into the back corner. I grinned. Almost everything I needed to build a new pillow fort network was right there in front of me.

"Hello, everyone!" Ms. Sabine trilled as our class tromped in. She was wearing turquoise-and-purple overalls today, topped with a massive straw sun hat and a collection of jelly necklaces. "Come in, come in! We're starting this summer with—yes, yes, come in, gather round—a collage festival! I've arranged some exciting supplies on the tables for you. Find a place, dive in, and let your imaginations run wild!"

There were a few eyes rolled at her enthusiasm, but everyone found chairs around the long, beat-up tables and began gluing construction paper, dried pasta, seashells, string, and bits of wood to cardboard squares.

Charlene steered me to a spot at the end of the farthest table.

I looked up and down the heaps of junk, relieved at the lack of fabric. Phew! That meant the scrap bin might still be just the way it was last summer when Abby found that patchwork quilt. All I needed was an excuse to search it.

I raised my hand as Ms. Sabine walked by. "Could I maybe use some different materials?" I asked. "I've always felt inspired by, you know, fabric . . . and cloth . . . and stuff."

"Oh, hello," Ms. Sabine said, the smile dropping from her

face. "You're the girl who broke the treehouse, aren't you? Quite the way to win yourself a place in Camp Cantaloupe history, dear." Charlene's head snapped up beside me.

Ms. Sabine examined me for a moment like I was a strange form of modern art she was trying to decide if she liked. Then her face split into a smile and she leaned in. "I'm not supposed to say," she whispered over the clacking of her jelly necklaces, "being a teacher and all, but when I heard what you did, I said to myself, 'Now there is an independent spirit!' Taking your destiny into your own hands! Pursuing your dream of seeing the moose! It's a sign of a courageous risk taker who trusts her instincts, and that's the first thing you need to become a great artist. Even if I am heartbroken to lose the treehouse."

"Um, thanks," I said, trying to keep up. Charlene, whose circle of cardboard was already half covered in even rows of dried pasta, was looking furious. "So, can I use some scrap fabric?"

Ms. Sabine stood up, throwing both arms over her head. "The world is yours, dear. Or at least, the contents of this cabin. Follow your inspiration!"

I nodded in thanks, turned my back on Charlene, and went to check out the rest of the room. After a bit of searching, I found the famous scrap-fabric bin crammed between one of the paint shelves and a tower of empty plastic buckets.

The clamor and chatter of the rest of the cabin seemed to fade away.

Okay. This was it. My entire plan hinged on finding what I needed somewhere in here. This had to happen.

I pulled out the top piece of fabric and held it up, spilling little scraps all over the floor.

"Careful!" sang Ms. Sabine from across the room. "Any mess made here, you clean up yourself!"

"She should clean up what's left of the treehouse, then," Charlene said loudly.

Ms. Sabine tsk-tsked, but a ripple of laughter ran through the class. I ignored them all and resumed my search.

There was way more material crammed in the bin than it looked like from the outside. I dug and dug, and the pile around my feet grew and grew, until finally—*yes!*—right at the bottom, hacked and fraying but still mostly intact, I found the tail end of a patchwork quilt.

I ran my fingers from square to square, until with a jolt I found the one I was looking for: soft green velvet shot through with gold thread. Thank all that was good whoever made this quilt used a repeating pattern. Another square of fabric from the First Sofa had survived! And I was holding it in my hands.

I had to contain an actual whoop of joy. For once everything in this place was going right! I just had to get through the rest of this impossibly long day, stay awake until everyone fell asleep, then sneak out again and break in here so I could start building forts. It was a tallish order, even for me, but the clock was ticking, and I was not about to leave Abby hanging.

Director Haggis came to see me during dinner that night—sloppy joes, not cucumber casserole, thank the ghost moose. "I thought you should know Mr. Hernandez called," he said. "He's having car trouble and won't be able to get here until tomorrow. It's a real shame." Director Haggis didn't look like it was a real shame. He looked like it was a massive relief.

"Oh, too bad."

"Yes. I know you were probably looking forward to seeing him," Director Haggis said. He paused. "Oh, well." And he walked away, whistling.

After dinner, the littlest kids sang us songs about woodchucks and tadpoles around the barricaded campfire. And then we all headed for bed.

Charlene had apparently decided that her buddy duties stopped at the cabin door, and most of our cabin got pulled into a disagreement about some video game I'd never heard of, so I got a little time to myself before lights-out.

I pulled out a book, trying to pretend I was off on a grand adventure like I should have been, but I couldn't keep my mind on the page. After reading the same paragraph five times in a row, I finally had to admit that what I really needed was someone to talk to. Someone who would understand just how frustrating it was being trapped here. Someone who would appreciate the brilliant plan I'd come up with to fix things. Someone to confirm I was doing good.

What I needed was Abby.

But Abby was gone, possibly in mortal danger, and I couldn't even send her a postcard.

Except, hey, I could still write one.

I dug around in my bag, pulled out a postcard with a cartoon map of Orcas Island on the front, propped myself up on my pillow, and poured out my troubles to my best friend.

Dear Abs,

It's been almost twenty-four hours since you disappeared through the trapdoor, and everything here is terrible. In case you couldn't tell, I'm still stuck at camp. Everyone hates me for breaking the treehouse (oh, yeah, it collapsed, by the way) (on me) (which is why I couldn't follow after you), and Director Haggis assigned CHARLENE to be my BUDDY and watch over me and guard me everywhere, and we have to do a scene together in drama, and there are police searching the woods for you, and basically it's gonna take all my secret-agent skills to sneak out tonight and launch my rescue plan. It'll work so long as everything goes to plan. Obviously. Because that's the plan.

Hope you're not trapped in a fire pit or ancient Greek
labyrinth or

Or what? I tapped my pen on my knee, staring around
the cabin. Why couldn't I think of more dangers Abby could
have run into? Why was my brain so full of camp stuff? What
was this place doing to me? I tapped some more, then put the
pen back on the paper.

an even worse summer camp than this one. If things can
just work around here for once, I'll see you soon. Somehow.

Love,

Mags

I finished writing—wrapping all the way around the edges
of the card in tiny letters, because it turned out I had a lot to
say—just as our counselor called a truce in the video-game
argument and told us all to get ready for bed and lights-out.

I tucked the postcard into my pack beside my socks. It
would make a nice welcome-home present for Abby once I
got her back. Which, depending on what the kids at NAFAFA
knew, could be as soon as tonight.

SIXTEEN
Abby

The Little Lagoon echoed with the sounds of me and Joe laughing and hugging and shouting all at once.

"What did you—"

"—the same time!"

"But how—"

"—is this island—"

"—should've brought a surfboard!"

"Enough!" hollered Antonia as she and Helene caught up to us. Joe and I quieted down. The singing and music had stopped too. Everyone was watching.

"It appears the castaways know each other," said Helene. "That certainly is . . . convenient."

"This is Joe," I said, flapping a hand and completely unable to stop grinning. Joe looked just the same as the last time I'd seen him. Well, he wasn't wrapped up like a blanket burrito and lying in the back of a pickup truck with a broken leg, but he was still tall and balding, with eyes that crinkled when he smiled. "He's my best friend's uncle." I whapped him on the arm. "How did you get here?"

"We can all get our answers in a moment," cut in Helene. "First we must follow procedure and get this party officially started. Take your places, everyone!"

There was a cheer from the crowd.

"I raised Helene to run a very efficient party," Antonia told me as we got in our floaties and pushed off from the shore.

In no time Antonia, Helene, Joe, and I were floating in a little clump at the center of the lagoon near the musicians. The others crowded around us, holding hands and linking arms to stay together on the gentle movement of the water. I grinned as I caught sight of Ariadne, calmly drifting through the crowd on a small floaty shaped like a sunflower.

Helene got to her feet, balancing perfectly on her inflatable walrus. The ring of keys swung at her side. "Welcome, everybody," she called. "Welcome to this emergency party. Thank you for coming. Is everybody floating comfortably?"

The crowd cheered.

"Did everybody sing a song?"

The crowd cheered again, and the musicians played a few bars of a jig.

"Does everybody love this crew?"

The loudest cheers yet.

"Right, then." Helene clapped her hands. "Party business. We are here to introduce two new people who have somehow joined us here in our home. I know we all have hundreds of questions about who they are, where they came from, and how they got here, so we are going to get everyone on the same page as efficiently as possible!"

More cheers and snatches of song from the crowd. They sure did seem like they were having fun.

"First, we have Castaway Number One," Helene announced, stepping onto the beverage raft and holding out a hand to Joe. "Come on up and say hello."

Joe was wobbly on his giant floaty rubber ducky, but with Helene's help he got himself onto the raft beside her. "Please tell our crew who you are, Castaway Number One," Helene said, "and share a little about yourself."

"Uh, sure," said Joe, squinting around at the floating crew in their fancy hats and outfits. "My name's Joe," he called. "I'm thirty-eight. I'm a whale scientist. I mostly study humpback whale songs and other marine mammal noises."

"Woo! Whales!" shouted a voice out in the crowd, and everyone cheered. Joe joined in, his boa waving in the breeze.

"And where did you come from, Joe the Whale Scientist?" asked Helene. She sounded like a TV interviewer.

"I've lived all over the world, depending on where I'm researching," said Joe. There was an "ooooh" from the crowd. "But just recently I've been back up in Alaska, at this bay where I've been studying for a while. I had a big discovery there last year, and got some awesome grant money that let me come back this year with cutting-edge equipment. It's been super fun!"

Antonia led a round of applause.

"And how, Joe the Successful Whale Scientist who was recently in Alaska, did you get here?" asked Helene, spreading her arms wide. The floating crew leaned in closer.

"Well, it all started because of that new equipment," said Joe. "There are no whales up in that area yet, and I was doing a baseline recording of the bay, just to have a sample of what it sounded like on its own, and I kept getting the strangest readings. I kept hearing Atlantic porpoises chattering, but very faint, like they were coming from the other end of a long tunnel. I thought there must be something wrong with the machinery, but everything tested out fine. So the only thing to do was investigate the bay itself. I got out my scuba gear, swam down to get a look, and found a door."

"A door?" I said, sitting up too fast and almost tipping my teacup. Antonia shushed me.

"A door!" said Joe. "Just standing open in a frame at the bottom of the bay. And there was all this sediment getting sucked right into it, like a current. I swam in to get a closer look, and whoosh! I got pulled through. Then suddenly I was in a big bubbling surge of water, shooting for the surface. I barely had time to look around and realize I was a long way from home before I was being hauled in and arrested." He turned to Helene. "By you!"

Helene bowed, and the crew whooped and cheered.

"All right," she called to the crowd. "Did everyone hear Joe's story?"

"Yes!" replied the crowd.

"And did everyone believe it?"

"Yes!"

"And does everyone understand exactly what happened?"

"Yes!"

"I don't," I said to Antonia, and got shushed again.

"Thank you so much, Joe. Please return to your seat," said Helene. Joe waved to the applauding crowd, lifted a foot, misjudged the distance to his rubber ducky floaty, and fell face-first into the lagoon.

As the crew nearby jumped in to help him, Helene held out a hand, inviting me up for my turn on the beverage raft.

"Presenting Castaway Number Two," cried Helene, when everything had settled down. "Same introduction, please; your name and a little bit about you."

I looked out into the watching crowd, taking a second to

let it all sink in. Two days ago I was at home, eating pan-cakes in my pajamas with my dad and brothers and Tamal, Samson purring on my lap. Now I was at a party, with all these pirates—or whatever they were—floating in a lagoon on a strange little island in the middle of who knew where. And oh, look, the other chickens were up from their nap and pecking around the shore. And there went Ariadne on her floaty to say hello to them.

My heart gave a serious Maggie-missing pang. She should have been here for this.

"Um, okay, hi!" I said. "My name is Abby. I'm twelve and a half years old, and I, um, have an amazing cat named Sam-son." It was the first thing I thought of.

"Woo! Cats!" shouted the same voice in the crowd, and everyone cheered.

"And where did you come from, Abby, Keeper of Sam-son?" asked Helene.

"Well, I live in Seattle," I said. "But I just started summer camp at Camp Cantaloupe on Orcas Island, which is near Seattle. I was there with my best friend, Maggie."

"Woo! Maggie!" shouted Joe, who was back on his rubber ducky and soaking wet. Antonia shushed him.

"And how, Abby, Keeper of Samson, Friend of Maggie, and Goer to Camp Cantaloupe," Helene said, spreading her arms wide, "did you get here?"

The crowd all leaned in again to listen. I told them what I'd told Antonia and Helene, adding a few more details about the Shipwreck Treehouse, and the fall, and my confusion as I'd arrived on the island. "And when I got to my feet," I finished, "I was standing on that big stump over in the trees. And there was no sign of any way back."

There were no cheers. No whooping. The whole crew, from shore to shore of the lagoon, was utterly silent.

"Thank you, Abby," said Helene, her eyes going as bright and sharp as her mother's. "That was a well-told story, but there is one important detail you appear to have left out: if the trapdoor has been part of that treehouse for as long as you say, how did you and your friend manage to be the first to open it?"

There was the question. The tension around the lagoon spiked. I could feel it humming in the air. I adjusted my green eighties headband, wondering if the Italian duchess who'd owned it before ever faced a situation like this.

"Um, that's sort of a long story," I said.

"This is sort of a long party. Please tell us."

I took a deep breath and told them everything. It took me ten full minutes to recap the events of the previous summer. There were audible laughs from the crowd at first as I laid out the basic facts about the pillow fort networks, but that all stopped when I got to the part about Versailles. The idea that there had been kids running in and out of le Petit Salon ever since the room was locked seemed to utterly shock them. And when I told them about the Oak Key hanging beside the door all this time, and how generations of kids had tried it out on the locked door of le Petit Salon from the inside, they all but fell off their floaties.

"So yeah," I said at last. "That's what happened last summer. Then this year we brought the key to camp with us and tried it out. And that's how I ended up here, meeting all of you." I gave Helene a smile. She didn't return it. She and the rest of the crew looked like I'd hit each of them in the face with a pie. They were, from one side of the lagoon to the other, entirely and completely agog.

Finally Antonia coughed, and Helene glanced up.

"Protocol!" Antonia whispered.

"Protocol," said Helene, almost to herself. "Yes." She gave her head a shake. "All right," she called. "Did everyone hear Abby's story?"

"Yes," replied the crowd.

"And did everyone believe it?"

"Yes ... ?"

"And does everyone understand exactly what happened?"

There was an outbreak of murmuring and heads ducking together.

"Sort of!" shouted the lady in the T. rex outfit who'd

answered Antonia when we arrived.

"That will have to do," said Helene. "Now, Abby, there is one last thing, which I think will explain why we are all so shocked by your story. My mother tells me you've heard the full tale of Captain Emily. You should know that over the years Captain Emily's last words have become enormously important to this crew and this island. They've shaped our traditions and customs since the day we lost her. But we aren't all in complete agreement over them. My mother, for example, has interpreted Emily's words to mean someone must stay in the Palace forever, maintaining what remains of the home the first crew built." She looked over at Antonia. "No matter how much her own family would like her to join them below."

Antonia shook her floofy-hatted head defiantly from her floaty. "Captain Emily distinctly said, *'Look after the Palace for me,'* dear. I don't see how that could be plainer!"

"She also said, *'Keep the crew safe,'* Mama," Helene replied. "And it would be easier to keep you safe if you would just let the Palace go and move below!"

"I keep myself safe!" Antonia shouted, her voice echoing over the lagoon. I looked around, expecting the crew to be as uncomfortable as I was with all this family bickering, but the faces I could see looked bored, and kind of annoyed. Apparently this wasn't the first time the crew had heard this argument.

Helene turned back to me, shaking her head. "Anyway, Abby. In the Island Underneath, we have our own important tradition, this one based around the captain's ring of keys. Captain Emily gave them to her first mate along with her last words, and the ring of keys has been passed down from first mate to first mate ever since." She pulled the key ring off her belt.

"I am the current first mate, and these are the keys." She gave them a jangly shake. "These are the keys to all the doors that were saved and all the doors that sank into the sea. All except one: the one Captain Emily lost. For first mates, and the whole crew of the Island Underneath, finding the final key and putting it alongside the others on this ring has become almost a quest, something we have dreamed of without success for a very, very long time." The tuba player blew three sad notes. "So what I want to know is this: do you still have the key you call the Oak Key with you, and may we have it back?"

The whole crew sat up very straight on their floaties as the tension rippling in the air went right off the charts.

"Oh, sure," I said. "It's no use to me anymore, right?" And that was true, now that the trapdoor at Camp Cantaloupe was open. It wasn't like the key went to anything else. Ben and some of the other pillow fort kids might want it back for nostalgia's sake, but it sounded like Helene and the crew were its real, proper owners.

After hundreds of years, the Oak Key was finally coming home.

I reached into my pocket, wrapped my fingers around the cool metal of the key, and pulled it out. Helene held out her hand. I placed it on her palm, and she smiled. It was a sweet smile, full of a sort of little-kid wonder, like I'd just told her she could fly. She looked down. The sun reflecting off the water shimmered across her face.

The smile disappeared.

"Is this . . . a very bad joke?" she said.

I looked down, too, and my breath caught.

The key in Helene's hand wasn't silver—it was a dull, dark gray. And it wasn't carved with oak leaves and a shining sun, it was plain and smooth. It lay there like a dead leech, out of place and wrong, across her half-curled fingers.

This was not the Oak Key. I'd never seen this key before in my life.

SEVENTEEN
Abby

The party had collapsed into chaos.

Helene and Antonia were in a huddle with half a dozen crew members on the beverage raft, all talking at once. The new key was being passed from hand to hand around the lagoon, frantic questions and arguments following in its wake. And Ariadne had somehow managed to invite the other chickens onto her sunflower floaty, which was spinning farther and farther from the shore while the chickens piled on top of each other, trying not to get knocked off.

I was back on my teacup beside Joe, checking my pockets for the thousandth time. Where the cucumber casserole was the Oak Key? And how on earth had I picked up a brand-new one instead?

It was clear that not getting the Oak Key had been a

massive disappointment for all the crew, but especially Helene.

I had to try and figure out what happened. What would Maggie do here?

Maggie would tell me to retrace my steps.

First things first, then. I definitely went through the trap-door with the Oak Key in my pocket. I landed on my back in the dark and freaked out a bit. I pushed on the slats and panels of the sofa. I heard the key fall out and hit the floor. I reached down and found it. . . .

"By my knees!" I said out loud.

"What?" said Joe. The sun was starting to dry him off after his plunge into the water, and wispy little hairs were standing up from his head.

"The key! Sorry, I was just remembering." Fireworks were going off in my brain. "When I was shoving my way out from under the sofa, I heard the key hit the floor, and it turned up way down by my knees. I figured I'd just kicked it or some-thing, so I stuck it back in my pocket. But what if I picked up that new key instead?"

Joe frowned for a second; then his face lit up. "Oh! I get it! And you think you left the Oak Key there in its place?"

"I must have. And then that means . . . hey, Antonia! Helene!" The mother-daughter pair broke off their conver-sation on the beverage raft and looked over. "I think I know what happened!" And I told them what I'd told Joe.

Antonia and Helene looked at each other, then back at me.

"You dropped it in le Petit Salon?" said Helene.

"And just happened to find a new one?" said Antonia. "Shouldn't one of your pillow fort friends have found this other key lying around a long time ago?"

"That's the best part." I flapped a hand at them. "Remember how you said Captain Emily was all sad because she lost the Oak Key in the sofa cushions? What if King Louis did the same thing with that other key—"

"We've named it the Iron Key!" interrupted one of the crew. I realized everyone was leaning in listening again. A lady on an inflatable wine bottle held up the new key and waved.

"Sure, fine, cool," I said. I had to get my theory out before I forgot it. "So, what if King Louis lost the Iron Key in the sofa cushions too, and when he went looking, he found the Oak Key and was all 'Whoa!' and kept it instead because it was cooler looking. And so the Iron Key stayed in the cushions and maybe worked its way into the secret back panel, which didn't get opened for hundreds of years until I got trapped under the sofa and started kicking and shoving!"

There was a pause while all the floating crew members sorted that out. "So," Helene said finally, "the key we want is lying under a sofa in Versailles, and the key we have goes to . . . what, exactly?"

"The door to le Petit Salon!" I shouted, so excited I kicked my feet in the water. "The Iron Key is the key to the little room! We found it!"

"*You* found it," said Joe. We high-fived. Oh my Samson. Maggie was going to completely freak out over this.

"And what does that mean?" Antonia asked. "Having the key to le Petit Salon?"

"It's super, *super* important to the pillow fort kids," I said. "And to the people who study Versailles. Maggie told me the tour guide they overheard said that's why no one's broken down the door or forced their way in. They decided to let the mystery stay a mystery. Only now it's not a mystery to us! We have the key!"

"But not the key we *need*," said Helene, frustration clear in her voice. I blinked. "It's the Oak Key we want, Abby. We almost had it, but you lost it again. And if the door that led to the sofa is truly destroyed, this time it may be lost forever."

The bobbing crew all murmured their agreement, and the bartender couple raised their glasses sadly. Ariadne and the chicken tower floated by. Even they seemed serious now.

"But, hang on, we have the key to that little room, right?" said Joe. "Why don't we just head over there, unlock the door from the outside, and go in to look for the key Abby dropped?"

"Ha!" Helene's laugh sounded almost exactly like Maggie's. "You think it would be that easy, do you?"

"Yes?" said Joe.

"Do not be ridiculous, Joe," Helene said. "We have no loops to Versailles, and the logistics of traveling there over land and sneaking into that room without detection would be extraordinary."

"Maybe we don't have to get in from the outside," I said. Ooo, more brain fireworks! "You said you still have the other doors, right? The ones that were saved when the ship was sinking?"

Helene raised her eyebrows. "Of course. The looped doors are how we get food and clothing and supplies and everything else. They're how we visit our children at school. They're the only way off this island. They're how we survive."

"And they all go to real palaces and castles around Europe?"

"They do. But as I just said, there are none leading to Versailles now that the door you came through is apparently broken beyond repair."

"No, that's totally not a problem! We don't need a door—we can get in through the pillow forts. Kids from around the world do it all the time."

I got hit with two confused frowns. "I don't see how that would be possible," said Antonia. "There are none of these magical pillow fort contraptions on this island."

"But there are in the palaces!" I said. "Or, well, there *were*. Maggie told me about it. Louis linked the First Sofa to palaces all over Europe so he and his friends could sneak around and visit each other. What if some of those forts are still there, hidden in palaces that you all have loops to? No one uses them anymore, and I never heard anything about them being monitored. We can use the *loops* to get to the *links*." I grinned and couldn't stop myself saying it. "By our powers combined!"

Their eyes slid out of focus as they worked out what I was saying. Antonia looked at Helene. Helene looked at Antonia. Ariadne's floating chicken pile collided with the musician's raft, and a feathery sort of invasion began.

"It could work," said Helene.

"It has potential," said Antonia.

Helene shrugged. "Then it's worth a try. Anything to recover that key." She got to her feet and shouted, "Ahoy!" Her voice echoed crisp and clear around the lagoon.

The floating pirates snapped to attention. "Ahoy!" they all shouted back.

"We have a plan to retrieve the Oak Key!" Helene declared. Everyone cheered. One of the chickens pecked out a happy riff on the xylophone. "It's too late to clean up from this party and get started today, but tomorrow morning we will begin investigating the looped palaces for signs of magical pillow forts, which, according to Abby, should link back to the sofa in le Petit Salon, where Abby believes she dropped the key. So, did everyone hear that?"

"Yes!" shouted the crowd.

"Does everyone understand it?"

"Not really!"

"Oh. Well, does everyone believe it anyway?"

"Yes!"

"Excellent." Helene turned to me. "And you'll know how to use one of these pillow forts if we find one, Abby?"

"*When* we find one," I said. Because we had to. This whole wacky island adventure thing was fun, but I'd already been missing from camp way too long. And it looked like my only chance of getting anywhere near Camp Cantaloupe—or North America in general—was through the First Sofa. If I could get there, I could find the link to the NAFAFA Hub, ask for help, and get back to Maggie's and my summer before my face ended up splashed across the news.

"Joe has to come too," I said, pointing over at him. "Once we're in le Petit Salon, we can probably find him a way home through the network links, too."

"Ooh, that would be great," Joe called, air-cheers-ing me with his glass. "I have all my research and equipment and everything to get back to before the humpback migration starts, and I'm pretty sure I left the milk out on the counter in my cabin."

"Fine," said Helene, nodding. "Joe will come too. So we have our mission! Tomorrow morning we will meet and begin our visits to the palaces, and—yes, Abby, one more question?"

I lowered my hand. "I was just wondering how exactly we're going to sneak through all these palaces. I mean, it'll be daytime. Won't there be people there? Guards and tourists and stuff? Won't they get suspicious if they see us poking around looking under pillows?"

"We've got ways to deal with that, don't worry," said Helene. "But you and Joe will need to be thoroughly coached and prepared beforehand, so you'll have to be up early for training."

"Yay!" said Joe. "Training!"

"That means you should come below after this meeting, Abby," Helene continued. "It will make things easier in the morning, and we have plenty of spare rooms."

"No!" I said. Going below now would mean leaving Antonia behind alone. And from what I'd heard she'd had more than enough of that in her life. "I want to stay in the Palace. It might be the only chance I get!"

"Ooh, can I stay in the Palace, too?" piped up Joe.

Helene looked surprised, but she shrugged and turned to Antonia, who was gazing into the distance with a thoughtful frown.

"What do you think, Mama? Could our guests stay with you tonight?" Helene asked. "I'll be doing the formal training myself, but maybe you could give them some classic protocol pointers before sending them below for the mission?"

Antonia seemed to come back from a long way away. She drew herself up, her cape shimmering in the sun and the feathers in her hat waving in the sea breeze. "Certainly the castaways can stay in the Palace," she said. "But I won't be sending them below in the morning."

Wait, huh? I looked over at Joe. Was Antonia about to start making things difficult? Did she expect Helene to find the pillow fort and Oak Key by herself? Was I going to end up doing that dusting and cleaning after all?

"What do you mean?" asked Helene. "Why not?"

"Because Abigail says she can get us into le Petit Salon," Antonia said, her voice echoing around the lagoon. "And thanks to her we also have the key that will open the door into Versailles itself. Until today I never had any real hope of fulfilling the last of Captain Emily's final wishes—none of us did. But with Abigail here, that's all changed." She looked over at her daughter. "We have a chance to take a second swipe at Versailles, Helene, and really make them notice. And I refuse to just stand by and watch. So the reason I'm not sending the castaways to the Island Underneath tomorrow is because I will be bringing them down myself." She looked over the hushed crowd, her eyes shining. "I'm going on the mission with you."

EIGHTEEN
Abby

The shock of Antonia announcing she was going to pay a visit to the Island Underneath completely upended what was left of the planning party. It was all Helene could do to squeeze in a formal closing sea chantey and start herding the crew back home.

Antonia and I returned to the Palace, bringing Joe and the chickens, who had adopted Joe as their leader after he saved them from toppling into the water during the post-Antonia-announcement excitement. Ariadne was still up at the lagoon, enjoying a nice quiet float by herself on someone's inflatable saxophone.

Joe loved the Palace. He ran around like a little kid, yelling about how cool everything was, until Antonia got him under control and gave him a proper tour, making sure he was caught up on the Captain Emily story along the way.

Helene came up a while later, bringing an early dinner and something for me: the Iron Key.

"We decided you should hang on to it," she said at the smile on my face. "It's no use at all to us here. Just make sure you don't lose this one!"

Dinner turned out to be summer risotto with pesto and fried squash blossoms, plus caramelized pineapple-honeycomb ice cream for dessert. It was honestly the best food I'd ever had in my life. I'd always thought my dad was the greatest cook in the world, but this was on a whole other level.

"Where did you all learn to make food like this?" I asked, shoveling cheese-crisped squash blossoms into my mouth. "I mean!" I could barely speak. Hopefully my expression was getting the point across.

"Twelve of the crew members have trained in palace kitchens," Helene said. "They rotate being in charge of meals. It's gotten quite competitive. Which turns out well for everyone."

"Seriously," said Joe, around a mouthful of ice cream.

After dinner and dishes, Helene said good night, and Antonia insisted Joe and I go check out the stars before heading to bed. As soon as we stepped out from the boulder pile, I was glad she had. They were unbelievably, stunningly glorious. They splashed across the sky from horizon to horizon, white and blue and silver, so bright I could see my shadow in the sand. We'd only been up there for a minute before I saw my first shooting star, its reflection gliding through the waves.

I had a sudden flashback to climbing into the Shipwreck Treehouse, and the view of stars over the ocean I'd gotten before everything fell apart. Now here I was on a different island, in a different ocean, preparing to break into a bunch of European castles in a quest for a key I'd had and then lost.

For the hundredth time that day I thought of Maggie. Hopefully she was doing okay. Hopefully she was avoiding Charlene. Hopefully she wasn't attempting some completely impossible rescue mission while there was no one sensible there to stop her.

Joe and I kicked back on the beach, listening to the waves and staring up at the rainbow-dust-colored Milky Way for a long, long time. But eventually the yawns got the better of us, and we headed back in, full of starlight and ready for bed. Helene had helped us clean and prepare two mini-bedrooms: one with a dark blue four-poster bed for me near the kitchen, and one done all in red-and-gold plaid for Joe, just past the second library. Antonia was in the best bedroom way down near the fireplace, and we all yelled good night to each other from our separate wings of the Palace.

Joe's light went out almost immediately, but I sat up a little longer with my camp journal, doing my best to cram everything that had happened into a letter for Maggie.

Dear Mags,

Hiiiiiii! Okay, so last time I wrote you, I thought I was alone here. And whoooo was I wrong!

I'm still on the island, but now I'm in a blue four-poster bed, in a palace that's all crammed into a sort of underground basement. There are chickens keeping guard outside. There's no way I'll be able to write down everything that happened, so here are some useful facts from today:

—A long time ago a bunch of nice-sounding pirates led by someone called Captain Emily found this island, which has magic trees that you can build links with.

—The tree links only go one way at a time (huge pain), so they made this super-complicated system to get a network going so they could sneak into palaces and steal stuff, and they called the links loops.

—After they lost their ship, they lived in a big palace on the surface, but they tore it down when spy planes were invented or something, and most of them live under it(?) now. Not sure what that means. I get to go check it out tomorrow.

—Guess what! Your uncle Joe is here, too! He says he went through a door he found in his bay up in Alaska and now he's here somehow! (I still have lots of questions about this.) Tomorrow we're going through the looped doors to check out some palaces (real ones) and see if we can find any pillow forts left over from Louis's original network. It's partly a mission to get back the Oak Key, which I totally dropped in le Petit Salon, and partly so Joe and I can maybe work out a way home.

—We have no plan for what to do if we don't find any pillow forts.

—There are waaayyyy more kinds of pool floaty than I thought there were.

—We need to find Joe a hat, because he already has a sunburn on top of his head.

Okay, enough useful facts. I never got my nap earlier, and I've been awake for ten thousand years and I'm in the fanciest bed ever and it's super comfy and goooood niiiight.

See you so soon, hopefully! We'll find out tomorrow!

Abs

NINETEEN
Maggie

I woke up with a start. The moon was blasting past the blinds on the other side of the cabin. Cantaloupe! I must have dozed off. I fumbled for my watch . . . 12:35. It was late. Much later than I wanted.

I began pulling back the covers and stopped dead. Charlene's bunk was empty.

I glanced around the cabin. *Okay. Don't panic.* She was probably just in the bathroom.

What to do? It was either head out now or lie down again, wait for Charlene to come back, keep waiting until she was fast asleep, *then* sneak out. Oof, that was not going to work. I might really fall asleep again if I had to lie there pretending I was. And tonight was my only chance. Another day of no Abby, and this place would be crawling with search-and-rescue officers, just like Director Haggis had said.

I was on my feet in three seconds, across the cabin with my supply pack on in eight, and padding out into the night in twelve. Charlene would notice I was out of bed when she got back, but hopefully she'd assume I was up to use the bathroom, too. I couldn't delay my mission another minute. I had to get to the Hub.

It felt weird sneaking out without Abby by my side. The night before it had been wonderful, all shining stars and pine-scented wind and the bubbling excitement of shared adventure. Tonight, the moon felt like a searchlight trying to pin me down. A chilly, mud-scented breeze was coming off the lake. Tree shadows stretched across the field like bars, and the cabins lurked in the darkness like they were hiding something.

Well, at least it didn't look like they were hiding the local police or squadrons of flashlight-waving counselors. If anyone was out searching for Abby, they weren't anywhere near camp. Maybe it was a good thing I'd overslept, after all.

My achy ankle wasn't happy about going on another mission, but it only slowed me down a little as I worked my way toward the classroom cabins, using all my super-spy skills to stay hidden. I was almost starting to enjoy myself when there was a snap of branches in the woods.

Faster than you could blink, I darted behind the nearest

pine tree and peered around the side. There was something, absolutely definitely a great big *something*, in the woods on the other side of the field. Everything went very still, except for the cold breeze breathing down the back of my shirt.

Another branch snapped in the silence, then another, and I heard a low, rumbling groan. I'd only met it once before, and in a totally different setting, but that didn't sound like the ghost moose of Camp Cantaloupe to me. Did they have bears on Orcas Island? Wildcats? Giant northwestern shadow leeches?

My fingers dug right into my piney friend's sticky bark as the creature charged out of the trees and burst into the moonlit field.

It wasn't the ghost moose. And it wasn't a bear. It wasn't even a wild cat.

It was Charlene Thieson, driving a golf cart.

She steered her little vehicle across the field, an empty rolly bin bouncing along behind her, and disappeared behind the maintenance shed.

What. On. Earth.

What was Miss Teacher's Pet doing? There was no way she was even supposed to be driving the camp golf cart, let alone at night, let alone through the woods.

A strange feeling danced across my brain, and it took me a second to realize I was impressed. Charlene knew the risks of sneaking out the same as I did, and here she was joyriding around camp after midnight.

I watched the maintenance shed for a solid three minutes, but Charlene didn't reappear. Hmm. The arts and crafts cabin was right in between us. If I was careful, I could make it. Just so long as Charlene stayed put.

It took all my best moves to dodge and dive from one dark place to another, zigging and zagging, but I made it to the arts and crafts cabin without a hitch. The window I'd cleverly unlocked during class was still in shadow. I slid the heavy frame up, wincing as it screeched, and heaved myself through.

Well, mostly through. The window came screeching back down just as I got my hips onto the sill, smashing my bag into the small of my back and trapping me like a bug. And right then, with my front half flailing inside the cabin and my legs kicking wildly behind me, someone spoke.

"You're doing that wrong, you know."

I jumped. Well, I spasmed against the frame.

"I can't believe you don't know how to sneak in a window," the voice said.

Ugh. Charlene. Of course. Any second now she'd start screaming for the counselors, and I would never live it down as long as I lived. Maggie Hetzger: the girl who broke the Shipwreck Treehouse, lost her best friend, and got stuck in a window in the middle of the night, all in her first two days at camp.

I kicked at the air, half hoping to hit her, but Charlene dodged my feet easily and came up beside me, peering in.

"What are you doing?" she asked.

"What does it look like? I'm trying to get free." I kicked and wiggled some more to demonstrate.

"But why are you trying to get through this window in the first place?"

"My business," I snapped. "Not yours." I was so annoyed at getting caught. This never would have happened back home. Why did plans *never* go right at this camp?

Charlene rapped her fingernails on the sill. "Well, speaking as your buddy, I think it is my business."

"Oh, yeah?" It was tricky trying to talk to her over my shoulder. "Then I guess it's *my* business to find out why I just saw you driving out of the woods in a golf cart."

The fingernails stopped.

There was a long, long pause. I did a little experimental kicking, but Charlene ignored it.

"You never saw that," she said finally.

"Did."

"Nope," said Charlene.

"Yup."

"Can you prove it?"

Shoot. She knew I couldn't. I kicked the air again.

"I'll take your silence as a no," Charlene said, sounding satisfied. "But what were *you* doing, running from tree to tree like a frightened bunny? It looked really weird."

My cheeks grew warm in the darkness. Of course she'd been watching.

"I was using advanced evasive maneuvers," I said. "You wouldn't understand. Now are you going to stand there interrogating me all night, or are you going to help?"

Charlene went silent again, leaving me feeling totally vulnerable. My future at this camp was in her hands. Along with my only hope of ever getting Abby back.

For one terrible moment I was certain she was going to leave me there, trapped. But then the window gave a screech, and the pressure on my back lifted. Freedom! I tumbled into the cabin with a thud that made the paint cans rattle. I got to my feet.

"Thanks," I said, testing my cranky ankle.

Charlene was still holding the window up. "No problem."

There was an awkward silence.

"So, yeah," I said. "Bye."

"Oh, no," Charlene said. "I'm your buddy. I'm coming in with you."

"What? No, you can't . . . I'm only—"

But Charlene did a little hop, threw one leg over the sill

like she was climbing on a bicycle, pulled herself neatly through, and dropped silently to the floor. The window slid shut behind her, as smooth and soft as velvet.

Dang, that looked pretty cool. Why was Charlene Thieson good at sneaking through windows?

We faced each other in the darkness. A thin line of moonlight sliced along the floor between us.

"So. What are you here for?" asked Charlene. Her blond bob cut floated eerily above the heather gray T-shirt she wore to sleep in. It was weird seeing her without her Safety Monitor sash.

"Nothing."

"Nothing? You snuck out of bed, used 'evasive maneuvers' across the field, and broke into the arts and crafts cabin in the middle of the night for nothing?"

I nodded.

"Okay," said Charlene. "Well, here's the thing: either you tell me what you're doing, or I start screaming my head off until every teacher and counselor in this camp comes running. And what do you think will happen then?"

The moonlight inched a little farther between us.

She had me. I'd never win if it came down to her word against mine. She could say she woke up and saw my empty bunk and came looking for me and found me breaking into this cabin. She could say I was sabotaging art projects or stealing glitter and tempera paints. She could say anything she wanted, and Director Haggis would believe her. She could get me sent home. She'd probably even get an award for being such a good buddy and checking up on me.

And if I did get sent home, my mom would have to fly back from her medical conference early, and she'd hear the news about Abby and insist on contacting Mr. Hernandez—the real one—and he'd cut his honeymoon short and fly home too. And Abby would be stuck where she was forever, because I'd never get a proper chance to rescue her.

Charlene had me cornered. And what was worse, she knew it.

"I was just . . . coming here to . . . work on my collage?" I tried. "No, no, you're right!" I held up both hands as Charlene, clearly not buying it, opened her mouth wide. "I'm here to . . ." Half-truth time again. A tiny plan was slapping itself awake in my brain. "To build a fort!"

"A . . . fort," said Charlene, suspicion drenching her voice.

"A pillow fort!" Time to employ some character-based deception. I made my voice wobble just the tiniest bit. "'Cause I don't know anyone here besides Abby, and I'm, you know, not good with new people. And everyone hates me for what happened with the treehouse. So I was just gonna build a pillow fort in here tonight and curl up and pretend everything was okay for a while."

I bit my lip, worried I was overdoing it. Although it was all mostly kind of true. The best secret agents and spies always based their stories in truth. It made the untrue bits harder to see through.

"I believe you, actually," said Charlene, eyeing me. "Abby said you built pillow forts last summer. Seems like that's your thing."

"When did she tell you that?" I asked. *Warning, warning!* Alarm bells started clanging in my head.

"During camp. You wrote and told her about it in one of your postcards, didn't you? I remember 'cause I thought it was weird how much mail she was getting. I made her read me some of them."

That sounded like exactly the sort of thing Charlene would do.

"So, a fort," she said, stepping over the line of moonlight and clapping her hands. "Where do we start? Do we grab a bunch of pillows? Or find a blanket and make a circle of chairs? What do we need?"

"*We?*" I said. "There's no *we* in this project."

"Oh, there definitely is. As your buddy, I'm supposed to help you transition into the camp experience. That's what Director Haggis told me. And if I'm stuck being your buddy, I'm going to be the best one possible, even if that means missing out on sleep to help build this pillow fort for you to be sad in."

Ugh. Why was Charlene so . . . Charlene?

Although this *might* turn out to be perfect. I needed two forts to make the link anyway. "Well, I guess," I said. "But if you're staying, you have to build your own place. I'm not sharing." Charlene rolled her eyes, but she nodded. "Cool," I said. "Then we start by taking the cushions off the sofas...."

It was dark in the back of the cabin, even with the moonlight, but of course Charlene knew where to find a safety flashlight kept by the door. We used it as little as possible in case someone saw, but it made the building process much easier. I built a simple symmetrical fort and tucked in the patchwork-quilt scrap I'd hidden during class, while Charlene slapped together a lopsided pillow monstrosity draped in a paint-splattered sheet. In a matter of minutes, we were done.

"Welcome to Fort Buddy, buddy!" said Charlene, sticking her head out from inside her fort, which was glowing softly from the flashlight. "Your forts always have names, right?"

"I am so not calling it that," I said, tugging my backpack of supplies into mine.

"Well, what's yours called? Maggie's Gloomy Place?"

"Ha, ha." I pulled a pen from my pack and threw it across to her. "Here, in case you need it. Every fort should have a pen."

Charlene tossed the pen over her shoulder without looking at it. I smiled. She didn't know it, but she'd just accepted a token from my fort, which meant we were linked. And that meant it was time to find the link and start attracting NAFAFA's attention.

"So, Maggie," said Charlene, propping her chin on her hands. "Now that you're safely in a pillow fort, do you want to talk to your camp buddy about why you're feeling sad?"

Ugh. Really? I was here for a rescue mission, not a therapy session.

"No, I don't want to talk about it," I said, shifting the pillow to my left and feeling around. There was sofa behind it. "Do you want to talk about why you were driving that golf cart through the woods by yourself?"

"No. And you still can't prove you saw that."

"Okay, then."

Charlene frowned at me, then peered up at the dark ceiling. "You know, I never got sad *my* first year," she said thoughtfully. "I was eight, and I loved sleepaway camp from day one. I don't think a lot of the other kids were as confident as me, but I helped them through it."

"Mmm," I said, checking the next pillow, and the one beside that. No link yet.

"Not everyone is good with people like I am, of course." Charlene seemed totally unconcerned that I wasn't responding to her terrible pep talk. "Abby almost is. She wasn't scared on her first day either. Or homesick. It was weird—all of us were talking about it, how she just seemed to fit right in. It was like she'd been coming to Camp Cantaloupe forever."

I twisted around to check behind the second-to-last pillow, silently praying to the First Sofa to do its thing before I was stuck at this camp with my Safety Monitor buddy forever. And there it was: a square of Charlene's pillow fabric. Finally!

I knocked the pillow over.

"Uh-oh," said Charlene, looking over her shoulder. "My fort's collapsing already. Good thing you're not in here or it would be a complete wreck like the treehouse!" She laughed at her own joke and sat up to repair the damage. I felt the pillow reappear under my hand.

I knocked it over again.

"Hey," I heard Charlene say. "What?" She reset the pillow.

I knocked it over.

"Is there a problem?" I called.

"It's this pillow—it won't stay put!"

Hello, pillow.

Goodbye, pillow.

"Uh-oh," I said, echoing Charlene's tone. Before she could put the pillow back again, I pushed myself through the link right into her fort, inches from her face. "Is there anything I can do to help?"

Charlene screamed.

"Wait," I said. "I *am* wrecking your fort. Sorry!" And I pulled back into mine, spun around, and gave her a sarcastic salute from the entrance.

It took Charlene several minutes to calm down.

"How is this happening?!" she said over and over. "What did you do?" In the end I had to crawl out and sit against one of the tables, waiting patiently as she went back and forth, back and forth, testing out the first link of our brand-new network.

"Okay," she said finally, propping herself up in the entrance to her fort. "Okay, okay, okay. You *have* to tell me how this works."

Briefly, I told her. I told her about the First Sofa, and the scraps of First Sofa fabric, and the rules and mechanics of networked pillow forts. She didn't look nearly as sure of herself when I finished. She looked a lot like Abby reacting to the news we were all going to have our cantaloupes confiscated.

"So this was why you snuck out here," she said as I returned to my new base. "You weren't just building a fort because you were sad. That was all a cover story for . . . this."

"Guilty," I said.

Charlene frowned. "But what was the point? Why did you want two forts that are . . . linked . . . so close together?"

I considered my answer. Telling her the rest would mean

telling her Abby wasn't actually camping somewhere in the woods trying to get rescued by the ghost moose. It would mean telling her about the trapdoor in the treehouse, and how we got the key, and above all, it would mean admitting I had no idea where Abby was now, and that I was building these forts in order to ask someone else for help.

And I was feeling too smug about Charlene's astonishment to admit that just yet. So I told her part of the truth.

"I needed two forts because I'm trying to get someone's attention," I said. "There are kids who monitor linked-fort activity, and they have answers I need. I can't go to them, so I built these forts to make them come to me."

"What kids?" asked Charlene.

Right on cue, a pillow to my right flopped open, and a young girl poked her head into the fort.

It was my turn to scream.

It was Kelly.

TWENTY
Maggie

"Will one of you please stop squealing and tell me what's going on?" Charlene demanded as Kelly and I hugged for the hundredth time.

We broke apart, grinning. I couldn't believe how good it was to see a friendly face. Even one I'd just seen before leaving for camp. Honestly, after everything that had happened since, it felt like years.

"This is my friend Kelly!" I said. "But what are you doing here? When did you get into the networks? And how?"

"The day you left," laughed Kelly. She looked awesome. When Abby and I had met her in her hospital-room fort last summer, Kelly was a friendly nine-year-old with wide eyes, a big heart, and even bigger plans to become an astronaut and bring hundreds of cats with her into space. And as we'd kept visiting her into the school year, and celebrated with her when she got to go home, and hung out with her at least once a month since, Kelly had only gotten louder, and happier, and more excited about pretty much everything. It was glorious. "And you'll never guess how I joined NAFAFA!" she went on, whapping me on the arm. My heart twinged. She'd picked up that habit from Abby.

"How how how?"

"It was after you and Abby dropped off Samson and all his stuff. I put Creepy Frog in my pillow fort for him, and I was moving things around so he wouldn't get his snaggle-paw caught so much, and one of the pillows fell down and there was *another fort*! And this kid with a clipboard showed up right away, and then there were lots of other kids, and everybody was talking at once. They wouldn't let me through until they figured out how I was linked in, and it turned out it was—" She paused dramatically. "Creepy Frog!"

"What?" I goggled at her. "Creepy Frog couldn't have linked you anywhere. He's not a token, he's just a stuffed animal."

"That's what I told them! But then they checked and found out there was a *feather* stuck in him. And Miesha remembered how she was covered in feathers from the big Hub pillow fight when she came over to give you the key last summer, and she says one must have gotten stuck to Creepy

Frog while you all were chasing that rat out of your fort!"

Ho-ly. Shipwreck. That was incredible! I caught a glimpse of Charlene beside me, her entire face from her bangs to her chin set on utter disbelief.

"And your new link led where? To the Hub?" I pressed on.

"Yeah!" said Kelly. "Right there!"

"So all this time we could have gotten back to the Hub just by building another pillow fort and putting Creepy Frog in it?"

"Totally!"

That was some serious news. Abby had taken her fort down in case any new kids we met at school thought it was immature or something, but I still had one in my bedroom, and so did Kelly. What a missed opportunity. We could have been running our own network all year!

Although, actually, we never did find out what happened with the NAFAFA election after we got cut off. Last I knew, Noriko was aging out as head of the Council, and Miesha was using us as leverage to get Ben's vote for her. I didn't even know if the west coast was still up for grabs, or who got elected leader. That could make a big difference in whether being linked in to NAFAFA would be fun or not.

Plus, if we'd shown up in the Hub during the school year, Ben would definitely have insisted we give the Oak Key back. And then we would have had to let everyone in on our discovery about the matching lock at Camp Cantaloupe, and I bet anything they would have insisted on coming here with us and taking over the whole mission.

Hmm. Maybe getting cut off had been a blessing in disguise. Maybe everything had worked out perfectly. Apart from the current situation with Abby missing, of course.

"So do you have your own new network, then?" I asked Kelly. "Are you running the west coast?"

Kelly shook her head. "Nope, I'm in Ben's network."

"Ugh! So he did get it. I'm sorry. He must be super smug."

"He is. But Miesha's head of the Council now, so she's been keeping him mostly under control."

"Yay, Miesha! And whew. What's Ben's new mega network called?"

"The Really Enormous Great Plains-Pacific Sofa Realm. You should see his banner in the Hub. It's kind of amazing."

"Well hey, why don't we go see it now?" I said. "Why are we just sitting here talking through the link?"

"Maggie, I'm so sorry, but I'm only here to say hi. They said in my training we're not allowed to bring anyone into the Hub without an okay from the Council. It's part of the new rules they set up after last summer."

"Why? What happened last summer?"

"You and Abby!"

"Oh. Right."

"They call it the . . ." Kelly screwed up her face, thinking. "The Hernandez-Hetzger Protocol. You two kind of caused some problems."

"Ha. That's fair. But look, Kelly, I really, *really* need to talk to Miesha and the rest of the Council. Abby's in trouble, and I need their help. And if you're saying we can't come into the Hub, then how am I supposed to—"

"Oop!" said Kelly, looking back over her shoulder. "Hang on, here comes someone else."

She scooched to one side, and a small boy in silver sunglasses appeared beside her in the gap.

"Maggie Hetzger!"

"Ben," I said, my heart sinking. Of course I'd reach out to my friends in NAFAFA and end up talking to my only enemy.

Charlene was spluttering behind me. I continued ignoring her.

Ben had grown a little in the last year—he was, what, ten now?—but he still looked like a character from a kids' book, overalls and all. And he was still carrying around that clipboard, stacked so high with papers that the clippy part looked ready to fall off. He was even pinker in the face than I remembered and breathing hard, like he'd just been running.

"Where," he hollered, his shiny sunglasses fixed on me, "is my key?"

"Firstly, hello to you, too," I said. "Secondly, it's not your key. The Oak Key belongs to everyone."

"Not to *you!*" Ben shouted. "You're not even a member of NAFAFA!"

"And thirdly," I pressed on, deciding I might as well get the big news over with, "I don't have it anymore. It's lost."

Ben's face locked in frozen horror, then drooped like a melting ice-cream cone.

"*Lost?* Wh-where did you lose it?"

I filled him and Kelly in on our adventures, right up until Abby fell through the open trap door when the fort collapsed, taking the key with her into the dark unknown.

Charlene had found her voice by the time I was done.

"So *Abby* wrecked the Shipwreck Treehouse?" she said. "And you're letting everyone at camp think it was you?"

"We both wrecked it," I said, annoyed. There were bigger issues than my camp reputation to think about here. I turned to Ben. "The important thing is, Abby and the Oak Key went through that door without me, and now it's smashed to pieces. I don't know how to figure out where she went, so I need you to let me into the Hub and help me find her."

Ben looked like he wanted to laugh and scream and cry all at the same time. "And what makes you think I'm willing to do that, Maggie Hetzger?" he said, his voice going squeaky. "You lost my key! Why should I do anything for you at all?"

"Because Abby is missing in some sort of . . . I don't know, *other* network because of that key. You're the ones obsessed with it, so you should help find her! Get your members to search the forts. Check with the other Continental Councils. Dig through the Archives for leads on where she went. You can't just do nothing!"

"And *you* can't just expect NAFAFA to drop everything and look for her!" Ben shot back. "This is not my responsibility. And believe me"—he flapped his overstuffed clipboard in the air—"I have plenty of those these days!"

"But what if she's hurt? Or trapped? Or in mortal danger?" I said. "What if she fell into an undersea bunker full of armies of diamond-plated scorpion crabs, and they made her talk and found a pillow fort to break into, and now they're only minutes away from a full-scale invasion of the Hub? I don't understand how you can possibly believe this isn't your problem!"

"Because it's *not*, Maggie Hetzger." Ben pushed his sunglasses up firmly. "I'll let the rest of the Council know that you've lost the Oak Key and inform you when we make a decision. I'll even allow you to keep this new network up until then. But that's all."

"No, no, no!" I was already shaking my head. "Not good

enough. I know Miesha will want to help find Abby. Tell her I want to talk to the whole Council face to face." I pointed a finger at him. "I mean it. Go tell her now."

Ben smiled. It was the same unpleasant I-know-better-than-you smile I remembered from the summer before. "The thing is, Maggie Hetzger," he said, "your little fort here is in my network's territory, so I control what access you get to NAFAFA and the Hub. Even Miesha would back me up on that. And I'm saying no."

Ugh. He was so smug. I couldn't even look at him.

But the truth was I did need him on my side. He could ruin everything if he wanted. He could shut down my new network. And I had no backup plan if this didn't work out.

"Fine," I said, trying to keep my face calm while I strangled one of the pillows. This was so unfair. I hadn't even gotten to use any of the gear in my supply pack tonight! "If that's how things are, I guess I'll just have to wait to hear back from you."

"That's how things are," Ben said. "I'm glad you recognize the situation. And since you don't have my key, there's no point in wasting any more of my time with this conversation. Come on, Kelly, let's go. We've got incident reports to write." He nodded to Charlene and me and backed out of the link, still smiling smugly.

"Kelly," I whispered as she pulled me into a goodbye hug.

"Make sure Miesha finds out about this. Tonight. Please. Abby's my best friend in the whole world."

"You got it," she whispered back, her eyes wide. "I don't want Abby to be lost either!"

I gave her a silent high five, and we pushed our pillows into place together. I looked at the closed link, my stomach knotting.

For the second night in a row, events had not gone how I'd planned. I'd never imagined I'd make contact with NAFAFA but be denied entry to the Hub. Why on earth did I keep ending up still stuck at camp?

I crawled out of my cramped fort into the darkness of the cabin, and Charlene followed. The moonlight had moved, splashing over a macaroni-and-seashell portrait of Abraham Lincoln on the wall.

"So," Charlene said. She cleared her throat. "Now what?"

"Now we wait, I guess. We just have to hope Kelly tells Miesha. She can handle Ben."

Charlene stared at me.

"Sorry," I said. "I mean we're hoping the girl we just met tells this other girl who outranks Overall Boy what's going on, so she can make him do what we want and help us rescue Abby."

"Oh, okay," Charlene said. "Sounds good. Should we take the forts down now and set them up again tomorrow?"

I shook my head. "They need to stay up so Miesha can contact us through the link. We'll have to convince Ms. Sabine to leave them alone somehow."

"That's easy," said Charlene. She crossed to the supply shelves and grabbed two pieces of paper, scribbled on them with a marker, then returned and pinned one to each fort.

"ART IN PROGRESS," I read. "PLEASE DON'T TOUCH. MAGGIE AND CHARLENE."

"She'll never take them down now," said Charlene. "We can tell her it's a conceptual installation piece or something. She'll love it."

"Perfect!" I said. "Thanks."

We looked at each other in the darkness. We'd definitely covered some ground tonight—shared experience and all that. Things between us were . . . different.

Charlene scuffed the floor with her shoe. "So, back to the cabin now?" she asked. I nodded. "You'd better let me climb out first then," she said. "I don't think that window likes you."

Outside, the moon was sliding behind the trees, camouflaging us in dappled silver light as we made our way along the edge of the field.

"Hey, what *were* you doing on that golf cart?" I said after a minute.

Charlene stopped. So did I. I could almost hear her deciding whether to trust me.

"Okay, fine," she said. "But you have to promise not to tell anyone." I raised my hand and promised. Charlene took a deep breath. "I was on the golf cart because I was stashing all those confiscated cantaloupes in the moose trap I've got hidden in the woods."

A strange feeling swam through my brain, like I was going backward through that spinny link from my old pillow fort up to Uncle Joe's in Alaska.

"Will you say that again, but slower?" I said. Charlene repeated her unbelievable sentence. "But . . . but what? Why? How? Explain."

Charlene sighed. "Way back when I started here, I didn't know a single person, and camp was so big, and I was so little, and I was totally scared. I know I said I wasn't earlier"—she raised a hand, cutting me off—"but I was, okay? Then they told us the ghost moose story at the end of the first day and I was like, yes, I am so here for this. The idea that there was this big, fuzzy, friendly moose patrolling the woods and keeping watch over my cabin at night was what got me through. It became like my personal guardian, even though I'd never seen it. I believed *so* hard.

"After a while I made real people friends, and by my second year I was a pro Cantalouper and on Litter Patrol and everything. I still wanted to see the ghost moose—like, I really, *really* wanted to see it. But I never did. Friends of mine claimed they'd seen it, and we heard all the stories over and over about the campers it's rescued, and I was always like, 'Why not me? Why am I not getting to see it? I'm the perfect Cantalouper! I want that spot in camp history too! I *need* it!' So near the end of my third year, I got this idea and started building a moose trap hidden in the woods."

"When you say 'moose trap,'" I said carefully, "do you mean an actual trap? Like with a snare or something?"

Charlene's bangs bounced as she nodded. "Yeah. Well, not a trap that could hurt the moose, just somewhere it would get stuck so I could see it. It all started when we were out doing science drawings and I found this little hill with a big tree on top. The dirt was all washed out from under the tree, making a tiny cave, and I thought if I lured the moose in there, its antlers might get caught in the dangly roots. Then I could say hi and maybe get a photo. I started sneaking out at night to work on it—digging out the cave, making it more of a trap—and stashed at least one cantaloupe in there the whole time I was at camp. More if I could get them."

"But no sign of the moose?"

"Nope. By the start of my fourth year, I was getting super frustrated, so I tried staying in the cave at night, acting lost. I danced the camp dance in there. I retold the legend of the ghost moose word for word. But still, nothing."

"You'd think just the cantaloupes alone should get it to show up," I said. "That's how the story goes, anyway."

"Right?" said Charlene. "But nothing. That's why this year I was like 'You're twelve. Let the ghost moose go, Charlene.' And I almost did. Only when Director Haggis announced he was confiscating everyone's cantaloupes, eight-year-old-me took over my brain and yelled, 'That means every cantaloupe in this camp is about to be up for grabs!' And I was like, sure, why not? Give it one last try. Go for maximum impact. So I volunteered to help collect them, spied on how that teenage counselor drove the golf cart, snuck out tonight, and brought the entire rolly bin of cantaloupes right to the cave."

Holy. Turtle. Poop. Rule-following, counselor-helping, tattletale-ing Charlene Thieson was actually a superspy-level secret rebel.

"And you know what's surprisingly hard?" Charlene went on. "Stacking cantaloupes. That was annoying. But they're in there, and I'm going to check the trap in the morning and see what I've got." She shot me a glance. "The thing is, I'm not sure I really believed it would work. After all this time, I'm kind of used to being disappointed. But now I know all this weird pillow fort stuff you're doing is real, then maybe that means . . ."

"The Camp Cantaloupe ghost moose is real," I said firmly. "I've seen it. And I bet you will to. It definitely sounds like you've earned it."

Charlene's expression was hard to read, somewhere between relieved, excited, and uncertain.

"Thanks," she said.

A soft whispering began as the breeze picked up, shifting through the trees, curling through my hair and ruffling Charlene's bangs.

We stood in silence just long enough for things to get uncomfortable. Was I supposed to say something now? Was she? Then an owl hooted overhead, and we both jumped like frightened bunnies, and together we headed for the cabin.

I smiled a little as we tiptoed through the door. I still had plenty of headaches to deal with here at camp, but after tonight, being stuck with Charlene as a buddy didn't seem like one of them. After tonight, I didn't mind quite so much.

Back in my bunk I used a splotch of moonlight on the wall to write two postcards' worth of updates to Abby.

Dear Abs,

Okay, first things first—I'm sorry you're not rescued yet. I'm working on it!

I tried out Plan Patchwork tonight to try and get to the Hub for backup, and you'll never guess what happened. KELLY turned up! She's in NAFAFA now because Creepy Frog had a feather stuck in him! (Will fill in details when I see you. Bad news update, though: Ben got the west coast, so she's in his network. Good news update: Miesha is head of the Council, and Kelly's gonna tell her what happened and that I need help finding you. Hopefully they'll check in somehow tomorrow. Ben tried to ruin everything AGAIN, of course. He wouldn't even let me in the Hub. He's so much worse than last year.

Also Charlene caught me sneaking into the art cabin so I had to let her in on everything. I'M SO SORRY. Turns out she's actually okay, like you said. She told me she's got this secret cave out in the woods that's also a trap for the ghost moose, and tonight she stole that rolly bin full of everyone's cantaloupes and drove them out there to use as bait. So that's pretty cool.

I hope you're safe, wherever you are, and not too bored and lonely. Keep hanging on—I'll get you back soon.

Love,

Mags

TWENTY-ONE
Abby

Morning on the island came way too early. It started with Antonia singing a jaunty sea chantey at the top of her lungs, then dropping a basket of homemade Cheerios on my bed and demanding I get up and help Joe feed the chickens.

There were puffy white clouds clumping like popcorn along the horizon, and the morning wind was brisk off the sea. The chickens stayed close to Joe as we did our walk from the boulders to the Ship Door and back.

Antonia had tea and toast waiting for us. She was wearing gray slacks and a fitted emerald-green jacket today, with her hair in an elaborate twist. For someone who lived alone in a basement in the middle of the ocean, she sure did know how to dress.

Helene arrived just as we were finishing. "Excellent," she

said, at the sight of us. "Mama . . ." She smiled nervously. "Are you ready to go below?"

"I said I was, didn't I?" said Antonia, all business. "Shall we take the elevator?"

Helene blinked. If she'd been hoping for some sort of mother-daughter moment, it didn't look like she was getting it.

"How long has it been since she went below?" I whispered to Helene as we followed Antonia and Joe out the double doors.

"Thirty-five years," she whispered back. "All because of me. I grew up in the Palace, and Mama expected me to live there forever and take over after her, keeping the old traditions going. But I had other plans, and when I turned seventeen I moved below. She's never forgiven me. I come up every week to visit and help clean the parts of the Palace she uses—that's why I came up yesterday—but Mama's refused to leave the surface even for a day."

"So this is a really big deal," I said as she tugged the doors closed behind us.

"You have no idea," said Helene.

I'd expected Antonia and Joe to be climbing the steps up through the rocks, but they were standing at the other end of the courtyard beside the bench.

"I called it already," Antonia said over her shoulder as we

approached, and a moment later there was a faint ping, the rock face slid smoothly to the side, and there was a shiny, perfectly normal elevator waiting for us.

"Howza-who now?" I said.

"Yes?" Antonia said. She looked at the elevator. "I'm sorry, do you not have this technology where you come from?"

"Well, yeah," I said. "Of course. But not in boulder piles. And why's the door hidden if there's no one else here? Who's it being hidden from?"

Antonia and Helene shared a look of surprise.

"It's just the way things were done," said Antonia. "To retain the island's natural beauty."

"No expense was spared on any aspect of the Island Underneath, Abby," Helene said, as we filed into the elevator. The door closed. "The crew had centuries of palace loot piled up, and building a secure, sophisticated, attractive new home under the island wasn't something they were going to cut corners on."

"So this place we're going is pretty fancy, then?" I asked.

"That's one word for it," said Helene.

The elevator hummed to a gentle stop and the doors pinged open, revealing a long stone hallway.

Helene took the lead. I counted twenty-three bluish white lights set into the stone walls before the hall ended and we stepped out into a shimmering, wonderland that made my heart do fifteen backflips and my brain parachute right down into my feet.

We were underwater.

When Helene and the crew kept referring to the Island Underneath, I'd been picturing fancy caves. And I was partly right. The rock wall of the island curved away on either side, elaborate doors and windows and balconies cut right into it, all linked together with a network of rope ladders, plank spiral staircases, and catwalks. It looked like a cross between a jungle gym, an old-timey ship, and a city set into a cliff. I craned my neck way back. Actually, it looked a lot like the Shipwreck Treehouse.

But that was nothing compared to the forty-foot-high glass wall rising from the carpeted floor in front of us, curving up and back to connect with the cliff face overhead. Because on the other side of that wall was the entire ocean.

Sunlight danced through the shifting currents, full of seaweed and jellyfish and bubbles. Schools of bright fish curled past the glass. A hammerhead shark swam past the glass! There were rays and octopuses and sunfish and eels, barnacles, anemones, and turtles. It was magnificent.

Between that and the marble statues, curvy armchairs, and tropical plants filling the area between the walls like the lobby of the world's fanciest hotel, this was up there with the NAFAFA Hub for the most epic, awesome, amazing, spectacular, unbelievable place I'd ever seen in my entire life.

"Oh," said Antonia, scuffing vaguely at the floor with the toe of her shoe. "I see you've changed the carpeting."

A few crew members scattered around the armchairs and catwalks waved as I turned in circles, trying to take it all in. I waved back.

"Welcome back, Mama," said Helene. She was watching her mother warily. "Do you, uh, want to take a look around, or . . . ?"

"I want to be sure we have everything we need for today's mission," Antonia said. "I didn't come down below for the first time in half a lifetime to be caught unprepared."

"Of course," said Helene. "I'll get someone to show you to—"

"I remember the way," interrupted Antonia. "I will see you at the doors shortly." And she swept off along the rock wall, heading for the closest spiral rope staircase.

"Oh. Good," said Helene. "Bye, Mama."

There was an awkward silence.

"Um, I'd like someone to show me around," I said brightly, trying to shift the mood. I elbowed Joe.

"Yes! Me too!" he said. "I still haven't had the full tour yet."

Helene sniffed, forced a smile, and nodded.

"We don't have time to see *everything*," she said. "Because this"—she waved around at the underwater glass cavern-lobby-atrium—"wraps all the way around the island. But I will show you the highlights."

We put the glass wall on our right and started on our way, Helene pointing out rooms in the rock wall as we walked. We passed a library, a game room, a whole long row of sleeping quarters. It was all cool, but it was hard to tear my eyes away from the three-dimensional underwater dream world happening on our right. Especially when more sharks showed up.

The ocean wall curved and rolled, following the shape of the island, and our path curved along with it. "We're near the lagoon now," Helene said. She pointed to a shiny door in the rock wall. "That elevator goes right to it."

"Why's it so much bigger than the other one?" Joe asked.

"The lagoon is neutral territory; it's the only part of the surface Mama allows us to visit freely without asking her permission. We go up there pretty often, so we need room to carry plenty of people."

"And their floaties," I said.

"And their floaties," agreed Helene.

Past the lagoon the floor sloped up, and outside the window the open ocean gave way to rocks and a wide reef stretching out from the roots of the island. The water here was so thick with plants and animals, it looked like one of those nature shows on TV. And right in the middle of everything was an old-timey wardrobe perched on a chunk of rock and coral, its barnacle-covered door spewing out a steady stream of bubbles.

"Ha! That looks like the treasure chest in the fish tank at my dentist's!" I said. And it totally did. When I was little, Matt and Mark told me that the dentist shrank kids who wouldn't floss and trapped them in there, and the bubbles were them screaming for help. I think they were trying to make me cry, but all that ended up happening was a lot of excitement when I climbed into the tank to rescue the kids.

"Hooray!" said Joe, running over and pressing himself to the glass. "That's it! That's how I got here!"

"Through that?" I joined him and peered past a starfish clinging to the wall above my head. "Wardrobe McBubbleton out there?"

"Yup. Hi, buddy!"

"Okay, so question." I turned to Helene. "You said the doors all led to furniture in palaces. Why did Joe's lead to some wardrobe out here on the reefy-do?"

"Answering that means another story," warned Helene.

"Woohoo!" cheered Joe. "Story time!"

I plopped down on the carpet, my back against the great glass wall, and looked up expectantly.

"Right, well we have to go back to the moment the original crew got stranded," Helene began, smiling. "Remember, they'd been on the run for months, then in the final battle they lost their ship, several of the looped doors, and Captain Emily."

"They were probably pretty heartbroken," Joe said.

"They certainly were!" Helene nodded. "But they also realized they had a problem: the looped doors that sank with the ship still worked. They were all locked, sure, and it might take centuries for the sea to open them, but it was only a matter of time before the furniture they looped to was going to start pouring out freezing North Pacific water." She looked back out at the wardrobe. "Can you imagine? A chest of drawers or a bookshelf in some royal Spanish bedroom just starts gushing saltwater, fish, seaweed, and who knows what all, and no one can do anything to stop it."

Joe and I whistled.

"So the door I went through was one of the ones that sank with the ship," said Joe. "I get that. And the ocean broke open the lock, I get that. But like Abby said, why's the wardrobe it looped to back here at the island? And out in the water? Why isn't it in some Spanish palace bedroom place?"

"Once the crew realized the problem," said Helene, "they decided to retrieve all the furniture that was at risk. It would only have taken a couple of pieces spewing seawater for folks to realize it was happening to furniture presented by the unknown ambassador, and that might have led all the palace dwellers in Europe to destroy their unknown ambassador gifts as a precaution, and then the crew would be stranded. With no ship, and no other way off the island, those links were—and still are—the crew's only lifeline. Even today we're completely dependent on them for all our basic needs.

"The initial plan was to bring the furniture back and store it here on the reef where it wouldn't pose a danger. But that turned out to be difficult. It's a lot harder getting a nice piece of furniture *out* of a palace than it is getting one *in*. They had such a hard time retrieving the wardrobe, they decided it just wasn't worth the effort for the rest. So the head carpenter and a few of the others went around posing as the world's clumsiest appraisers, and one by one, they broke the remaining drowned-loop furniture to bits. They got a little famous for it, actually. There was an opera."

"That is wild," said Joe. "And when did the lock on my wardrobe buddy break?"

"About twenty years ago. One moment it was normal, the next the doors flew open and all these bubbles started erupting toward the surface. We threw a party for it. It was very exciting."

"Having North Pacific water pouring through there must be causing some fascinating disturbances in the marine environment," Joe noted, putting on his sciency voice.

"Oh, it is! The sea life around here has really boomed since."

"And Orpheus, the Pacific humpback, heard the whales singing in the Atlantic and started singing back." Joe got a dreamy look in his eyes. "Singing back through the drowned door."

"That explains a lot," said Helene. "We've been wondering why whales keep turning up and singing at the wardrobe. Sometimes we gather here and sing them chanteys, in case the whales are lonely. It's good to know they've just been making long-distance calls."

Joe and I agreed that it was good to know.

"Hey, what about the door that led to the sofa in le Petit Salon?" I said. "The crew left that one behind to sink too, right?"

"Naturally. With the key lost, there was no point bringing the door back to the island."

"Then why didn't the clumsy appraisers destroy the sofa it went to?"

"Oh, they tried," said Helene. "But when they arrived at Versailles, they found King Louis's private study was guarded day and night. In the end they had to go away and just hope the door with the Oak Lock wouldn't open for a long, long time."

"And it didn't," I said quietly. Not until Mags and I had arrived on the scene. Oof, more Maggie heart pangs. We'd been part of this centuries-old pirates-and-palaces wild furniture saga without even knowing it. We really should have been learning about it together.

I climbed to my feet and our little group continued on, Joe looking back over his shoulder at the wardrobe. The floor sloped down after the reef, and Helene pointed out more doors leading to a mess hall, a movie theater, a bowling alley, and a storeroom stacked floor to ceiling with barrels.

"Oh, now, you have to see inside this one," she said, pointing us over to a plain metal door I would never have noticed. She tapped a keypad set into the rock beside it, and we stepped inside.

Oh. My. Covert ops. Maggie would have completely flipped over this.

We were in a round, windowless room, lit by red track lighting and glowing banks of computers, display panels, and screens hugging the wall. Buttons, switches, and cables gleamed everywhere, like we'd stepped onto the bridge of a TV starship crossed with the secret lair of some futuristic super-spy.

"Welcome to the command center for the island," said Helene, waving us to a platform in the center. She pressed her palm to a waiting tablet. Immediately a large screen against the wall reset, losing its columns of numbers and showing a map of an oblong green dollop surrounded by blue.

"Ooh, is that us?" I asked.

"Yes, that's our island," said Helene. "Ready for one last dose of storytime?"

"Yay!" Joe and I said together.

"Excellent. So, for the first two hundred years or so, the pirates had an easy time keeping this island secret. It's quite tiny, and ships crossing back and forth over the Atlantic didn't usually travel at this latitude, so they weren't likely to run into it. There were a few near misses in the late 1800s, though, and that's when the crew first began thinking about maybe possibly having to hide their Palace out of sight so the looped doors could be safe.

"But the twentieth century made the decision for them. First there were planes going overhead, then massive ships with powerful sensors, then satellites with their super-targeting cameras. The crew had to protect the island, and fast, so they threw everything they had into building a state-of-the-art, self-contained underwater base. Over the last fifty years we've removed every sign of life from the surface of the island, except the stumps, which we can't hide, and the Ship Door, which is a monument to Captain Emily. We've been safe from discovery so far, and we're all just hoping it stays that way. That was why you two arriving back-to-back caused so much excitement. It was practically an invasion."

"Incredible," Joe said. "But hang on, what about modern ships? Can't they take their own readings nowadays, even apart from satellites? Some of the whale research boats I've worked on have been pretty high tech, and they're not even top of the line."

"Very true," said Helene. "But we've managed to convince the world's geodata centers that this place has been thoroughly explored and found useless. We planted the information years ago, adding in some information about hazardous conditions for shipping routes, and it's been passed on as fact ever since. That's kept most ships from getting too close.

"And we do have some high-tech defenses of our own. Look, I'll show you. See that screen there? That red dot? It's a British navy ship that's getting too close. I've been monitoring it the last couple of days, and this is as good a time as any to redirect it."

She tapped a pattern on the tablet, and another monitor lit up. There was a snazzy trumpet fanfare, and something gray and silver flashed across one of the screens in a burst of bubbles. Over on the map, a silver dot appeared, heading right for the red dot of the ship.

"What on earth was that?" I asked.

"Florence," Helene said. "Our mechanical dolphin."

Joe and I looked at each other.

"You have a mechanical dolphin," I said slowly. "Named Florence."

"Yes."

"And she chases away ships?"

"Florence sends out interfering signals to rechart the ship's course past the island or show a dangerous weather anomaly happening in this area, depending on which sensor equipment the ship is using."

Up on the screen, the silver dot was already halfway to the ship. "Whoa," I said. "She's fast!"

"Top of the line," said Helene. "I designed her myself."

"Why did it play a fanfare when you activated her?" asked Joe.

"Because she's a mechanical dolphin named Florence who guards a secret island!" I said. Come on, that part was obvious. "It'd be weird if she didn't have her own fanfare!"

Helene gave me an approving nod.

There was a soft ping from a speaker somewhere overhead, and a familiar voice fuzzed into the room.

"Hello? Hello! Helene? Castaways? Can you hear me?"

"Hello, Mama," called Helene, speaking to the ceiling. "We're here. I was just showing Abby and Joe the control center."

"Lovely," Antonia's disembodied voice replied. "And when were you planning on doing some actual work? Everything is in place at the doors, but we'll need at least an hour of protocol training to get our visitors ready. I didn't come all the way down here to let them ruin this mission with their complete ignorance of how to do a proper courtly curtsy."

TWENTY-TWO
Abby

Three rope ladders and one swingy plank bridge later, Joe and I were standing in a long door-lined hallway with Antonia, learning how to behave inside a palace.

For a full hour she briefed us on things to do and not do, things to touch and not touch, what to say if we were spoken to, and the proper way to walk into and out of a room.

"I don't see why we need to know all this," I said. "We're just checking out places Louis might have had links to; we're not actually going back to the 1700s."

Antonia shook her head. "You will see why you need this protocol training soon enough," she said. "Oh, that reminds me. How's your Russian?"

I blinked at her. Joe and I looked at each other.

"No Russian? Ah. Well, I assume your other languages are decent, then?"

We both shrugged.

"I know some Spanish," I said. "But not, like, palace Spanish."

"I took two years of French in high school," offered Joe.

"*Bon*," said Antonia. "So you can carry on a simple conversation?"

"All I remember is how to ask where the bathroom is," said Joe. "And say, 'I am an American and I speak no French.'"

Antonia grimaced. "Well, let's hope neither of you has to say a word to anyone while we conduct this mission, then. Now, bowing and curtsying lessons!"

Helene, who'd been fussing with Florence, arrived just as our lessons were finishing, and she and Antonia headed for one of the hallway's many doors. "Stay here and give me fifty more bows and curtsies each," Antonia called as they disappeared. "Then follow after us, and we'll get you set up with supplies."

"I wonder what that meant," said Joe as we finally finished flailing and followed them. "What are our 'supplies'?" We stepped through the door into a simple square room, and Joe got his question answered.

One entire side of the room was lined with rack after rack of clothes. There were dresses with massive skirts covered in lace and frills and bows, silk pants in every color imaginable, velvet gowns, wildly elaborate wigs, tiaras, necklaces, satin slippers, buckled shoes, military jackets, three-cornered hats, and trays of sparkling jewelry.

In the very center of the room was an old-timey wooden door, just like the one up in the grove of trees, standing in its frame with a lock holding it closed and everything. I stepped forward to take a closer look, but—

"Ah, good, you're here," said Helene, sweeping out from behind a curtained alcove at the end of the racks of clothes. I gasped, for good reason. Helene was wearing a bloodred crimson gown with built-in hips that had to be five feet wide, covered with bows and ruffles. A glittering net of white jewels curled around her neck and shoulders, and she'd capped the whole look off with a two-foot spiraling gray wig decorated with silk gardenia flowers. She looked stunning.

"Well, what are you staring at?" she said. "Pick an outfit and get changed. We want to get this show on the road."

But Joe and I could only stand there gaping, and it got worse when Antonia appeared from behind another curtain, her tasseled heels clopping softly on the wooden floor. Her dress was similar to Helene's, but in black, with a high collar decorated with silver and gray feathers. She'd accessorized with elbow-length ivory gloves, and her wig was a cloud of pale blue studded with tiny golden stars.

Antonia adjusted a bow on the back of Helene's dress and raised her eyebrows as Joe and I stayed rooted to the spot, staring.

"Yes?" she said. "You have questions?"

"What is . . . how . . . why . . . ?" I managed. I tried again. "What's up with the costumes? You look amazing, but how will they help us search for pillow forts? Won't they make us totally noticeable inside the palace?"

"Yes, that's the point," answered Helene. "We learned long ago that sneaking around palaces is an art, and the easiest way to get caught is to try to stay out of sight. There are always guards, and nowadays cameras, looking for just that sort of thing. So we make good use of the three hundred years' worth of fine clothes we've collected and just pretend to be period reenactors. It works like a dream, and no one bats an eye."

"Really?" I said.

"Really," said Antonia. "Think about it. If you were visiting a palace, or a security guard working in one, and someone walked by dressed like this . . ." She did a full turn, letting the beaded midnight-satin trim of her dress spin. ". . . wouldn't you think that person probably had a good reason for being there?"

"Oh, totally," I said.

"I get it!" said Joe, snapping his fingers. "Because who else would go to all that trouble?"

"Exactly," said Helene. "And now it's your turn. Everything in this room is appropriate for the destination on the other side of the loop, so please choose an ensemble quickly and get dressed. Abby, if you don't want to select a wig, I can help you with a period-specific fancy updo."

"What palace are we visiting first?" I asked as I headed over to the treasure trove of glamorous clothes.

"My very favorite," said Antonia, a real smile appearing on her face for the first time that day. "Somewhere I haven't been in far too long. It's part of the Hermitage Museum now, but when Captain Emily first visited, it was known as the Winter Palace, the preferred home of Her Imperial Highness Catherine the Great, Empress of All the Russias."

TWENTY-THREE
Abby

Joe and I emerged from our dressing rooms at almost the same time. He'd picked out a swoopy coat made of green silk covered in gold embroidery, matching shorts that cinched tight around his knees, white-and-gold stockings, sparkly buckled shoes, and a sleek brown wig. "I haven't had hair like this since I was in grad school," he said, running a hand happily over his head. "And Abby! You look so splendid!"

"Thanks!" I said. I felt splendid. I was wearing a wide-hipped dress like Antonia and Helene, but mine was in the softest, sleekest teal velvet the world had ever seen, with cream ribbons at the sleeves and neck. I'd also found a big chunky necklace of lapis blue stones, purple satin shoes—*purple! satin!*—and, because everyone else was doing it, a big white wig shaped like a muffin.

How on earth could Antonia refuse to come below for so many years? If I lived on the island, I'd be down here dressing up every single day.

While Joe and I were admiring each other's outfits, Helene brought out her ring of keys and unlocked the door in the center of the room. She held it open politely for her mother, waving us in, and as we filed after Antonia, I caught a look at the carved lock. There was no sun surrounded by oak leaves here; this lock was patterned with honeycomb and three delicate bees.

Helene came behind, closing the door after her, and for a moment the four of us stood pressed together in the dark. There was a creak, and a crack of light appeared, Antonia's silhouette framed against it. Another creak, and she slipped out, carefully angling her wide-hipped dress. We followed, blinking as we emerged.

We were in a library. Enormous bookshelves—like the one we'd just stepped out of—lined three sides, with a grand doorway on our left facing a huge wall of windows to our right. Everything was old-fashioned and lush. There was golden piping where the walls met the ceiling, a seriously expensive-looking woven carpet, intricately carved chairs and sofas, and a chandelier making it all gleam. Yep, we were in a real palace.

And whoa. This had once been someone's actual home.

I wouldn't have minded moving so much if it could be to someplace like this. Although Samson would be a terror on that fancy carpet.

"Let's begin our search," said Antonia. "Everyone please remember your palace protocol."

And so the great pillow fort hunt started. The searching part was easy, since all we had to do was walk from room to room, casually looking under sofa cushions and tugging pillows off chairs, but I had the hardest time staying focused on our task. The palace was mind-blowingly beautiful. I kept catching myself gawking like a tourist at the impossibly grand rooms, or pressing my nose to the windows to stare at the sun-drenched gardens full of roses and fountains and statues.

There were red velvet ropes blocking most of the doors, but we just sauntered around them. Once or twice guards walked through, looking all official with their hands behind their backs, but Helene gave each of them a smile and a deep formal curtsy, and they smiled and nodded and went right on by.

We searched room after room, pillow after pillow, but there was no sign of a fort, and no sign of a link.

We were inspecting a long gallery lined with little sofas when the first actually exciting thing happened on our mission. A tour was coming through, and the guide, speaking in a language I didn't understand, brought his group to a stop beside me just as I was leaning over to peer under a cushion. I wheeled around, startled, and instinctively dropped into the world's worst curtsy. The guide spoke to me. Oh, no.

I gave a weak smile back and looked in panic to the rest of my party along the hall. Joe's eyes were huge. Helene was making frantic hand gestures I didn't understand. Thankfully, Antonia came to my rescue.

She swept over and addressed the tour guide in what sounded like his language, then turned to the group and launched into some sort of dramatic story. The crowd smiled, then laughed, then made sad noises. Antonia came over to Helene, Joe, and me in turn, apparently introducing us. I tried to match my expression to Antonia's sad tone when she reached me, and the crowd all tilted their heads and said "Ohhh!" in a comforting sort of way. Whatever she was doing, they were loving it.

The story went on for a good few minutes, until Antonia wrapped up with a showy flourish of her hands and a perfect curtsy so deep she had to hold on to her wig. The group applauded enthusiastically. The tour guide gave Antonia a very deep bow, and they moved on.

"Whew!" Antonia said, wiping her forehead and taking a seat on one of the sofas. "That was fun!"

"What language were you speaking?" I asked.

"Polish. My grandmother taught me."

"And what did you tell them?" said Joe. "They looked totally captivated."

"The guide asked Abby what we were all looking for," said Antonia, leaning back against the cushions. "So I made up a story to explain. I said there was an old Winter Palace legend of a young down-on-her-luck Russian princess who lost a valuable necklace one night during a ball. The necklace was a treasured family heirloom, and she and her poor widowed father—that's you, Joe—had nothing else left of value in the world. So she begged two strangers for help, and those strangers"—she indicated herself and Antonia—"were each recently widowed and down on their luck too, and they helped her search. And by the end of the night, they had found not only the necklace, but enough other lost and forgotten treasures to set all four of them up for life. And they all went to live together and formed a new dynasty, and down-on-their-luck Russian girls still dream of losing a necklace at a ball in hopes the same thing might happen to them."

"You really just made that up?" I said, impressed. That was almost a Maggie-level story! "That's amazing!"

"Thank you, Abigail." Antonia got to her feet. "Or should I say thank you, Princess?"

We continued our search for another hour, but in the end, after walking up and down way more marble staircases than my feet had been prepared for, Antonia and Helene sadly announced we'd searched every corner of the Winter Palace that was likely to be hiding a pillow fort.

We took a shortcut through the glittering jewel box that was the throne room and emerged back in the library where we'd started. Antonia opened the secret panel in the bookcase, and one by one we stepped into the darkness, appearing a second later in all our tired glory under the blazing sun on the stump amid the trees on the breezy surface of the island.

TWENTY-FOUR
Maggie

The awful hubbub of the rise-and-shine loudspeaker shattered my sleep again the next morning. I sat up, blinking. It felt like five minutes, tops, since Charlene and I got back from our art cabin adventure.

And speaking of Charlene, her bunk was already empty, the sheets and blankets tucked in all neat and crisp. Whoa? Why was she up? Did she change her mind and decide to go tattling on me to Director Haggis? Was I in serious trouble here?

But I was wasting my worries. Charlene stomped in a few minutes later, and I heard her telling the counselor she'd been doing early-morning Litter Patrol. She shot me a disappointed look as she came over.

"I went out to check the moose trap," she whispered, although there was so much yelling in our cabin in the mornings there was no point. "And *nothing*. Even with all those new cantaloupes I added!"

"Boo," I whispered back. "That's rough. Once we have Abby back, I'll work up a real plan for you."

Charlene shrugged grumpily and headed out to brush her teeth.

Roll call took forever. Breakfast took even longer.

Finally, after an unending eternity of scene rehearsal in drama class—though I was sort of having fun playing the king, the lady with the string, and the monster all at once— we were on our way to arts and crafts.

I checked the back of the room as soon as we walked in. Phew! Our forts were still there. Ms. Sabine clapped her hands as we all settled into our seats.

"Attention, please," she said. "Before we begin today, I'd like to draw everyone's attention to these extraordinary art pieces at the back of the classroom! Will the artists please reveal themselves?"

Charlene and I raised our hands. The other kids looked at each other in surprise.

"I was just blown away when I saw these here this morning," Ms. Sabine said. "I'd love it if you'd both share your artistic inspiration with the class!"

I glanced over at Charlene. What were we supposed to say? But she was smiling. She gave me a nod that clearly said *I got this.*

"Well," she said, taking a deep breath. "It was your whole direction of 'collage' that gave us the inspiration, Ms. Sabine. . . ." And she was off. She talked for three whole minutes about our artistic perspective, our reflective intention, and our form-focused interpretive analysis. It was seriously impressive. The more Charlene talked, the more Ms. Sabine lit up, and by the end she was practically clapping with delight.

"Oh, I can't even tell you! I just . . . I am overwhelmed with excitement!" Ms. Sabine declared, making the glassy-eyed class jump. "And now I would love it if Maggie could share with us the part about the fabulous letters!"

The what? Charlene looked just as confused as me this time.

"I'm sorry?" I said.

"The letters!" said Ms. Sabine. "I took the liberty of examining your art installation just before class, and I discovered the absolutely brilliant meta-narrative you've created within the piece. Forget the moon, children, I am over the solar system about these! You *must* read them out to us."

She hurried to the back of the room, ducked into my new fort, hurried back . . .

. . . and pressed a handful of large silver envelopes into my hands.

Oh. My. Catastrophe.

Silver envelopes. With my name on them. These were letters from NAFAFA.

And they had all been opened.

"Go on, dear," urged Ms. Sabine. "We're waiting! Oh, I just adore letters!"

Every single person in the classroom was looking at me. Ms. Sabine perched herself on her desk and gave an encouraging nod. The silence pressed in; I had no choice. Slowly I pulled the paper from inside the top envelope, but Ms. Sabine stopped me.

"No, dear, no," she called, flapping a hand. "Not like that. Read them in order, please, starting at the bottom. It's marvelous how you even thought to include that detail, building the letter pile from the bottom up, like they'd been dropped there one by one!"

I gulped. *Deep breath, Maggie.* It sounded like Ms. Sabine thought Charlene and I had written these. So long as she kept believing that, we might be able to contain this. I turned the stack upside down and pulled out the first letter.

To: Maggie Hetzger
From: Murray, Captain of the Northern & Arctic Alliance
Timestamp: 8:17 a.m. Hub Time

MAGGIE! Hi!!! How are you? Miesha called a Council meeting this morning and said Kelly slipped HER a note that Ben met with you last night and was keeping it a secret. Ben got all grumpy, but Miesha made him stop, and he told us you're at camp, and Abby is missing after using the key from le Petit Salon in some sort of treehouse, and she could be anywhere and you're trying to find her and how are you always SO GOOD at messing up the NAFAFA schedule???

Sounds like you're up to date about Ben getting the west coast, and Miesha being head of the Council now. But did you know Carolina is also on the Council as head of the east coast? It's a good group, but Ben's managed to push through a lot of reforms, like that timestamp dealy at the top here, and some things are pretty different. I don't know what we're going to do to help you with the Abby thing, but everyone who's not Ben agrees we have to do something. Hope I get to see you whatever we end up doing! Hope you're having fun at camp, too! I mean, considering! Bye!

I looked around at the class. The other campers were staring blankly at me. Ms. Sabine was beaming from her desk. She silent-clapped her paint-stained hands and gestured for me to keep going.

To: Maggie Hetzger
From: Miesha, Head of the Council of NAFAFA and Queen of the United Southern Gulf-Pacific Fortresses
                    Timestamp: 9:31 a.m. Hub Time

Dear Maggie Hetzger,

Everyone says Abby Hernandez is lost somewhere in some sort of treehouse network. Sorry to hear that. We've all been brainstorming ways to help find her. The only thing we know for sure is that the key you used has been hanging in le Petit Salon as far back as our records go. (Until I gave it to you.) So that's our main clue.

Ben's got a meeting with a representative of the European sofa fort network in le Petit Salon in half an hour to try and find out any background info that might be useful. Maybe they know something we don't. I'll be gathering a team from my network and digging through the Archives for references to the key or Versailles or anything else we can think of. And all the networks are asking their members with treehouses to check them for strange girls named Abby just in case.

Please stay calm and do everything you can to keep your new forts up and running. I hope we have good news for you soon.

I tore the next letter open without looking around. What if they'd found something?

To: Maggie Hetzger
From: Miesha, Head of the Council of NAFAFA and

Queen of the United Southern Gulf-Pacific Fortresses
Timestamp: 10:06 a.m. Hub Time

We have a major problem, Maggie Hetzger. Ben just came running back from le Petit Salon with the lost key in his hand. When he stopped laughing and screaming "PRECIOUS!" long enough to talk (seriously) (I know), he told us he found it lying there under the First Sofa. Just hanging out. He also said the sofa looked like it had been pushed around, and some of the pillows were knocked over. He canceled his meeting with the European representative, and now he's refusing to help with the search for Abby, since all he wanted was the key anyway.

I've called another emergency meeting of the Council. If you're sure Abby Hernandez had the key when she fell through that door, then it looks like it led to le Petit Salon, and for some reason she dropped the key there and left it behind. She's not in the room now, which obviously means she left through one of the pillows. Six of them lead to the different Continental networks' Hubs, but the rest lead to King Louis's original palace network from three hundred years ago. The European Council says those are super off-limits, since some of them lead to dangerous dead ends or big-time tourist attractions (apparently) (weird). So let's hope she's not stuck in one of those, because problem.

Although if she is in one of the other Continental networks, I've got no idea why they haven't let her contact us yet. That's kind of suspicious.

I'll let you know how the meeting goes.

"Is this, like, a play, or something?" one of the girls from my cabin asked. I looked up. I'd forgotten there were other people in the room.

"Something like that," Charlene said. She was watching me intently, her eyes as big as Litter Patrol badges. She knew we didn't write these letters. She knew every word of them was true.

"So are we not doing collages today?" said a boy at the back of the room, his half-raised arm dangling over his head. Ms. Sabine waved her hands for quiet.

"Just keep listening, children," she said. "We're almost done. I hope you're all getting inspired by the scope of this project!"

There were two letters left.

To: Maggie Hetzger
From: Carolina, Director of the Forts of the Eastern Seaboard
Timestamp: 11:22 p.m. Hub Time

Maggie Hetzger. We have another serious problem. Miesha had her dog, Sprinkles, visiting for the meeting today, and your friend Kelly got very excited and decided to bring Abby Hernandez's cat in to meet him. Sprinkles really loves cats, but it seems like not all cats love him, and anyway now they're both in hiding.

Miesha has barricaded herself in the Archives to avoid the cat hair. She is VERY unhappy Kelly let him into the Hub, and has ordered us to have the cat found and gone as soon as possible, since he could do real damage if he gets lost in the networks. So far no one's having any luck. It's hard to find a cat in this place.

We may end up needing your help on this.

Finally, the last one.

Maggie! It's Murray. (I couldn't find the right form. I'm not sure what time it is.) I'm writing because HONESTLY HOW DO YOU DO THIS? As far as anyone knows you and Abby aren't even HERE, but you've got us all running in circles.

Obviously we need to meet in person: please be in your fort at the same time tonight—

I stopped dead. Why did I just read that part out loud? I scanned the room nervously, but most of the kids were looking out the windows or scratching paint off the tabletops, clearly bored out of their minds. A flash of prickly outrage shot through me. This was important, top-secret stuff! Who did these kids think they were to just be zoning it out?

—or as close as possible to the same time, so we can get you back into the Hub and join forces to find all the missing cats and people you keep sending into the networks.

And of course it'll be awesome to see you anyway! I'm on Snack Committee today. I hope you like gummy bears!

There was total silence in the cabin as I finished, but my brain was roaring with everything I'd just learned. The trapdoor had led to le Petit Salon! Ben had the Oak Key! Samson was loose in the networks!

"Oh, wasn't that *wonderful*?" Ms. Sabine trilled. She was on her feet, hands clasped together. "I just *adore* how you two managed to turn your fear over your missing friend into such a multifaceted epistolary project. Class . . ." She addressed the entire room. "I've made a decision. We will finish work on our collages today, and tomorrow Maggie and Charlene will direct us all in starting letter-and-fort projects of our own. Homework for tonight: think of some issue or obstacle you want to address creatively, and at the end of the week we'll share and read our letters aloud. Yes? But for now, please continue giving your collage masterpieces your all. Remember, art is how you feel!"

There was a general round of grumbling. Ms. Sabine

swept over to Charlene and me.

"Goodness, you two," she said, putting an arm around each of us. She was wearing all orange today, and up close she smelled like construction paper and Earl Grey tea. "In all my years of teaching, I've never seen such a fiercely independent project. I'm guessing you snuck in here before breakfast and 'delivered' the letters so you could activate the meta-narrative of the project by 'receiving' them in class? Genius!"

Charlene and I kept catching each other's eyes and looking away quickly, but Ms. Sabine was too excited to notice.

"I wonder, dears, if you'd be willing to share this divine project with more than just your classmates?"

I looked at her warily. "What do you mean?"

"Well, many of our younger campers are having a hard time with homesickness this year. To be honest, I've never seen so many bad cases; it's like a plague! And I think this might be the perfect solution. I mean, take you for instance, dear." She beamed at me. "This is *your* first year, isn't it? I'm sure you're feeling homesick. Plus you've got the stress of everyone hating you for destroying the Shipwreck Treehouse, *and* your best friend is lost and missing somewhere in the woods! If anyone has the right to feel terrible, it's you!"

I blinked. Okay, that was a lot all at once.

"But look how well you've handled it!" Ms. Sabine went

on. "You've used art to deal with your grief and regret and lack of control. Art!" She shouted the word to the rafters, squeezing us in tight and positively vibrating with enthusiasm. "If you two can convince the homesick kids to conquer their fears using this wonderful project, and they write and tell their parents how much fun it was, then maybe *I* can convince Director Haggis to give me a grant for the art department! Maybe I can get a decent cabin! Maybe we can finally afford crimping scissors!"

Charlene looked wary. "What sort of letters would we be helping these little kids write?" she asked.

"Well, it's your project, dears. But they could write pretend letters from their parents, maybe, or siblings, or friends back home. Those are good ideas, right, Maggie?"

"They could write letters from their pets, too," I offered.

"Pets!" Ms. Sabine threw back her head again, her eyes closed in bliss. "I knew this would be perfect. I'll write up a lesson plan tonight and tell Director Haggis about it tomorrow, and we can get started!" We got one last Earl Grey–scented squeeze, and she released us, heading for her desk. She stopped and turned back. "Oh, of course that will mean you'll be missing your swimming and archery lessons next week in order to be here for the younger children's art classes, but you won't mind that, will you?"

I didn't mind. I was too caught up in the Abby situation

to even be able to think about next week, but Charlene spluttered, her face turning red.

"Excellent, excellent," sang Ms. Sabine. "Now, if your
independent project is at a good stopping point, I'm dying to
see what you two world-class artists can come up with in the
exciting realm of collage!"

TWENTY-FIVE
Maggie

Charlene and I finished our collages just before the end of class, which was kind of a miracle considering we spent most of the time whispering about everything we'd learned from the letters. Charlene had thousands of questions about NAFAFA, the Council, its politics, and the Hub, and by the time we headed off to lunch, I'd answered enough of them for her to be more or less ready for the meeting that night.

I realized I hadn't thought twice about Charlene coming to the meeting. It seemed obvious that she should. And it was nice to have someone to keep secrets and make plans with again. It felt like home.

Charlene and I were going over our sneaking-out agenda, eating corn chips and ignoring the—ugh, there it finally was in person—cucumber casserole we'd been served, when the chatter around us died away ominously. Charlene's mouth snapped shut.

Director Haggis was crossing the mess hall, flanked by two grown-ups in official-looking green uniforms with patches on their sleeves that said WASHINGTON STATE SEARCH AND RESCUE. They stopped at our table.

"What? Did you find something?" Charlene practically yelled, leaping to her feet. Her Safety Monitor sash caught the corner of her tray, knocking it into mine. A handful of casserole slopped onto my lap, and I jumped up too.

"That is not how we greet visitors at Camp Cantaloupe, Miss Thieson," Director Haggis said, turning his eyebrow V on her. "But yes, we did find something." A little gasp ran through the room, and I stopped swatting at the congealed cucumber slices oozing down my pants. Everyone leaned in, listening.

Charlene looked like she might faint. I understood why. We both knew there was no chance the search teams had found Abby, and the only other thing they could have found was Charlene's moose trap hidden in the woods. Maybe they'd spotted tracks from the golf cart, and put that together with the stolen cantaloupes to figure out whose cave it must have been.

"And . . . um, what did you find?" Charlene asked.

"A letter," answered one of the officers.

"For Maggie Hetzger," said the other.

"From Abby Hernandez," said Director Haggis.

The silence was so complete I could hear the last slice of cucumber slip off my shoe and splat onto the linoleum floor.

A low murmuring began, building to chatter, then uproar. The Girl Who Went Missing had somehow sent The Girl Who Broke the Treehouse a letter, and apparently everyone had something to say about it. Some of the kids at our table rolled their eyes and started telling everyone to ignore us, since it was probably just part of our overachiever art project.

"Perhaps we should talk with Maggie Hetzger in private?" suggested one of the officers, speaking over the noise. Director Haggis nodded and held out a hand, inviting me toward the exit.

My brain went completely numb. Leaving a shocked Charlene still standing over the mess of the lunch table, I followed Director Haggis to the door, the officers falling in behind me.

What was going on? How could there possibly be a letter for me from Abby? She hadn't been gone long enough, and the trapdoor had taken her to le Petit Salon, not a post office. Or had another letter turned up in my arts and crafts fort just since class, and Ms. Sabine or someone had seen it? Only no, that would mean Abby was safe in the NAFAFA networks, and then why wouldn't she just come back to camp herself?

I looked up, realizing I hadn't been paying any attention to where we were going, and discovered we were outside my cabin. Director Haggis opened the door and I went in, the officers' shoes thudding on the floor behind me.

"Now, Miss Hetzger," said Director Haggis. "You will notice these officers have acted in their official capacity, and—"

"Looked through Abby's stuff!" I said, pointing. Abby's bunk had been stripped, and all her things were spread out on the floor. "You had no right to do that!"

The taller of the search and rescue officers gave me a sympathetic smile. "Actually, Miss Hetzger," she said, "we do. Your friend Abby has been missing for a long time now, and everyone is very, very worried about her. You more than anyone, I'm sure! That's why we thought it would be worth taking a look at what she brought to camp, because any clue, no matter how small, might help us find her."

"That's how we located this," the second officer said, pulling an envelope from the pocket of his uniform. "It was the only unusual item. And it's addressed to you."

He held it out, and I took it, my stomach swooping. All three grown-ups were watching me closely. The envelope was a normal envelope, with four words written across the front: *For Maggie, in case.*

For Maggie, in case. What did that mean? In case what? I flipped it over.

"You didn't open it," I said in surprise.

"Director Haggis suggested we let you read it first, Maggie," said the tall officer. "We just hope you'll tell us if there's anything in there that can help us find Abby."

"Got it." I looked back down at the letter. More than anything in the world—well, almost anything—I wished they would all go away and let me read it on my own. But that clearly wasn't going to happen.

For Maggie, in case.

I ripped open the envelope, took a deep, slow breath, and unfolded the letter.

Dear Mags,

If you're reading this, we tried the Oak Key in the trapdoor, and nothing happened. Maybe the lock didn't open, or the magic didn't work, or something else went wrong, but basically we didn't get the great big adventure we wanted, and now, if I'm right, you're sad.

You're probably pretending to be sick so you can be sad alone in our cabin, and maybe you're mad at me for still going to activities, and that's why I'm writing this letter here at home before we leave. (Samson's asleep on my left foot right now. He says hi.) This is my just-in-case letter.

And what I want to tell you is we can still have fun! Don't forget we planned to be here together last summer, but now we finally ARE here, and we've wanted this for a literal year, so to be honest I'm only gonna let you mope for a little while before I fill your bed with water balloons or something and make you get involved with camp. Because Mags, I really need Camp Cantaloupe this summer.

I haven't talked about it much, but it's been SO weird helping my dad and the twins pack up our house. And you know I love Tamal, and he's gonna fit in great, but having him move in with us, and becoming a whole new kind of family starting over in a whole new house, that's a lot of stuff changing all at the same time. And to be super seriously honest, I've been feeling pretty sad about it.

What I want is just a chunk of time where everything stays the same, and that's camp. And obviously the main person I want to hang out with at camp is you. So quit moping! Get out there and try things! Take some risks!

Samson's stuck to one of the moving boxes now, and I have my foot back, so I'm gonna wrap up.

You're my best friend in the whole world, Maggles, and I know we're gonna make this a summer you and me will never forget.

Love,

Abs

P.S. I've got a treasure-hunt mission to help cheer you up. When I was at camp last summer I made you a necklace in art class, and I hid it in a secret place as a sort of guarantee that you'd be here with me this year. When you get the chance, head over to the tree marked on the map, climb to the third branch up from the ground, and look in the gap in the trunk. Unless Scrabbles McFloof (this squirrel I became enemies with last year) stole it over the winter, you should find it.

I looked up, surprised to find the room had gone all blurry, then blinked down at the paper again, trying to make out the map sketched at the bottom. I sniffed loudly. I could smell the cucumber casserole drying on my shoes.

"So? What does it say?" Director Haggis asked impatiently. "Does the letter relate to Miss Hernandez's disappearance?"

I shook my head. "It's a letter Abby wrote me before we came here," I said. "In case I got . . . homesick." It was mostly true, kind of. And it was the best story my brain could come up with under the circumstances. I might have seemed frozen on the outside, but inside I was swimming for my life against a tidal wave of feelings.

Abby had written me a letter, just in case. Abby had made me a necklace and hidden it so she could surprise me with a treasure hunt. Abby had thought ahead about how I'd feel at Camp Cantaloupe, and what I might end up needing, and what she could do to make sure I got it.

I'd never done anything like that for Abby. Not on my own. Not just out of the blue. Not once.

And Abby had written that she'd been feeling sad lately. I'd had no idea. I'd never imagined she might be unhappy about moving, or worried about Tamal moving in. I only had my mom, so Abby's family always seemed big and fun and wonderful to me, and I figured she'd be over the moon about getting even more of it.

Only I guess the new stepdad and the new house *would* be a lot of things changing all at once for Abby. And maybe I should have thought about how that felt. And what that might mean she needed. And how I could help her get it.

She shouldn't have had to write a letter to get me to notice.

I had the *best* best friend in the world, and I had not been keeping up my side of things. At all.

"Miss Hetzger?" the tall officer said in a much gentler voice than Director Haggis. "Maggie?"

I looked up again and opened my mouth, but no words would come out. I couldn't even manage another deep, slow breath.

It took me a minute to realize I was crying.

TWENTY-SIX
Maggie

Thirty seconds of crying turned out to be all Director Haggis could take, and he raced out of the cabin, shouting a reminder to reunite with my buddy when I went back to lunch. The officers were a lot more professional, and they waited quietly as I sat on my bunk and sobbed.

Five minutes later I was splashing water on my face in the bathroom, waving goodbye to the officers, and heading back to the mess hall. Charlene was waiting for me on the front steps.

"Hey," she said, jumping to her feet.

"Hey."

"So . . . what happened?"

I told her about the letter.

"Oh." Charlene looked very relieved. "Yeah, that sounds like something Abby would do."

"She also hid a treasure last year for me to find. Look." I showed her the map, with its rough outlines of the cabins and a big X on one side of the field.

"That looks like the oak tree behind the drama cabin," said Charlene. A group of screaming first-year kids ran out of the mess hall and down the steps past us. "We've still got half an hour of free time. Should we try to go get it now?"

"Obviously," I said, hiding a sniff, and we set out across the field.

It looked like Scrabbles McFloof had gone into retirement, because the necklace was right where Abby said it would be. It was a simple design, just three clay beads molded to look like cantaloupes, with M&A painted on them. I sat on the branch, holding it and thinking, while Charlene, who was being super cool about all of this, kept watch beside me.

So many times last summer I'd stretched out on my roof at home, staring out west and thinking about Camp Cantaloupe, and how much fun Abby was having without me. Had Abby actually been sitting up here too sometimes, looking east?

A gust of wind swept across the field, pushing into the trees and blowing through my hair. I pulled the necklace on.

"Hey," Charlene said, elbowing me. "Look." I looked and saw a new official-looking vehicle pull into the parking area beside the admin cabin. Three people got out, all in uniforms, their badges and dark glasses glinting in the sun. They looked professional and serious.

"Ooh, that's the sheriff's office," said Charlene, squinting at the car.

We watched as Director Haggis and the two officers I'd met earlier came to greet the newcomers. There was a round of handshakes and nodding. The new officers turned a slow circle, examining the camp, then stared out at the trees.

"Looks like they're going to be searching the woods again," I said. "What if they find your moose trap this time?"

"They better not," said Charlene. "But if they somehow find it and come asking questions, I can just talk my way out of it." She gave her bangs a flip. "I'm good at getting around grown-ups."

The group of grown-ups outside the admin cabin finished their serious nodding and went inside.

"When are you gonna tell me where this secret cave is, anyway?" I asked, sitting up a little to stretch my neck. Charlene had learned most of my deepest secrets in the last twenty-four hours. It was time we evened the score.

Charlene leaned over to my part of the branch and pointed into the woods. "That's the tree, there, see? The old, tangly one sticking out in that gap."

"That's close. And the moose-trap cave's at the bottom of it?"

"Yup." She sat up. "Hey, want to check it out? We're not supposed to go in the woods alone, but we know those search and rescue people are all inside, and we've got enough time if we hurry."

"Seriously?" I said. Miss Safety Monitor was surprising me again. Sneaking into the woods at night was one thing, but this was broad daylight.

"Yeah. Do you want to see it or not?"

I chewed my lip. I was already in plenty of trouble, but hey, they hadn't sent me home yet. And what had Abby said in her letter? *Get out there and try things! Take some risks!* No time like the present.

"Of course I want to see it!" I said. My official camp buddy grinned.

We climbed down and headed into the trees. Camp Cantaloupe might have had terrible lunch food and a tyrannical director, but I had to admit the woods surrounding it were perfect. The ground was a tangle of fallen logs, ferns, bushes, and saplings, with moss and tiny flowers covering everything. The big trees didn't start their branches until twenty feet up, so following the winding path was like walking through a cool, dim room full of sweet smells and birdsong, with a green roof stretched overhead.

We stopped at a bend. "There it is," said Charlene. "Shoot. Still no moose."

I looked where she was pointing. A sort of mini-hill rose

from the forest floor a little way off the path. Ferns and brambles grew around it, sharp slabs of boulders stuck out through the moss, and an ancient, crooked tree perched on top, its roots hanging over the edge of the mound and down the side like fingers.

I whistled, impressed. Somewhere in the woods behind us a bird whistled back.

"Good call picking this spot," I said as Charlene led the way off the path. "The moose would definitely get its antlers caught if it tried to go in there."

The bird whistled again, louder. I glanced up at the sky and replied.

"We shouldn't stay long," said Charlene, ducking down and pushing a tangle of ferns away from the roots. "It's risky in the daytime. But here, come and see."

My new bird friend whistled a third time, closer now. I spun in a circle, hoping to catch a glimpse, my lips ready to whistle a reply . . . and saw something else instead.

"Go!" I said to Charlene. "Go! Go! Go!"

"What? Why?"

"Shhh!"

I ducked into the ferns beside her and pointed.

Five people were heading along the path in our direction: the two search and rescue officers I'd met over lunch, and the three scary-official new ones from the sheriff's. One of them raised his head, pursed his lips, and whistled.

My bird buddy was a grown-up.

"Ohhhh, no," breathed Charlene. "We cannot get caught out here. What are we gonna do?"

"Get inside," I said, pushing Charlene toward the cave.

"But there's no room in there! It's full of cantaloupes."

"Pretend you're a cantaloupe, then." I could hear footsteps. "Just until they're gone. We've got no choice."

I held back the roots as Charlene squeezed between them, then snuck one last look over the bushes. The officers had reached the bend in the path.

I ducked into the darkness. The hollow space Charlene had carved out under the tree was almost pitch black, and it smelled like wet earth, rotting bark, and the overwhelming warm melony sweetness of cantaloupes.

"Where . . . ?" I whispered, feeling around, my hands and knees and elbows bumping everywhere I turned. "How am I supposed to—"

"Shhh!" hissed Charlene. "Quit moving or you'll knock them over."

Even as she said it, I felt a rogue cantaloupe bounce against my shoulder. I fumbled it back into the pile, then scooched around until I was pressed against the dirt wall. It was the exact opposite of comfortable, but at least we were out of sight.

"Told you it was a false lead, Ron," said a voice suddenly,

so close to our hiding place I jumped, scratching my back on a root. "Just some local birdlife, like I said."

"Didn't sound like a bird," said another voice, which I guessed was Ron, my not-a-bird whistling buddy. "That whistle sounded human to me. A little kid, maybe."

I bristled in the darkness. I was twelve and a half years old. I was not *little*.

"Yeah, sure," said another, deeper voice. "You were going to come out here and find the missing girl on your very first sweep of the woods, thirty yards from camp. Right."

There was some scattered chuckling. Charlene shifted slightly in the cantaloupey darkness.

"I wish you had, though," a familiar voice said. It was the nice lady officer who'd been there when I read Abby's letter. "We've found no clues at all, and we've got, what, just over twenty-four hours? That about right, Officer Fields?"

"Just about. If we don't find this girl by then, it's goodbye, Camp Cantaloupe."

"Closed down?"

"Closed down. For good."

"Shame."

Charlene's gasp was as loud as mine, but she was smart enough not to whap frantically at the air, catching the precarious pile of produce with her hand. I wasn't.

In my experience disasters usually went down in super...

slow ... motion. But not this time. My friend the rogue cantaloupe clonked out of its spot, bounced off my arm, and went
rolling merrily out into the open, crashing through the ferns
as it went.

"What was that?" said Ron sharply. "Over there!" The
footsteps started up again.

Charlene made a tiny noise in her throat. If getting caught
on our own in the woods was bad, getting caught hiding in
a cave full of stolen cantaloupes was going to be a scandal.
Thank Samson's snagglepaw the rest of the pile was holding.
For now.

The footsteps crunched closer and closer through the
undergrowth, then stopped abruptly.

"What the—"

"Is that what I think it is?"

"What's it doing out here?"

"Ron, I think the big question is: why was it moving?"

There was silence. I could picture them all, standing over
the rogue cantaloupe, looking around for clues to where it
came from. And I could picture one of them spotting our hiding place. Then another. Then another. Five heads turning
together toward the only possibility.

Crunch. Crunch. Five sets of footsteps were headed right
for us. And then—

Fleedle-fleedle, fleedle-fleedle, fleedle-fleedle!

The crunching stopped.

"Who leaves their phone on the factory-default ringer?" said the nice officer.

"It's my work phone, Carla," snapped Ron. The ringing cut off. "Yes? It is.... Huh, okay.... What? Are you certain? That's a serious setback.... Yes, we'll be right there, but we found a clue in the woods not far from the main field.... A cantaloupe.... I'm sorry, what? ... Really? ... I see. We'll be there in five minutes."

Ron closed his phone.

"Who was that?" someone asked.

"The director, Mr. Haggis. He just heard from the missing kid's father. Still can't make it out here, something about car trouble and some sort of baking emergency. But the big news is he also heard from the search and rescue canine unit. They missed the ferry. Won't be here until later this evening."

"That's a serious setback."

"Literally what I just said. We need to regroup and come up with a new strategy for today."

"But what about this?"

"Mr. Haggis said it was nothing. He says the cantaloupes are an old camp tradition. All the kids bring them and leave them lying around, hoping to get the attention of some pretend moose. He said he confiscated most of them since they were becoming a health and safety hazard, but obviously someone slipped this by him and hid it out here."

"And it was moving because . . . ?"

"Probably a mouse or squirrel trying to eat it."

"Hmm, maybe."

"Hey, is this a first for anyone else? Standing around in the woods arguing over a cantaloupe?"

"Yup."

"Same."

"Beats paperwork, though."

"True. I'll take cantaloupe detecting any day."

"Okay, enough," said Ron, sounding fed up. "Let's head back. We've got a missing child to recover. And not much time to do it."

The footsteps moved away, and the woods grew still again. But Charlene and I waited a long, long time in our cave, pressed against the walls, the smell of cantaloupe and tree roots and fear wrapping around us, before we dared to creep out again, like stiff and very relieved bear cubs, into the light.

TWENTY-SEVEN
Abby

A steady wind was puffing over the island from the sea, disrupting the popcorn clouds and making the leaves of the Flappy Trees whisper over our heads. Another elevator hidden near the stump took the four of us back down to the Island Underneath, and we returned to the room with the Winter Palace door to change into our regular clothes. Afterward, we headed to the galley for lunch.

The galley was set on a rope-and-plank balcony overlooking the glass wall, and Joe was so busy shouting about all the fish and whales and turtles, he barely got to eat anything.

"We've spent the better part of the day just getting prepared and checking one palace," said Antonia, as I devoured the best grilled cheese sandwich I'd ever had in my entire life. "We'll have to push to get the other two in."

"Definitely," Helene said. "Though we did get the biggest location out of the way first."

"Where are we going next?" I asked, wiping my mouth.

"A classic, but a bit of a tricky one, seeing as the royal family still lives there. We're headed to Buckingham Palace."

The room housing the door to Buckingham Palace was a little farther down the hall where Joe and I had practiced our bowing and curtsying. Inside, it had the same basic setup, and I was surprised to discover the clothes along this wall were super similar to the ones we'd gotten to choose from before.

"Why aren't the clothes different?" I asked. "I thought there'd be more variety or something."

"History," called Helene from behind a curtain. "Older outfits provide the best cover, and there was remarkable consistency in the courtly fashions of the early and mid-eighteenth century. But we don't all have to dress like the courtiers did."

She reappeared, dressed in a simple dark gray dress with poofy skirts, a white apron, a high collar, and long sleeves. A round cap covered most of her head, and she'd perched a pair of tiny spectacles on the end of her nose. The ring of keys matched her outfit perfectly. "I'm a housekeeper, see?" she said. "And look, Mama makes a wonderful old sea dog."

Antonia had drawn back her curtain. She was wearing a

movie-quality pirate captain's outfit, complete with jacket, hat, boots, and belt. "This is the only time you are ever allowed to call me an old anything," she said, lifting her eye patch and frowning at her daughter.

Joe dressed himself in a blue-and-white striped tunic with braided edges and gold buttons, a black hat with three corners, ivory silk stockings, a dark blue coat with tails, and a silver cane. He looked like a fancy version of the guy on the Quaker Oats box.

After a long search that had Antonia tapping her pirate boot impatiently, I put together an outfit that was even prettier than the last one. The hips on this dress were only a few feet wide, thank goodness, but it did have a big bustley underskirt, so the shining silver fabric poured around me as I walked. I chose heeled silver slippers to go with it, a long necklace of blue stones that honestly might have been actual sapphires, and an elegant dark brown wig with a silver coronet perched on top.

"Everybody ready?" asked Helene. We all nodded. I adjusted my coronet. "Good. Now, please remember that this isn't a museum like the Winter Palace. This is a living, working building, so we'll have to be extra careful as we search. No talking to palace workers or tourists, you two." She pointed at me and Joe. "And no wandering off and getting lost. Remember your palace protocol, and we should all be fine. Oh, and since the day is getting on, I'm setting a two-hour time limit. We're leaving after that, no matter what."

Helene brought out her ring of keys again and opened the lock, which was decorated this time with roses. There was the usual gap of darkness after we shut the door, and then Antonia was pushing open the side of a massive china hutch and we stepped out into some sort of storeroom. Fluorescent lights buzzed overhead.

I did a little twirl, examining my gorgeous new outfit in the light. Helene looked down her glasses at me. "We need seriousness from everyone here, please, Abby," she said. "This is not a dress-up game."

We trooped after her out of the storeroom, along a plain hallway, up a set of concrete stairs, then through a door into what looked to be the public-facing, historical part of the palace. There were velvet ropes again, and informational signs, and a security guard.

The guard came right up to us.

"Morning, ma'am," she said, bowing to our leader. "How's the historical housekeeping today?"

Helene put her hands on her hips. "It's always difficult on rainy days," she replied, in a pitch-perfect British accent. She nodded at the window across the hall, which was being lashed with rain as dark clouds bumped each other across the sky. "Everyone gets a little housebound. It's all I can do to keep the family from declaring an absolute monarchy again!"

The guard laughed, and we moved on, smiling and nodding.

"They know who you are here?" Joe asked in a whisper as Antonia steered us past another velvet rope into a room full of squashy chairs and sofas. A knot of passing tourists snapped photos of us.

"I make a brief appearance once a week," Helene answered, lining us up beside a marble fireplace. "As far as most of these people know, I really do work here as a historical reenactor." She arranged us around the fireplace like we were deep in conversation, motioned us to act like we were talking, and started searching the chairs and sofas, pretending to be fussing over the state of the room. A small crowd gathered to watch, cell phones held up for videos.

And that was how we carried on, crossing the velvet ropes in room after room, miming theatrical conversations for the tourists while Helene pretended to clean and fuss and fluff pillows. Buckingham Palace wasn't quite as fancy as our first stop in Russia, but it was cozy being inside with the rain sheeting down the windows, and it was nice being able to understand some of the reactions from the crowd, including one little girl who tugged her dad's arm, pointed at me, and said, "Look, Daddy, it's the Princess of England!"

She kept her eyes on me while her parents read the informational signs, and when they moved on she looked back over her shoulder and waved. I winked and waved back, and she looked so happy I forgot all about how much the shoes were pinching my feet and the crinkly dress was itching like crazy.

I lost track of time, and there were no wall clocks in the historical parts of the palace, but it must have been close to our two-hour time limit when it happened.

We were finishing up in our third royal bedroom. A tour group had just left, and Helene was herding us toward a door at the back when a family arrived with two wide-eyed little girls. I couldn't resist the chance to be the "Princess of England" one more time, so I turned and waved. The girls gasped and waved back. One of them tugged on her mom's sleeve, whispering excitedly. The mom saw me watching.

"She wants to know if you're a real princess," she called. Ooh, Americans! I could talk to these people. Antonia coughed meaningfully behind me, but I was too caught up in the moment to remember all her lectures.

"Of course I am," I called. "I'm the Princess Abigail." I gave a deep curtsy, my best yet. One of the girls clapped, but the other tugged at her dad's sleeve this time, speaking urgently in his ear. Another tour group filtered into the room. I heard Joe shifting beside me.

"She, um, wants to know if she can grow up to be a princess too, someday," said the dad. The mom smiled and quirked an eyebrow at me.

"Oh . . . ," I said. Shoot. If only I had Maggie's imagination, or the talent to make up a story on the spot like Antonia. An idea suddenly sparked in my brain, and I crossed the room to kneel right in front of the little girls, the velvet rope between us. "You don't have to wait to grow up," I said, giving them my very brightest smile. "Because you already are. A princess is who you are inside."

"Really?" said the first little girl. Her eyes went wide, and she grabbed her sister by the hand and pulled her under the rope.

"Hey, wait!" I said.

The girls clambered onto the massive carved bed.

"Stop!" cried the mom. "Stop!"

I tried to go after them, but my shoes got caught on my dress as I stood and I fell spectacularly, taking the dad down with me.

"We're the princess! We're the princess!" sang the girls, holding hands, jumping up and down on the antique cushions and clearly having the time of their lives.

The dad and I staggered to our feet, but the whole velvet barrier was down and more kids were running excitedly into the room, climbing on furniture and touching everything.

Two palace monitors and the security guard we'd met earlier pushed their way in, ordering calm in loud voices. The guard took one look at my friends backed against the wall and gave Helene a scalding look. Antonia started forward to help restore order, but the guard called, "No! Please, just get out of the way," and began escorting screamingly happy children off the royal bedspread.

If the look the security guard gave Helene was bad, the look Antonia gave me was devastating. Ugh. My stomach curled itself into a ball of molten acid. I hated being in trouble more than anything in the entire world.

Helene marched us out through the door at the back of the room, around a corner, and down a flight of stairs. Another security guard rushed past us, heading the way we'd come, loud voices squawking from his walkie-talkie.

No one said a word as Helene swept us along, navigating the complicated hallways of Buckingham Palace like she could do it in her sleep, until we were back in the storeroom where we'd started.

"That," Antonia said, slamming the door closed behind us, "was a terrible mistake." The fluorescent lights made everything look washed out, but the angry red in her cheeks was clear. "Do you have any explanation for why you felt the need to endanger our entire mission like that?"

"I'm so sorry. It was those little girls," I said. "I just wanted to make their day, make them happy. I wanted to give them something to remember."

"You've certainly done that!"

"Hey, she tried to do a nice thing," said Joe softly.

"And that nice thing may have permanently damaged our relationship with this palace and our access to this city," Helene replied, her voice clipped. "If they look into this and start asking questions about who we all are, there will be serious trouble the next time I show my face." She clicked open the secret door in the hutch. "I'm extremely disappointed in you, Abigail. You know how important these loops are to us. You know we depend on access to these palaces for everything in our lives. We've put a great deal of faith and trust in you, and I believed you would show us the basic respect of following our instructions. Clearly, I was wrong."

And she turned her back on me and disappeared through the panel without another word.

TWENTY-EIGHT
Abby

The island looked as gloomy as London when we got back. The clouds from that morning had rolled in, and thick, heavy rain was smashing down, soaking our clothes in an instant and making the stump dangerously slippery. A rogue gust knocked my wig into the grass, and I tripped twice going after it, miserable right down to my wet, aching toes.

Our group stayed silent as we made our way down to the Island Underneath and back to the Rose Door cabin, where Helene flung her housekeeper's cap onto a chair with a squelch, open anger clear on her face, and disappeared behind a dressing curtain.

I wanted to melt into the floor. I felt completely horrible. Joe gave me a sympathetic smile from across the room as he pulled his curtain closed too, but Antonia claimed the only remaining alcove without a glance.

I was kicking off my sodden slippers when a voice fuzzed in over a speaker in the ceiling.

"Hello? Helene? Antonia? Are you there?"

"What is it, Cypher?" Antonia called from her alcove.

"We've got a serious problem," Cypher said. My stomach seized up. Had the news about my mistake traveled that fast? Did everyone on the island already know?

"What kind of problem?" asked Helene.

"Security, I'm afraid. Florence is malfunctioning. That ship she was decoying traced her command codes back to us. They're headed this way."

There was a thud from Antonia's dressing room. "There's a ship heading here?" she called. "You're sure?"

"Positive. And they're ignoring all of Florence's distraction and diversion signals."

Helene swore. "We'll be right there!" she yelled. Oof. There was no way this was helping her mood.

She reappeared wearing a zip-up hoodie and fashionable sweatpants. "I'm off," she said. "The third palace will just have to wait until tomorrow. Mama, will you bring Joe to the control room when you're both ready? His sonar expertise may be useful."

Antonia agreed, and Helene headed for the exit. She turned back in the doorway. "Abigail, stay here and do what you can to hang up our wet things. We may have just wasted a whole day chasing phantom pillow forts and ruining our relationship with an important palace, but that's no reason to take it out on the clothing archives." And she pulled the door shut behind her with a thunk.

Soon Joe and Antonia were dressed and dry, too, and following after Helene.

And there I was. Left behind. Alone.

I hated being alone almost as much as I hated being in trouble. I felt even worse now than I had last summer, when the NAFAFA Council attacked and my dad thought I'd trashed his entire kitchen as a joke.

Maybe there was some way I could make it up to Helene. Maybe I could fix things while she and the others tackled the problem with Florence and the ship. There must be some way of proving I wasn't a total goof.

I changed back into my own clothes, hanging my wet princess dress up as neatly as I could, then did the same for Joe's and Antonia's outfits. But when I pulled back the curtain to Helene's alcove, I got a surprise. There were her shoes and her housekeeper dress lying in a soggy heap. And there, sitting on a chair beside them, was the ring of keys.

I picked it up. Okay, now here was an opportunity.

Helene had said we'd wasted a whole day. She'd said the third palace would have to wait till tomorrow. So what if I went and checked another one by myself? Sure, it was a little risky, but I knew exactly where I'd gone wrong now. There was no way I would mess up again. And fine, it was kind of a long shot that I'd just happen to choose a palace that still had a functioning pillow fort link, but it was worth a try, right? For Antonia? And Helene?

The keys were heavy in my hand. There was the Honeycomb Key I already knew, and the Rose Key leading to Buckingham Palace. The other carved symbols clinked together: a falcon, a deer, a lily, a ship. My stomach swooped as I examined the tiny sails. That ship headed our way right now sounded like a real problem, but if it was giving me a chance to find the Oak Key and redeem myself, I'd take it.

Before I could change my mind, I threw the rest of Antonia's things on hangers and headed into the hall. The long row of doors set my heart thumping like Samson that time he got trapped with a catnip toy in the linen closet. I had no clue which palace Helene and Antonia had planned to check next, so the question was: How to choose?

I could always just pick a door at random, but that felt a little too reckless even for this plan.

What would Maggie do? Hmm. Maggie would let the universe decide by flipping a coin or something. I patted my pockets. I didn't have a coin, but I did have . . . the Iron Key.

I pulled it out, set it on the floor of the hall, and gave it a spin, watching it blur into a circle while I silently begged the universe for a break. The key hissed softly to a stop, pointing directly at the last door on the left.

I scooped up the key, darted down the hall, and headed through it.

This room was just the same as the others: long wall of clothes, changing alcoves at the back, a door in its frame in the center. I walked over to see which lock the universe had paired me with. The Deer. Huh. I had no clue what that meant.

The clothes in this room turned out to be different, and not in a fun way. They were less shiny and much more practical. I changed into a simple black dress with long sleeves, a lace-lined collar, a high waist, and thankfully, no weird hip extension dealies at all. Next came a boring but comfortable pair of flat slippers—because seriously, enough with the pinchy shoes—a brooch shaped liked a singing bird, and a shiny amethyst-and-silver bracelet.

There were only a few wigs, all too big for me, so I settled on a pale lavender hat with swooping pointy sides that tied with a ribbon under my chin. I probably looked like I had a piece of modern art floating on my head, but it was surprisingly comfortable.

Last but not least I tucked the Iron Key into a pouch in the waistband of my dress. Just in case.

My stomach began swirling as I stepped toward the door,

but it was too late to back out now. This was my one chance to save the day. I turned the Deer Key in the matching lock and pulled. The door opened onto darkness.

Okay, what did Maggie always say? Deep, slow breath, Abby. All I had to do was track down a linked pillow fort, retrieve the Oak Key from le Petit Salon, loop back to the Island Stump, and get down here again before the Florence crisis was fixed. Once I found the pillow fort, the rest would be as easy as feeding the chickens. And when Helene got back from the control room, I could hand her the ring of keys and casually mention that she might find an extra one on there if she looked.

Keeping that shining image of victory front and center in my mind, I stepped into the darkness.

The air smelled musty as I emerged, blinking, under greenish fluorescent lights, from another wooden box. Though at least this time it was one I could stand up in.

It looked like I was in a furniture storeroom. The place was crammed with bookcases, tables, dressers, chairs, and unidentifiable lumps under white sheets. I'd looped in through a heavily carved, bathtub-size wooden chest leaning on one end against the wall. A pink tag dangled from the lid, showing measurements and a few lines scribbled in what looked like German.

Great. German. I didn't speak a single word of German.

Well, not that that mattered. I'd learned my lesson in Buckingham Palace: I was not about to talk to *anyone*.

I adjusted my fancy hat, did a quick practice curtsy just to see how the new dress moved, and walked out of that room with my head held high.

I made it three steps along the hallway outside before I realized I still had Helene's ring of keys in my hand.

Oh, problem. I looked back toward the storage room, then down at the keys, then back again. What should I do? I was racing against the Florence-situation clock as it was, and there just wasn't time for me to loop through the chest back to the island, get down to the door room, drop off the keys, and loop back through the Deer Door to restart my search.

There was only one good option under the circumstances: I'd have to bring them with me.

The hall looked depressingly like some sort of business officey area, but a flight of stone stairs leading off it looked promising. I headed up, hooking the keys onto my belt and burning the route back to the chest into my brain.

One flight up I found the touristy area of the palace. The architecture was dark and heavy, but the deep red carpeting, carved stone arches, and elaborate paintings were similar to the palaces I'd already seen that day. Oof, three palaces in one day. This was not what I'd been expecting from my first week back at summer camp.

There was a visitors' map on the wall. It was in German, but from what I could make out I was somewhere called Schloss Charlottenburg. There were five floors, and I was on the one with the great hall. Hmm. I needed the floor with the lounges and bedrooms. Anywhere with lots of pillows.

I headed up one more flight. There was another map, but I couldn't make out if the little rooms on it were bedrooms or not. As I squinted at the tiny lines, a group of grown-ups speaking loud, bouncy Italian appeared at the end of the corridor. One of them pointed at me and shouted a greeting, pulling out his phone. Oh, no thank you. The last thing I needed right now was to end up in a tourist selfie fest. I escaped back to the stairs.

The next floor up was brighter and more delicate, and this time the visitors' map showed the clear outline of beds in a line of rooms on the far end. Victory!

I followed the arrows on the sign, passing from a gallery room to a music room, from the music room to a sitting room, and from the sitting room, at last, into a bedroom.

I'd passed a few tour-guide types along the way, all wearing green sweaters and black pants, and they'd nodded hello just like the guides at the other palaces. But the first bedroom came with a surprise: a security guard in dark blue, complete with walkie-talkie and badge. She looked very serious.

Keep your head up, Abby. Pillow fort search time. I could

already see at least six spots that had pillows and blankets together. I gave the guard a deep curtsy, receiving the ghost of a smile in return, and stepped over the velvet rope. The guard shifted slightly.

Carefully, methodically, I began lifting and adjusting every pillow around the room, starting with the bed, then moving on to the chaise and two sofas standing against the wall.

The guard coughed. I ignored her, focusing on staying in character as I pretended to fluff pillows and smooth creases. She coughed again, very clearly, and I had to look up.

She spoke in German, asking me something, nodding back toward the rooms I'd come through.

I blinked at her. The guard frowned.

She spoke again, definitely asking more questions, and stepped away from the wall.

Oh, boy. This was bad. Why were there no tourists here to give me cover? But I was going to stick by what I'd learned at my last palace disaster; no talking unless I had absolutely, positively, utterly no choice. I smiled again, held up my hands in a sort of general "Oh, well" gesture, and headed for the next room over, all my fingers crossed.

The guard followed, watching as I stepped over the velvet ropes into an even more elaborate bedchamber, with a humongous bed and mountains of sofas and squashy furniture. She let me begin my fluffing and smoothing and discreet searching uninterrupted, but as I poked behind a velvet-and-chintz sofa cushion, I heard her speaking in a low voice into her walkie-talkie, then the crackly buzz of someone responding. I sped up.

There was more buzzing on the walkie-talkie as the guard asked a question and got a curt, one-word reply. I looked up just in time to see her hurrying back to the first room.

Oh, doom. She was definitely suspicious of me. And all signs pointed to her going to get backup. Think, Abby, think. Deep, slow breath.

Could I hide? Nope, hiding wouldn't solve anything. Could I get out the way I'd come? No, that's where the security guard was. My only option was to find some other way back downstairs to the chest or escape through a pillow fort link. And so far, the links were leaving me hanging.

Why did I try to do this on my own, again? I'd barely gotten started and I was already trapped and cornered with the authorities on the way. And the authorities would make me talk, and find out I was American and not supposed to be here, and they'd get in touch with my dad and ruin his honeymoon and he'd have to pay to get me flown home and everything would be awful.

And what about my new friends on the island? I had the ring of keys, and if I got caught and arrested I'd have no way of getting it back to them. And without it they had no way of getting off the island, bringing their kids home from school, getting food supplies, or anything else.

I really was living one of Maggie's worst-case scenarios this time. I'd just single-handedly ruined everything. For everyone. All at once.

Only . . . hold on, wait. That line between those two paintings. Was that . . . was that a door?

I darted over, kicked the wall, and nearly shouted with joy as a panel swung open, revealing a powder room featuring an old-timey sofa draped in pillows and blankets.

The snap and hiss of the walkie-talkie sounded in the room behind me, then sharp, quick footsteps. A voice called out. Another answered. And another.

I was completely trapped.

Almost hyperventilating, the ring of keys jangling like an alarm at my side, I began pulling pillows off the sofa at random. Honestly, why did Maggie always include near-misses and narrow escapes in those games we used to play? It sounded fun in theory, but in real life this was *terrifying*.

The footsteps were past the rope, speeding into a run . . . and . . . yes! Thank you, everything forever! A blue silk pillow came away in my hand to show a faded brown pillow beneath it, and when I shoved that one forward, there was darkness instead of more sofa.

I jumped feet-first into the link, almost crying with relief, and caught a half-second glimpse of the security guard racing into the room as I pulled the blue silk pillow back into place and slammed the brown pillow shut as hard as I could behind it.

TWENTY-NINE
Maggie

Charlene and I were very late for volleyball after our adventure in the woods, but when I told the teacher the search and rescue officers had wanted to talk with me about Abby, and that Charlene had come with me because she's my official buddy, he accepted the story and told us to just join a team and get spiking.

The rest of the day dragged by even slower than the day before. Though there was some excitement after dinner when the search and rescue dogs arrived, and their poor handler had to make a run for the admin cabin to avoid being swamped by hundreds of kids wanting to say hello.

I couldn't stop thinking about what Charlene and I had heard from inside the cantaloupe cave. If our plan didn't work, this might be the very last day of Camp Cantaloupe for everyone here. Forever. All these kids were walking around living their last day of summer camp. And none of them even knew it.

Finally, finally it was lights-out, and Charlene and I started counting down the minutes until we could sneak out and head to the NAFAFA meeting. It was easier to stay awake this time, knowing she was staring up into the darkness too, waiting. I brought my flashlight under the covers and wrote Abby one last postcard before we set out.

Dear Abs,

The search for you is getting serious. Today the officers went through your stuff, which made me mad (don't worry, I put it all back), and they gave me the letter you wrote me. The one in case the key didn't work. And Abs, thank you. So much. And for the necklace, too. You're my best friend in the world, and I miss you, and I promise to be a better friend when you get back. Which will hopefully be tonight, since Charlene and I are heading out in a minute here for a meeting with NAFAFA so we can join forces and rescue you.

Updates from today: Charlene and I had to hide in her moose trap in the woods when the search and rescue officers came by. We finally got served cucumber casserole for lunch, and most of mine ended up on my shoes. Your squirrel enemy didn't steal the necklace you made me (obviously, since I'm wearing it). And Ms. Sabine wants me and Charlene to do this big art project with the first-year kids next week to help cure them of homesickness.

This time I'm gonna make it out of this camp, Abs. You'll see. I won't be stopped again.

See you soon,

Mags

It was another perfect night of blazing stars, whispering trees, and bright moonlight. I followed Charlene—in her Safety Monitor sash this time, in case we ran into any authorities—out of the cabin and along the edge of the field, keeping a careful eye out for the search dogs, my faithful supply pack tugging at my shoulders.

Summer camp sure was turning out to involve a lot more covert operations than Abby had let on in her postcards last year.

"Hey, whoa, stop!" Charlene hissed, holding me back as we rounded the corner of the mess hall. I peered around her head. There was still a light on in the admin building. And worse, the windows of the arts and crafts cabin were blazing.

"Seriously?" I groaned. I should have known it wouldn't be easy. The stakes were too high.

"Maybe Ms. Sabine just forgot to turn the lights off," whispered Charlene. "Let's go see."

We snuck up to the side of the cabin. One of the windows

was open a crack, and I could hear music. Ballroom dancing music. We peered in.

It looked like the scene of some massive art explosion. Ms. Sabine, wearing a collage crown, a paper-chain necklace, and a rapturous smile, was spinning around the room with a brush in one hand and a bucket of paint in the other. There were canvases on easels and pieces of cardboard set up everywhere, and whenever she passed one she'd attack it furiously, splashes of paint flying, then dance away.

Charlene looked at me, and we both choked down laughter.

"Well, *that's* going on, I guess," I said. "But it's almost time for the meeting. How are we going to get past her?" I watched Ms. Sabine do a pirouette, knocking over one of the easels. She laughed, drizzling paint on it from overhead, and kept on dancing.

"We need a good distraction," said Charlene. "Any ideas?"

Both of us jumped as there was a knock at the cabin door, just around the corner of the building. Ms. Sabine didn't hear it. The knocking came again, and we ducked as she stopped dance painting and looked up. The music clicked off, and a moment later we heard the door squeak.

We peered back over the windowsill. Director Haggis was standing in the doorway, his mouth hanging open.

"Is . . . is everything okay, Eleanor?" he asked.

"Everything is wonderful, Hector," Ms. Sabine said, waving her paintbrush like a magic wand. "I was so inspired by the extraordinary artistic creativity shown by some of my students today, I simply *had* to dig in deep and see what I could create. I have to say so far I am thrilled with the results!"

Director Haggis eyed the paint-splattered easels, the upended tables and chairs, and Ms. Sabine's paper-chain necklace.

"Well," he said. "I'm glad everything is . . . all right." He ruffled his mustache. "I wish I could say the same for this camp. I just got off the phone with the sheriff. That woman asks some tough questions, and she's made it clear she's going to shut us down by tomorrow afternoon if that missing girl hasn't shown up. Anyway, when I saw your lights on, I thought I should stop by to make sure there wasn't some new disaster happening here."

Ms. Sabine, who had been peeling paint off her forearms, looked up, beaming. "And I'm so pleased you did!" she said. Clearly she hadn't been listening to a word he'd said. "Because I've got a curriculum proposal I desperately want to share with you!" And she launched into an enthusiastic description of the project she'd condemned Charlene and me to. I was fighting back a giggle at the bewildered look on Director Haggis's face when Charlene elbowed me hard in the ribs.

"Ow! What was that for?"

Charlene was pointing frantically toward our sofa forts at the back of the cabin. I looked and saw a girl wearing silver sunglasses and a baseball hat over her cloud of curly black hair getting to her feet.

Carolina! Wow, she'd really grown over the last year.

My eyes zoomed to the grown-ups, but they hadn't spotted her. Carolina looked around, taking in the chaos of the room, then turned her sunglasses to the window. I raised my head a fraction of an inch higher and waggled my eyebrows. Carolina stood there, cool and calm, then gave a brief nod, ducked down, and disappeared from sight.

Charlene and I ducked down too.

"That was close!" she said. "Who was that?"

"Carolina. She's from the Forts of the Eastern Seaboard network. Well, she runs it now, I guess, which means she's on the Council of NAFAFA. She must have come to get us for the meeting." I frowned, angling one eye over the windowsill again. "She probably went back to tell everyone how we're trapped out here."

"Do you think they'll be able to help?" asked Charlene.

"I'm not sure," I admitted. "I mean, the Council can't just crawl out of our forts and politely ask Ms. Sabine and the director to leave, can they?"

"Nope. So that means it's up to us to get those two"—Charlene pointed a thumb at the window—"out of there."

"Totally. We need that good distraction you mentioned."

"Or just a decent plan," said a voice. And with no warning at all, Carolina materialized out of the night between us.

Charlene screeched.

"What was that?" Director Haggis's voice said.

The three of us pressed our backs to the wall as footsteps crossed the cabin to the window. "Just an owl," said Ms. Sabine. "Anyway, as I was saying . . ."

The footsteps moved away, and we relaxed. I turned to Carolina.

"How on earth did you get out here?" I whispered. "How did you get by the grown-ups?"

Carolina shrugged. "I told you last summer I was training to be the world's best secret agent," she said. "This was a chance to practice. I think I'm getting pretty good."

"Super good!" said Charlene. "Hi, I'm Charlene."

"I'm Carolina. Nice Safety Monitor sash. Ben would really like that." They shook hands.

"So, yes," I said. "Hi. You said we need a decent plan. Do you have one?"

"Yep." Carolina leaned in close. "That man in there sounds like he's more worried about finding Abby Hernandez than anything, because a missing kid will ruin his camp. So you and your responsible sash"—she pointed to Charlene—"are going to knock on the door and tell them you saw her from your cabin window."

"Ooo, and I bet they'll want to go see!" said Charlene. "Yes!"

"Perfect!" I said. "You lead them into the woods, and by the time you decide you didn't see anything after all, we'll be long gone."

"I can do that." Charlene nodded. "And then I double back here and come to this meeting with you?"

Hmm. Carolina and I couldn't wait around for Charlene to do all that and get back. There wasn't even a guarantee she'd be able to get away from Ms. Sabine and Director Haggis. It was a bit unfair, but she'd have to miss the trip to the Hub.

"Actually, what we need most is someone to hold things down here at camp," I said, thinking fast. "It might take us a while to find Abby, so someone will have to cover for us and get in the way of the authorities. Obviously you're the best person to be in charge of that. You'll be the only one here who knows the truth about Abby, and the Shipwreck Treehouse, and the forts and letters and all of it. Plus no one knows Camp Cantaloupe like you. No one could do it better!"

Charlene smiled. "I am good at fooling grown-ups," she said. She agreed to the plan, and after a last-minute conference with Carolina, she got to her feet, rounded the corner of the cabin, and knocked on the door.

The conversation went down just as we'd predicted. Charlene told Director Haggis that she'd gotten up for a glass of water and was sure she'd seen Abby wandering through the woods near camp. Director Haggis was overjoyed, and he and Ms. Sabine agreed it would look best if they rescued Abby themselves. Pausing only to grab the emergency flashlight and turn off the lights, they hurried after Charlene.

"Oh, this is all awfully dramatic, isn't it?" I heard Ms. Sabine say happily as they ran past.

"I'll show that sheriff who's *really* dedicated to the welfare of my campers!" cried Director Haggis.

Carolina and I watched until their flashlight beam was a safe distance away, then crept into the cabin. "Thanks for coming to help us out like that," I said as we picked our way through the knocked-over easels and splatter-painted chairs. It was kind of a miracle I got only a few smears of glitter paint on my pajama pants. "I'm pretty sure you're a great secret agent already."

We crawled into my fort, and I had a sudden flashback to the summer before, when I'd followed Carolina into the Hub for the very first time, the night my whole world changed.

I smiled. My summer at Camp Cantaloupe might be in total chaos, but at least this time as I headed into the Hub, I knew exactly what I was getting myself into.

At least I thought I did.

THIRTY
Abby

I lay back, gasping in the darkness, finally releasing my death grip on the faded brown pillow.

That. Was. Way. Too. Close.

Gradually my heart stopped hurling itself against my ribs, and I felt around in the darkness. Wooden slats and panels, cold floor, squashy pillows. Victory! I was back under the First Sofa, and without the backpack it was a lot easier to navigate. Although the wings on my hat were kind of a nuisance as I scooched my way out.

The room was dark, but a bright sliver was coming from behind one of the curtains. I headed over and pulled it open. A line of medium-quality sunlight sauntered through the dirty window, and I got my first look at le Petit Salon.

And yup, that was it. A small, dusty room with marble

floors, paneled walls, a carved door on one side, curtains and windows on the other, and the poor, lonely, sagging sofa. The First Sofa. The source of all this pillow fort nonsense. And, if I was lucky, my missing key.

I knelt down, fumbling under it as best I could. My fingers found cold marble, dust bunnies, and a couple curled-up dead spiders, but no key. I searched again, and again, and again. Finally I had to face facts: if I really had dropped the Oak Key under there, it looked like somebody else already found it.

Disappointment punched me in the stomach. Of course it wouldn't be that easy.

I got back to my feet, staring down at the sofa. Who had the key? Only pillow fort kids could get in here, and it sounded like only Council members ever bothered. Maggie had said le Petit Salon was something most pillow forters saw on their first day and never visited again, like a hometown tourist attraction. And I couldn't blame them. Who would want to hang out in here? There wasn't anything to do. They couldn't even open the door.

But hey ... I could. ...

I looked over. The grimy sunlight had reached the handle, highlighting the keyhole and the legendary lock. A tingle ran down my spine.

Should I ... ?

Yes. The answer was yes.

I pulled out the Iron Key, crossed the room, and fit it neatly into the lock that hadn't been opened in almost three hundred years.

I took a deep breath. I turned the key.

The lock clicked open.

For five long seconds I stared at it, then laughed. I was acting like Maggie, expecting something dramatic to happen. So much for the prophecy about the person who opened this door. So much for step seven of Maggie's big summer plan, ushering in a golden age and revealing the deepest secrets of pillow forting and all that. In the end it was just plain old me.

Although, to be fair, I was wearing a very fancy hat.

I pressed down the handle and pulled. With a creak that sounded like a scream in the silence, the door eased open a few inches, then a few more. Light stabbed me in the eyes. I squinted out into a wide hallway full of white marble, gold detailing, and beautiful silver dangling lights. I'd seen my fair share of palaces in the last twenty-four hours, and I could tell this one was a stunner. It almost put the Winter Palace to shame. I looked both ways down the hall, but there was no one around. A metal sign standing beside the door read LE PETIT SALON in swirly writing.

So, yes, more victory. I'd opened the famously closed

door. Whee. Maggie would probably have made a speech to mark the occasion, but since I was all on my own, there wasn't much point.

I returned to the room and eased the door closed, trying to minimize the squeaking. It had just clicked shut when a loud clunk sounded behind me. And the only thing behind me was the First Sofa.

Someone was coming into the room.

I yanked the Iron Key out of the door and stared around wildly. Where on earth was I going to hide?

Turned out I wasn't. Before I could take my third step toward the curtains, a girl launched herself out from under the sofa and got to her feet. She was about my age, with golden-brown skin and a sleek black ponytail. She wore trendy jeans, silver hoop earrings, and a ferocious gaze.

"Hello," she said, looking me up and down from hat to slippers. "Who are you supposed to be?" Her accent was hard to place.

"I'm Abby," I said. "Abby Hernandez."

"Oh," said the girl, as if that explained anything. "Did Ben send you? Is he not willing to show his face?"

"Ben?"

"Your Council member. The overalls one."

"Oh, that Ben."

"Yes, that Ben. Where is he?"

"I don't know."

The girl exhaled angrily. "Well, when you see him tell him he's in trouble with the entire European network. I told everyone how rude he was at our last meeting, and they are furious."

"What happened at your last meeting?" I asked. So this girl was from the European pillow fort networks. Interesting.

"It was appalling! I was here—early, of course, because that is polite—and I heard Ben coming through the sofa, only he stopped halfway through and screamed."

"Screamed?"

"Like a peacock! And then he came bursting out of the sofa with the lost key in his hand, waving it like an Olympic torch and running in circles, laughing."

Ugh! So *Ben* had found the key. That was a real worst-case scenario. If what I'd heard last summer was still true, that key was his entire world, and he wouldn't give it up easily.

"I don't know how he found it under there," Europe Girl went on. "It's been missing so long. But before I could get any details, he declared that our meeting was canceled, crawled back under the sofa, and linked away. I never even found out what he wanted to meet about, apart from there being some big emergency in your Hub. The whole event was an insult to every single member of the European networks!"

"Oh," I said. "Sorry."

Europe Girl drew herself up. "An apology is not good enough, Abby Hernandez. A breach of protocol between Continental Councils is a serious offense. Ben will have to appear before our Council and admit that he was rude."

"Okay," I said. Why did I keep running into people so obsessed with protocol?

"And wrong."

"Got it."

"And promise never to do it again."

"Sounds great."

She peered at me. "You are not bothered by this?" she asked.

I shook my head. "Ben's not my favorite member of NAFAFA."

"I take it you are not in his network, then?" Europe Girl said, a smile tugging up the edges of her frown.

"Oh, I'm not in any network," I said. "I'm just sort of visiting."

The smile became a look of horror faster than I could blink. "You—you are not a member of a proper network?" The girl staggered to the First Sofa and leaned on it for support. "You're just . . . just nobody? And the North American Council is letting you wander around playing dress-up? Here, of all places?"

"Well, it's not like *that*," I said, frowning. "See—"

"No!" the girl cried, dramatically. She was starting to

remind me of Maggie getting way too into one of her adventure games. "No, I will not see! This goes against . . . this is utterly . . . I won't hear any more! You are all in trouble with Europe! All of NAFAFA is in trouble now!"

And she flung herself under the sofa and crawled out of sight.

Well. That had happened. What did I know now?

I was alone in le Petit Salon again.

And the European networks were mad at us.

And Ben had the Oak Key.

I had two choices. I could go back through the hidden panel to the island, tell Antonia and Helene how I'd tried and failed, and face their anger over my ruining things with the German palace and their disappointment at losing the Oak Key forever.

Or I could go after Ben myself. Right now. I could link into the NAFAFA Hub, track him down, and figure out some way to get the key off him.

One choice was sensible and responsible. The other was risky and reckless. I could practically hear Maggie screaming at me to take the second one. It was exactly the sort of secret-agent spy adventure she'd always dreamed of, and here was a real-life opportunity staring me in the face.

Well, hey, I'd come this far. How much more could go wrong?

I crawled back under the sofa and came face to face with

my first problem: which pillow led to the Hub?

Maggie had told me the NAFAFA pillow linked in from the Hall of Records, which, if I remembered her story right, was full of pale blue walls, marble pillars, mirrors, and golden lights. So all I had to do was look behind the pillows till I found that combination.

I started on my left, pulling the pillows aside one by one. The first led to darkness, the next to a science lab, and the next to a sort of lounge full of sofas and books and green and silver banners and pictures of snakes and skulls. Weird. I kept going, but nothing even came close to what I was looking for until I hit the seventh pillow.

Bingo! Golden light, marble columns, pale blue walls; this had to be it. It seemed brighter than I'd imagined, but that was probably just from me being in the dark for so long. I squeezed myself through the link and got to my feet, brushing off my dress and straightening my hat.

There was a dramatic gasp, and I looked up. A crowd of people, from wrinkly seniors to little kids in strollers, stood staring at me, their mouths hanging open. A red velvet rope hung between us. Oh, cantaloupey doom. This wasn't the NAFAFA Hall of Records. Where was I?

My eyes darted around. The columns and mirrors and golden lights were there all right, but judging from the padded window seat I'd just crawled out of, the ornate dressing table, and that huge four-poster decked in velvet, I was in some sort of ultra-fancy bedroom.

So why did I have an audience?

I turned back to the crowd, all talking and pointing now, and . . . smiling. They were all smiling. With absolutely no idea what else to do, I called up my palace protocol, forced a princessy sort of smile onto my face, and gave them my best curtsy.

And the crowd broke into applause.

THIRTY-ONE
Maggie

No words could ever describe how ridiculously happy I felt slipping through the link into the Hub. I was back in the game! I was back where I belonged! I got to my feet behind Carolina and looked around.

Whoa. My happiness burst like a popped balloon.

Things in the Hub had changed.

Last summer the NAFAFA Hub had been a chaotic wonderland of kids running wild through a maze of pillow forts, sofas, bookshelves, and tangly pathways, all lit up by the sunlike glare of the massive chandelier hanging in the center of the room. But now the golden chandelier was . . . off. It was dark. Dead. The Hub was stuffed with shadows.

A few lamps and twinkle lights dotted the main floor, just enough to show that the maze had been tidied, squeezed into a grid system radiating out from the Council platform like spokes on a wheel. A few kids bobbed in and out of the forts, and a few more walked the aisles, but there was a distinct hush over everything. It felt like a strict, unpopular library.

"What happened to this place?" I said, turning to find Carolina pulling a headlamp on over her baseball cap. She clicked it on, angling it down when the light hit my face.

"Ben happened," she said. "He had this big idea to put a dimmer switch on the chandelier a few weeks back. The idea was to save energy during quiet hours when no one's around. Of course it totally messed up the wiring. Repairs are taking forever." Her eyebrows rolled between her sunglasses and cap.

"Seriously? That's awful. And wait, hang on, what are quiet hours?"

"Another Ben innovation. He had plenty of conditions for finally voting Miesha in as head of the Council."

I looked at the chandelier, hanging like a dead squid in the gloom above the network banners. "So you've all been wandering around in the dark for the last few weeks?"

"We turn on track lighting for the aisles and everything during regular hours," Carolina said. "But it's definitely been annoying getting around."

"Why are you still wearing your sunglasses, then?"

Carolina gave me a flat look. "Because, Maggie Hetzger—"

"You're the Council of NAFAFA," I finished. "Yeah, yeah, I remember."

I followed her down the nearest path, heading for the platform, staring around at the unhappy transformation. It was incredible how different it felt.

The massive patchwork dome of sheets and blankets curving overhead was visible only right at the bottom edges, leaving a well of chilly darkness above us. On the far wall I could just make out the garage-door-size cushion that led to the collecting fort, where the NAFAFA kids gathered huge vats of coins—and, weirdly, Cheerios—that got lost in sofas. A little past that was one of the six huge tapestry doors, set at intervals among the pillow links lining the walls. Last year I'd learned that the tapestries weren't links like the pillows, but normal doors, leading to more spaces branching off the Hub. One of them led to the Hall of Records, which had the link to le Petit Salon. I'd never found out where the other five went.

The question I'd asked in my first-ever visit came bounding back: Where *was* this place? Like, in the real world, where was it? Under an airport? A secret government bunker? An abandoned mine? It would have to be a huge space, and right now it really did feel like we were underground. Or actually, with the dead-squid chandelier glinting in the darkness, like we were underwater. . . .

A sudden shout bounced down one of the aisles as we passed, and next second I was almost knocked off my feet by a hug from a very short astronaut.

"Maggie! Maggie! You're here!"

It was Kelly, wearing a homemade space suit, complete with helmet.

"Oof! Hi!" I said, hugging her back. "How's it going? And what are you wearing?"

"My space suit!" said Kelly, pulling off the helmet. Her face was shining as brightly as Carolina's headlamp. "Can you *believe* this place? It's so cool! I'm pretending we're in outer space. Look, those lights are the stars, and this is the alien planet, and the chandelier is the stealth spaceship trying to sneak up on us. Quiet hours are so much fun!"

"You like the Hub like this?" I asked, surprised.

Carolina waved a hand to keep us moving. "She's never seen it any other way. Kelly's only been in NAFAFA a few days." She smiled at the little astronaut. "But I think she's introduced herself to every single kid already."

"I *love* it here!" Kelly said, literally jumping along beside me. "I thought this summer was gonna be the best ever just 'cause I got to spend it at home! And then Abby was like, wanna look after Samson? And I was like, *yeah!* And now *this* is happening! I'm so sorry about losing Samson, though," she said, her face dropping. "He's here somewhere, but it's too dark to find him. Bobby says it could be bad for the forts if his snagglepaw gets caught on an important pillow or blanket or something. And Miesha and a couple of other kids are pretty allergic. I should have thought of that."

"It'll be fine," I assured her as the three of us reached the platform steps. "Samson always turns up."

"Come on, Maggie Hetzger," Carolina said. "Meeting time. And I think you should come too, Kelly, since you know Abby Hernandez. Maybe you can help us find her?"

"Yeah! Okay!"

Kelly skipped up the steps beside me to the Council table, where a cluster of desk lamps gave a decent amount of light. The four chairs were the same as I remembered, along with the banners for three of the four North American networks: the midnight-blue banner with its silver ship for the Forts of the Eastern Seaboard; the blue-and-green stripes and castle of orange pillows for the United Southern Gulf-Pacific Fortresses; and the polar bear on a mound of white pillows under a pink-and-purple sky for the Northern & Arctic Alliance.

The fourth banner was new. The Great Plains Sofa Circle's green banner was gone, and in its place was something only Ben could have designed. Massive blue-and-white waves were crashing in from the left of the banner, meeting a wall of wheat and long grass sweeping up from the right. Together they formed a ridge of mountains down the middle, with snow-covered peaks framed against a golden pillow radiating like the sun. In each corner was an elaborate ornamental clipboard.

"Wow," I said.

"I know, right?" said Carolina.

"What was this new network called again?"

"The Really Enormous Great Plains-Pacific Sofa Realm."

"Wow," I repeated.

"Yeah."

Carolina took her seat under the Forts of the Eastern Seaboard banner just as Ben appeared, stumping up the steps on the other side, a stack of clipboards in his hands.

I froze. The Oak Key was dangling from a shoelace around his neck, glinting in the light of the desk lamps.

This was too weird. I'd had that key in my hands only two nights before. That key had kept me going all through my first year of middle school, when it lived in a secret envelope in a secret box in a secret corner of my room. It made my stomach hurt to see it hanging around someone else's neck. Especially Ben's.

"Hello, Maggie Hetzger and everyone else," he said, dumping his clipboards on the table and barely glancing around. "I've got fifteen new members to impress, seven fort designs to approve, and a protocol presentation to prepare by this time tomorrow, so let's get this over with." He turned his sunglasses on Kelly. "Why are you here?"

"I invited her," said Carolina. "And I know she's in your network, not mine"—she held up her hands—"but she knows more about Abby Hernandez and the missing cat than any of us. Except Maggie Hetzger, obviously."

"Fine, fine. I've got too much else to deal with to argue about it," said Ben. He arranged his clipboards into a neat pile and looked around the platform. "But wait, where's Miesha? And Murray? Regulations say we can't have a meeting without the whole Council present."

There was a piercing whistle from somewhere behind me. Everybody's head swiveled. Way out in the darkness, one of the tapestry doors was partly open, with Miesha framed in the light pouring through.

"I have been trapped in here for twelve hours now!" she shouted across the Hub. "Is that cat still loose?"

"Yes, ma'am!" Carolina called back, ignoring Ben, who was making shushing noises. "Sorry!"

"Boo!" yelled Miesha. "Then on your feet, everyone. I've already got Murray with me. We're having this meeting in the Archives where it's safe from cats!"

"What?" Ben said beside me. "But protocol requires—"

"And is that Kelly in the space suit?" Miesha shouted.

"Yes! Hi!" screamed Kelly.

"Can you find Bobby, please, and get him here too? I need him to translate something!"

"Sure! Fun!"

"Will everyone stop yelling!" Ben yelled. "It's quiet hours!"

"What?" shouted Miesha.

"Quiet hours!"

"Hey, Carolina," Miesha called. "What's Ben saying?"

"He says it's quiet hours!"

"Quiet hours?"

"Yes! Quiet hours!"

"Oh! That's cool!"

"Yeah!"

"Hi, Maggie Hetzger!"

"Stop it stop it stop it!" shouted Ben, going past his usual pink to bright red.

Miesha waved and disappeared behind the curtain. We all got up, and while Kelly went to find Bobby, the rest of us tromped back down the steps, Carolina in the lead, and headed across the Hub to the tapestry door.

I'd seen the Hall of Records the year before—a beautiful, marble-floored hall full of golden light and famous pillows—and I was expecting something just as grand for these Archives I'd heard so much about. But I got a serious surprise when we arrived and Ben yanked aside the tapestry.

I saw right away why Miesha was so sure she'd be safe in there: no cat, not even one as good at finding trouble as Samson, could possibly get past the massive floor-to-ceiling iron door barring our way.

THIRTY-TWO
Maggie

"What's this all about?" I asked as Carolina heaved on a three-foot-long handle and the iron door groaned open.

"What?" said Ben.

"The door."

"What about it?"

"Why is it so . . . fortressy?"

He stared at me. "Because these are the Archives."

I stared back at him. "Oh."

And that was the end of that discussion. Carolina waved us through, and I took my first steps into the Archives of NAFAFA.

One of the things I loved most about the Hub, and the whole pillow fort world, was that every single space—fort, room, whatever—was different. Like, *really* different. Last summer I'd gotten to see the gilded Hall of Records, the noisy forest of pipes in the Collecting Fort, and the quiet calm of Bobby's den, with its blue sheet walls, neat books, and starry twinkle lights. Every fort, wall pillow, and tapestry out there on the floor of the Hub led to some place completely unlike any other.

But I doubted any of them could top the Archives.

The iron door clanged shut behind us, and I gaped like a third grader presented with a lifetime supply of ice cream.

We were standing on the edge of an Olympic-size swimming pool, stretching away to a pair of diving boards over the deep end. There were benches lining the room, and tile floors, and paintings of blue and white waves stretching from the floor to the heavy industrial lights hanging from the ceiling.

It would have been an impressive sight all on its own, only this pool wasn't filled with water. It was packed wall to wall with shelves, and the shelves were packed from end to end with papers, scrolls, and books.

"What the . . . ?" I said. I turned to the others, gesturing at the sunken library. "How is . . . ? I mean, *what*?"

Ben gave a sarcastic sigh, but Carolina answered.

"This is the Archives, Maggie Hetzger," she said. "The quick story is that a Council back in the 1960s decided to add a pool to the Hub, and they built this place. Apparently it was fun at first, but pretty soon they realized it would be tricky to keep filling it with fresh water and chlorine. Plus it meant someone always had to be on lifeguard duty. Some of the older kids started pushing to make it an over-ten-only pool, and added that big door as security, but the younger kids said that was a terrible idea and broke in and peed in the pool in protest. In the end they just drained it and gave up the whole thing."

"Wow," I said. "Also ew. So why did it get turned into the Archives?"

"Because the Archives were overflowing their last home," said Ben, deciding to join the conversation. "And once the pool was drained, someone from my network realized all this empty space was equipped with a natural filing system."

He walked over to the edge and tapped his toe on a patch of tiles reading 1.2 METERS.

"The depth markers," he said in full, classic Ben explainy mode, "crossed with the lane markers running long ways along the bottom, let us organize the archived materials on a grid. Older materials up here"—he pointed to the shallow end—"newest materials down there"—he pointed to the deep end. "It's the Archives, it works, it makes sense, it's old news. Now, where is Miesha?"

A sandy-haired head popped into sight climbing up one of the ladders halfway down the pool. A pair of silver sunglasses followed, and then the rest of what turned out to be Murray, a bundle of papers and a giant bag of gummy bears clutched awkwardly under one arm.

His milky-pale face went deep pink when I waved, and he hurried over to us.

"Hi, Maggie!" he said, fumbling the gummy bears. "Hey, I wanted to say . . . I'm really sorry if I sounded bossy in those letters I left you in your new fort."

Aw, Murray had been obsessing about his letters.

"You didn't, and it would be okay anyway," I said. "There's a lot going on!"

"Speaking of, do you know where Miesha is, Murray?" Carolina said.

"And where we're holding this totally against regulations offsite meeting?" added Ben.

"Both in the hot tub." Murray pointed with his head. "Come on."

Okay, both in the what? I was starting to feel as clueless and wrong-footed as I had on my first trip to the Hub almost a year ago.

Murray led us around the pool into a small side room, where the same industrial lighting lit up a raised hot tub that could have fit twelve, filled to the brim with adorable stuffed animals, rainbow-striped pillows, and Miesha, reading an ancient-looking book. She had a bowl of grapes and half a dozen soda cans lined up on the hot tub wall beside her, along with more books and stacks of papers. And hanging over all of it was a drooping canopy of honest-to-goodness Lisa Frank bedsheets, complete with multicolored turtles, kittens, pandas, and dolphins.

"Hi, everyone," Miesha said, barely looking up. She'd grown over the last year, too. She had a new pair of clear frames under the Council-member silver sunglasses gleaming against her deep brown skin, and her hair was up in rows of wavy braids. There was a sparkly green unicorn perched on her shoulder. "I'm almost done here. Take your shoes off and come on in."

"What . . . what is all this?" said Ben, setting down his clipboards.

"All what?" said Miesha.

"This!" He waved his hands. "I mean—all this . . . this!"

Miesha turned a page of her book. "Carolina, what's wrong with Ben? Is he gonna be okay for the meeting? Oh, hi again, Maggie Hetzger! How was your year?"

"Hi! Good!" I said, while Ben spluttered. "I like your hot tub!"

"Thanks. I've been hiding in here for so long, I decided to fix the place up. I sent some of my network helpers to get supplies."

"You're still doing that Lisa Frank thing, then?" I said, slipping off my shoes and perching on the side, my feet swallowed by squashiness.

Miesha put down her book and stretched, reaching her arms up and smiling around at the bright sheet canopy and the rainbow puddle of pillows and stuffed animals. She shrugged. "Yeah, I keep thinking I should grow out of it, but then I remember how into Lisa Frank stuff I was when eight-year-old me started here. And if eight-year-old me knew she was going to become head of the Council someday, this is exactly what she would have wanted to do. So I do it for her."

Murray and Carolina kicked their shoes off, too, and we all sank into the pile, spreading out comfortably.

"Are you just going to stand there and frown?" asked Carolina as Ben stood there, frowning.

"I want to say for the record that I am completely against us having a meeting under these circumstances," he said grumpily.

"Got it," said Miesha. "And as head of the Council, I'm starting the meeting anyway. And since you're not getting in the hot tub, you can be in charge of the whiteboard." She waved a hand at the opposite wall, where, sure enough, a whiteboard on a rolly stand stood waiting, complete with markers. "I thought we might need one," she informed us as Ben plodded over to fetch it. "In case things get complicated."

"They always do," I said.

"Can we please start?" said Carolina, who had burrowed in up to her neck. "This is totally comfy and I might fall asleep here otherwise."

Miesha sat up, brushing away her unicorn. "Yes, definitely, time for business. I officially call this meeting to order."

"Real quick," said Murray, raising his hand. "Is anyone else on Snack Committee?"

"Oh, I think I am," said Miesha. "There's more sodas over on that side."

When everyone had a soda, and the bag of gummy bears had been passed around twice, and Ben was stationed sullenly by the whiteboard with a dry-erase marker in his hand, Miesha got right to the point.

"We are here," she began, "to discuss the disappearance of Abby Hernandez into the global pillow fort networks. Now, we all know the basic facts: two days ago Abby Hernandez, carrying the Oak Key, fell through the trapdoor of a treehouse and disappeared, and no one's seen her since."

"And yesterday I found the Oak Key under the First Sofa in le Petit Salon," said Ben.

"Which is proof that that's where Abby Hernandez ended up," Miesha said. "So there are only three possible routes she could have gone from there." She jabbed a finger at the whiteboard, and Ben grumpily uncapped his marker. "Route one, she found the link back to the NAFAFA Hub and is somewhere in one of our networks."

"But that'd be super weird," I said. "Wouldn't she have made contact and tried to get in touch with me so I'd know she was okay?"

"Yeah," said Miesha. "Meaning we can pretty much rule that one out." Ben crossed out everything he'd just written.

"Route number two," said Carolina. "Abby Hernandez could have picked the wrong link and ended up in another Continental network's Hub instead."

"That one seems more likely to me," said Murray, around a mouthful of gummy bears.

"Me too," said Ben, still scribbling on the board. "It would explain why she's managed to completely disappear. Only it raises two more questions."

"Like which Continental network is she in," said Miesha, nodding.

"And why haven't they sent her back," said Ben.

"What's the third option?" I asked, raising my hand.

"The third option is the worst," said Carolina. "There are still one or two pillows under the First Sofa from King Louis's original network, sometimes called the Royal network. They lead to pillows in furniture in places kids are really, *really* not supposed to be. And if Abby went through one, and grown-ups caught her . . . ."

"She could be in serious trouble," said Murray.

"She could be stuck somewhere with no chance to escape," said Miesha.

"She could be in jail," said Ben.

I choked on a gummy bear. "But we'd know, right? We'd know if Abby ended up in one of those places."

"How would we know?" Murray said.

"Well . . ." I wasn't actually sure. "We just should, is all.

Doesn't anyone monitor those old links? Or check to see if someone's stuck in them? What's the point of having them at all if they're off-limits and dangerous? Why not take them down?"

"Because they're historic!" said Ben, looking scandalized. "They're part of our global pillow fort history."

"They're also the property of the European Continental network," added Miesha. "We can't touch them."

"Fine—let's ask the Europe kids to check them, then!" I said. This was exactly like last summer. All these layers of tradition and rules and regulations. When it came down to it, we were just a bunch of kids running around in pillow forts! Why did everything have to be so complicated?

Carolina shot Ben a look. "We would, but the European reps are refusing to talk to us right now. Ever since a certain *someone* walked out of his meeting with them three seconds after finding the Oak Key under the First Sofa."

"I was distracted!" said Ben, clutching the key in his free hand. "You couldn't expect me to sit through a meeting after that. It's not my fault those Europe kids are so obsessive about manners and formalities."

"You mean protocol?" said Carolina. "Dude, you have a literal clipboard covered in rules as part of your new banner! You are not one to talk."

"At least *I* know how to get things properly—"

"Hey! Hey!" Miesha said, waving a hot-pink giraffe over her head. "No fighting in the hot tub!"

"I'm not in the hot tub," said Ben. "And it's Carolina who—" The giraffe hit him in the face.

"Okay, seriously!" I said. This meeting was going nowhere. "Abby's still lost, we've got no clue where, and you're telling me no one here has any real leads at all?"

"We were kind of hoping you did, Maggie Hetzger," said Miesha. "You're the one who asked for a meeting with us. Although I did just find a tiny lead, maybe. We keep a bunch of King Louis's old papers in the Archives, and I *might* have found something about le Petit Salon." She nodded at the pile on the edge of the hot tub. "But it's in French, and I need Bobby to get here and translate it before we know if it's anything useful."

"See?" said Murray, smiling at me. "You've got all of NAFAFA running in circles again."

"And that brings me to a big point of order," said Ben. "Why should we care about this at all?"

Everyone blinked at him. Murray put down the stuffed hippo he'd been playing with.

"I mean it," Ben went on. "If she's lost, she'll find her way back eventually. Abby Hernandez isn't a member of NAFAFA. Her being missing doesn't really matter to us."

"It totally matters!" I said, shocked. "If we don't get her

back, then Camp Cantaloupe will get shut down, and her dads will have to come home from their honeymoon early, and they'll search and search but they'll never find her. And everyone will be worried and scared and I'll know the truth but not be able to tell anyone and that will be awful!"

"So what's *your* plan to find her, then?" Ben demanded. "Why were you so insistent on having this meeting?"

"My plan was to come here and ask you all for help!" I might have been yelling now. I wasn't sure. "Do you even know how hard it was to get here from camp tonight? How smart I had to be? How many obstacles I had to get past? I've got nothing to work with back there, but I thought here we could at least do *something*!"

Ben held up both hands. "But it turns out we can't, because your missing friend is your problem, not ours! Our only problems are finding Sprinkles"—Ben's anger gave way long enough for him to flash the dreamy smile he always got at the mention of Miesha's dog—"and getting rid of the cat that shouldn't have been here in the first place. We don't owe you anything."

"Hey now, that's not fair," said Miesha. "I did give Abby Hernandez and Maggie Hetzger that key last summer. NAFAFA is at least a little responsible for where things have ended up."

"You mean *you're* a little responsible," Ben shot back.

Miesha chucked a cupcake pillow at him. "I'm also head of the Council, and you know what? I say we're going to help find Abby Hernandez." She clapped her hands. "So—let's start by making extra-super sure she's not in our networks. That way when Ben goes and *apologizes* to the European reps—oh, yes, you will!—and asks them to search the Royal networks just in case she took route number three, we can say we looked everywhere before bothering them."

Miesha had stepped into full command mode.

"Murray, Carolina, Ben," she said. "Rally your troops and organize a search of your forts in the Hub and the closest branches of your networks. I'm still stuck in here thanks to that cat, so someone else will have to start the search in mine."

"Ooh, why don't I do that?" I said, my hand in the air. "I can totally help!"

Miesha's eyes flicked over to Murray. His face fell as he glanced back.

"What?" I said. "What is it?"

"Miesha and I were, uh, talking," said Murray. "Before you all got here."

"Yeah? And?"

"And we came to a decision, Maggie Hetzger," Miesha said, "about you."

I blinked. "Okay . . ."

"What you have to understand," said Murray carefully, "is that Ben is kind of maybe right about some stuff. You and Abby Hernandez seriously shook up our networks last summer. I mean, you remember, you were there."

"And now you two are at it again," said Miesha. "So Murray and I decided this time we're going to be clear about boundaries, before this gets even more out of control. And since Abby Hernandez and that cat are already running around in the networks or just plain missing, the only person we can still put boundaries on is you."

My heart suddenly felt like it was being squeezed between Director Haggis's eyebrows. What were they saying?

"So we decided—and I'm really sorry, Maggie," Murray said. "We decided that no matter what plan we came up with at this meeting, we can't actually let you help. We know from experience what happens when all three of you start running around. We remember."

The Lisa Frank canopy swam in front of my eyes. This was a bad dream. It had to be.

"So . . ." My voice cracked. "So what are you saying?"

"I'm saying, Maggie Hetzger," said Miesha, "as head of the Council, that your part in all this ends here." She gave me an apologetic half smile. "I'm sending you back to camp."

THIRTY-THREE
Maggie

"No!" I yelled, the sound echoing off the tiled walls of the hot tub room.

"Maggie—"

"No!"

"Mag—"

"No!"

"Maggie Hetzger, please sit down."

I looked around the Lisa Franked hot tub. I didn't remember getting to my feet.

"I am *not* going back to camp," I said, making each word echo around the little room. "I didn't sneak past counselors, teachers, and real-life professional search and rescue officers just so you could make your own plans and kick me out! That's not how this is going to work!"

How could Murray and Miesha think I would be okay sitting this out? I'd been planning all year for the adventure Abby and I were going to have through the trapdoor of the Shipwreck Treehouse. I'd imagined every epic, outrageous thing that could possibly happen, and mentally prepared for all of them. And fine, the plan had gone all wrong, and Abby had gone off on her own and I'd been left behind to catch up, but I was still more prepared for a high-stakes rescue mission than any other person in this room.

"I don't think I've ever said this before," said Ben, "but I agree with Miesha and Murray. Maggie Hetzger and Abby Hernandez caused enough damage to our networks last year. We can't risk having them both running loose again." He set the dry-erase marker on the whiteboard tray and crossed his arms, clearly fighting back a smile. "I vote to expel Maggie Hetzger, too."

"No!" I shouted again.

"'Expel' is a strong word," objected Murray.

"Kind of accurate, though," said Miesha.

"But Maggie can still help," Murray said, a plea in his voice. "She can run the base of operations back at her camp. That's important, isn't it, Maggie?"

"Charlene is already doing that!" I snapped. Man, I wasn't used to being angry at Murray. I turned to my last hope. "Carolina, please! Tell them I have to stay here. I can't go back without Abby!"

Carolina tugged on her baseball cap. "Nothing I can do, Maggie Hetzger. Even if I thought you should stick around, they've got three votes." She nodded at the others. "That's a majority."

This could not be happening.

I'd been cut off from my dream summer adventure when the treehouse shattered. I'd been blocked from entering the Hub when I made contact with Ben. And now the whole Council was voting to send me back to summer camp without any say at all.

I felt utterly betrayed. I felt achingly furious. I felt broken, abandoned, and shipwrecked.

And darn it, standing knee-deep in all these pillows and stuffed animals was making my feet sweaty.

I was opening my mouth to do some more shouting when the squeal of the iron door echoed through from the main room. There were running footsteps; then a boy sprinted into the hot tub room, stopped dead, and gave a scream of happiness.

"Maggie! Yay! Maggie Maggie Maggie!"

"Bobby!"

Finally, a real friend! Bobby's shiny black hair was longer than it had been last year, almost down to his shoulders. He pushed it out of his eyes and stretched over the little wall to hug me, smiling so big it filled the room.

"I came as fast as I could," Bobby said, waving at the

others with both hands. "Kelly said it was urgent. I love that space suit she's wearing, don't you? Did you know the helmet really works? She made it herself. Ooh! Gummy bears!"

"Thanks for coming, Bobby," said Miesha. "There's something I need you to translate. But first we have to say goodbye to Maggie Hetzger."

"No, you don't," I said. "I'm staying put." Bobby was here now. He'd back me up, and I knew Carolina was wavering. Maybe I could still swing this.

"Oh?" said Ben. He came over and sat on the edge of the hot tub, crossing his arms. "Well, then so are we. Right, Miesha? Murray? If Maggie Hetzger refuses to listen to the Council and go home, then we refuse to search for Abby Hernandez or ask the other Continental networks for help finding her."

Bobby looked confused, but Murray, Miesha, and even Carolina exchanged frowns, then nodded. "Yeah," said Miesha. "I hate to agree with Ben, but he's right. If you insist on staying here, Maggie Hetzger, then so do we."

"But . . . but don't you care?" I said. "Don't you care that if I don't get Abby back soon, Camp Cantaloupe is gonna be closed and all those kids' lives are gonna be ruined? Especially mine and Abby's?"

"Of course we care," Murray said gently. "And we want to find Abby Hernandez. But it's your decision now, eh?"

I stared around at them as the reality washed over me. If I stood my ground, Abby was guaranteed to stay lost, and Camp Cantaloupe was guaranteed to get shut down, and everything was guaranteed to be ruined. If I left, they would start the search, and there was at least a chance of getting Abby back in time and avoiding disaster.

They had me cornered.

Slowly, more reluctantly than I'd done anything in my whole life, I nodded.

"Thank you, Maggie," said Murray.

"I promise we'll get her back," Carolina said.

Ben smirked. There was a very prickly silence.

"I'm, uh, not super sure what's happening here," said Bobby. "And sorry to change the subject, but Miesha, I have some good news from the Hub: we found Sprinkles fast asleep in my fort. He looked so cute we left him there."

"Thank goodness for that!" said Miesha, as Ben squealed with delight. "Any sign of the cat?"

"Not since two minutes ago."

"Ugh. You and I will get to work in here, then. You three"—she pointed a stuffed silver dolphin at Ben, Murray, and Carolina—"will walk Maggie Hetzger home, and then Ben will go to le Petit Salon and beg the European Council for a meeting. Now get going."

Murray, Carolina, and I got up and put on our shoes, as

Ben, scowling and grumbling, collected his clipboards.

"Thank you for understanding, Maggie Hetzger," Miesha called from the hot tub. "I really mean it."

I gave her a heavyhearted nod, waved goodbye to Bobby, slung my supply pack back over my shoulders, and turned away.

We were almost out of the room when I remembered.

"Oh, hey, Miesha," I said, stopping and swinging my pack around to dig in one of the pockets. I realized with a jolt that it was the first time I'd used it. "These are yours."

The silver sunglasses Miesha had dropped in my fort the summer before flashed through the air as I tossed them back to the hot tub. Thorough testing by Abby and me had revealed they didn't work as a token to new links, and I'd thrown them in my supply pack and more or less forgotten about them. But since I was here . . .

Miesha caught them one-handed. "Ha!" she said. "Thanks for bringing these back! I don't really need them, but it's good to have a backup, I guess."

"Can I have my patchwork scarf, now?" I asked. The fiasco that had left Miesha's sunglasses stranded in my fort had also resulted in me losing the scarf Abby had made me in her first week at camp. The scarf that had started this whole saga. "I mean, you still have it, right?"

"Of course we do, Maggie Hetzger." Miesha waved a hand

toward the big room. "It's filed in the Archives."

I blinked at her. "My scarf is in the Archives? Why?"

"Because it's a historical artifact. The network you and Abby Hernandez started was the very first ever on the west coast. Since we had no way to get the scarf back to you, we catalogued it and filed it away. It's kind of an honor, you know."

"Oh." Maybe these kids thought having my scarf in the Archives was an honor, but I sure didn't. This felt like just one more example of them saying they had the right to make decisions for me, whether I liked it or not. "Well, I want it back," I said, loudly. "It's *my* scarf, made for me by my best friend. Who's gonna help me go get it?"

"No one!" snapped Ben, his toe hammering the tile floor. "I don't have time for this. I have *so much work to do!*" He rattled his clipboards with each word. "And filling out the paperwork for a withdrawal from the Archives is not getting added to my to-do list! Neither is standing around here arguing!"

"Please, just head back to camp, Maggie Hetzger," said Miehsa, showering stuffed animals as she got to her feet. "And I promise you I'll see what I can do."

I looked around for backup, but Bobby, Murray, and Carolina were all avoiding my eyes. Ben was glaring. Miesha gave me a smile that looked like a shrug. The decision had been made.

With my jaw clamped so tight I thought it might break, I reshouldered my pack and stalked out of the Archives, Ben and Murray following after.

Carolina came last, pulling the iron door closed with a clang like a bell signaling the final end of all my hopes and dreams for the summer.

The Hub looked extra dark and gloomy after the bright fluorescents of the Archives. It fit my mood. My guards switched on their headlamps, and we set off across the floor, marching along the wide, empty paths until we reached a golden wall pillow on the far side.

Carolina tugged away the pillow. "This is your stop, Maggie Hetzger."

I stared into the dark opening. On the other side of that pillow was the arts and crafts cabin. Camp Cantaloupe. Director Haggis. The search and rescue teams. Lights-out and morning roll call and cucumber casserole. And no Abby.

Somewhere in the darkness behind us there was a thump, then a muffled shout. Murray looked around.

"Come on, Maggie Hetzger," said Ben, clacking his clipboards. "The longer you stall, the longer it will take us to get started with our search."

Ugh. Ben was the worst. But he was right. I stepped toward the open link.

Another shout floated through the gloom. Then raised voices. Carolina turned, her headlamp beam joining Murray's.

"Hey, Ben . . . ?" she said.

"You just sit tight in your little fort," Ben said to me. "Maybe do some arts and crafts, and let the professionals handle this one."

"Ben," said Murray. There was definite yelling across the Hub, now, and the sound of running footsteps.

"I'll handle the European networks," Ben continued. "And we'll send Abby Hernandez back to you, and everything here can go back to being calm and orderly like it should—"

"Ben!" shouted Carolina, whapping him on the shoulder.

"What?" Ben snapped. "I'm trying to make sure—"

"Look!"

Ben looked, and I looked too.

A gap had appeared in the wall not far from the tapestry door to the Archives, and something was pouring through the gap into the Hub. Something white, and foamy, and bubbly.

There sure was a lot of it.

"Soapsuds?" said Ben. "The Arena! What the—" More kids were appearing now, popping out of forts, running down the paths, some yelling, some laughing.

Memories of my second visit to the Hub the summer before leaped into my brain, and the kid named Connor we'd seen emerging from a wall pillow, covered from the waist down in soapsuds after winning some kind of sporting event. If this was the same link, it was definitely malfunctioning. The foam was avalanching through in waves and already reaching the tops of the closest pillow forts.

"Back to camp, now!" Ben said over his shoulder, clamping his clipboards under one arm and darting for the aisle.

"We'll be in touch soon, Maggie!" Murray called as he and Carolina raced after Ben. "I promise!"

Ben was already shouting orders, and I heard every word loud and clear as the Council members reached the foam.

"The link! Shut the link!"

"What happened to the door pillow?"

"It's gone!"

"I'm in charge here!"

"Ouch! Where is it?"

"Who's in there? Ow!"

"Murray, go back, I can't—"

"My clipboards!"

"Why are you just—"

"Somebody find that pillow!"

The mountain of silver-white foam was growing bigger and taller every second. Unless they got the link shut fast, they'd have a major crisis on their hands.

But what could make a wall pillow open with no warning,

then disappear? I mean, it didn't just run away on its . . . own. . . .

Samson and his snagglepaw. It had to be! And that meant he was nearby!

I might not be able to find Abby on my own, but if I could rescue Samson out of all this mess, that would be one step closer to fixing everything.

Only I'd have to be quick to find Samson. And speedy. And I couldn't be quick and speedy all weighed down with worst-case-scenario gear.

In one deeply satisfying shrug I heaved my supply pack to the ground. I glared down at it. Three nights running I'd lugged that thing along with me, not to mention the months of careful planning that went into it, and all it had ever done was get me stuck in a window. I'd thought that pack would make everything better this summer, make me ready for anything, and so far it hadn't helped once.

"You go back to camp," I said, shoving the pack through the open link. "I've got a job to do here."

I pushed the golden pillow back over the link and stood tall, staring defiantly into the Hub. So what if the Council had ordered me out of their networks? So what if I was breaking their rules? I was done letting other people make decisions for me. I knew what I was capable of, and that was enough, no matter if a single other person was impressed. I could do this mission with no gear, no backup, and no approval. I was a world-class secret agent. All on my own.

I set off along the line of wall pillows toward the soapsuds fiasco, keeping my eyes peeled. More and more kids were arriving as the foam poured in, and some of the younger ones clearly thought this was the best thing that had ever happened in their entire lives. It was getting hard to tell if this was a disaster, a cleanup operation, or a party. I could still hear Ben and the others yelling, but it didn't sound like they were making any progress.

And then I saw it: a flash of movement, too close to the ground to be a kid, just down the next aisle. I raced after it.

Left at the comic-book shelf, right at the fort shaped like a birthday cake, right again at the glow-in-the-dark bouncy castle, and—darn it!

A large, round pillow lay alone at the next turn in the path, splattered with foam and ripped by a very familiar set of claw marks.

So where was Samson? He must be close. I just needed to look for . . . bingo! A patch of foam gleamed on the edge of an inflatable rocking chair outside a fort. Samson had definitely been here.

A girl carrying a badminton racket emerged from a nearby fort, whooped, and made a start for the foam. "Hey!" I yelled. She looked over. "Get this to Carolina or Murray if you can!" I said, lobbing the pillow at her.

The girl caught the pillow, looked back at me, shrugged, and raced off with it under her arm. Whew, one problem down. Hopefully they could get the link closed before the whole Hub was buried.

As for me, it was time to channel all my very best super-spy tracking skills into the chase of a lifetime. I had a cat to catch.

THIRTY-FOUR
Abby

There was no chance at all of escaping back through the window seat. There were already too many eyes on me and too many phones getting photos and videos.

I couldn't just stand there blinking forever, though.

The crowd finished clapping, and I crossed the room as calmly as I could, stepped over the velvet rope, and looked back to see where exactly the link had brought me.

I was in a museum. A banner arcing over the area I'd been standing in read:

★ SPECIAL EXHIBIT GRAND OPENING ★
THE BEDROOM OF PRINCESS NATALIA IMBRUGLIANA,
ON LOAN FROM CHRISTINEHOF CASTLE. THE
HERITAGE MUSEUM OF MONTREAL WOULD LIKE

TO THANK OUR SPECIAL UNDERWRITERS FOR
SPONSORING THIS HISTORIC LOAN.

Then what looked like the same again in French.

Montreal. Montreal? How on earth was I in Montreal?

"It's where she wrote all her books," a lady in a head scarf next to me was saying to her friend. "And her operas."

"And the brochure says it's supposed to be haunted!" The friend spotted me and reached out, squeezing my arm. "You were wonderful, dear! *So* creepy. And that surprise entrance!"

"Are there more 'ghosts' hiding in there?" asked the lady in the head scarf. "Oh, I hope so! Let's camp out here for a bit and wait to see them!"

I moved on.

"'The entire bedroom was carefully documented, packed up, and reassembled here in Montreal by trained historians,'" a bald man with a crinkly beard read from a brochure as I squeezed past him. "'Every detail has been re-created exactly as it was in her palace on the Swedish border.'"

A little girl tugged at his free hand. "Can we go in, Daddy?"

"No, honey. But let's stay here and watch for more people pretending to be ghosts."

Doom. If everyone was going to keep their eyes glued

to the exhibit, there was zero chance of me getting back through the link. At least not until the museum closed. That meant I'd have to hang around for hours, then hide from the guards, maybe in the bathroom with my feet up on the toilet seat. And I didn't have that kind of time.

How long would it take Helene and Antonia to discover the ring of keys was missing, and me with it? They'd probably go through the unlocked Deer Door after me, and scare the security guards again, and be arrested on the spot and thrown in some German prison. And Joe would go looking for them and be arrested and thrown in prison, too. And even if I somehow got back to camp, how could I ever explain that to Maggie?

I glowered at the exhibit. Honestly, whose bedroom has sky-blue walls, a golden chandelier, and marble columns? Overdoing it much? Way to be totally misleading.

I turned my back on my latest disaster and set off into the museum.

Of course this had happened. Of course I'd chosen one of King Louis's old-timey palace links. And of course the bedroom it led to had *just* been moved and reassembled on the opposite side of the Atlantic. I mean, why should anything be easy? I was only trying to be adventurous and brave so I could make things up to my friends on the island. Why should that turn out well?

The museum was crowded, and my outfit and I got lots of stares. I kept my head down and kept walking. So many strangers. Usually that didn't bother me, but I could have used just one friendly face right then. My dad, or the twins, or Samson, or—

Maggie?

I thought . . . over in that picture gallery, I could have sworn—

I pushed against the crowd, fighting my way into the next room, but a whole group of little school kids came roaring past, giggling at my hat, and by the time I made it to the picture gallery, there was no sign of her.

I found a free bench and slumped onto it. It couldn't have been Maggie, anyway. Maggie was at Camp Cantaloupe. Maggie was sleeping in our splintery cabin and eating terrible food in the mess hall and probably in some sort of feud with Charlene. I was the one trapped in this museum, tired, and all alone, and lost.

I blinked. Lost?

Hey, where was that darn moose, then? It was supposed to come rescue me, right? It rescued us last year up in Alaska. I pictured myself standing on the bench and doing the Camp Cantaloupe dance over and over, and almost smiled. That would really give people something to stare at.

But, ugh, there was no avoiding it: nobody and nothing

was coming to save me, and if anything was going to happen here, I'd be doing it completely on my own.

I got to my feet, looked sadly over at the next room, and locked eyes with . . . no way.

Was that actually . . . ?

I was across the floor in five seconds flat, pushing through the crowds into a gallery full of skeletons and animal skulls and plaster casts of footprints. But I only had eyes for my new friend.

It was stuffed, and it wasn't nearly as big as the one that had rescued us before, but it was still standing there in front of me: a moose. An actual moose. Maggie would have called it a sign.

I got right up close, staring into its glass eyes, hoping and wishing with every fiber of my being, my hands clenched in my dress. But nothing happened. No shiver of magic, no moosey snort, no rescue.

"Wow!" shouted a little girl beside me. She was craning her neck back to take in the next model over, her eyes huge. I looked up too. It was a woolly mammoth.

Wait.

A memory started hammering on the walls of my brain. I took another look around the room. Taxidermied animals, big taxidermied animals. And skulls, big skulls. And fossils. And a banner: AGE OF THE MEGAFAUNA.

The pieces clicked into place. Bobby! Montreal! Museum! That had to be the mammoth he'd brought Maggie to see last summer. The mammoth with the pillow fort inside it. A pillow fort that led back to the Hub.

Hope burst throught the clouds like a chicken on a sunflower floaty. The moose had actually worked! I wasn't lost anymore.

Now I just had to get inside the mammoth without being seen. I needed a distraction. But what?

"Mommy, why is that lady dressed like that?" I heard a little kid say nearby.

"I don't know, sweetie—maybe she's part of a special exhibit. Come over here and look at the dire wolves. See how many teeth?"

Yes! That was it! Thank you, little kid and cool mom. I *was* part of a special exhibit, if only by accident. Before I could think too hard about whether this was a good idea or not, I climbed up onto a display of plastic-molded footprints, clapped my hands, and shouted, "Attention, living visitors!"

The chatter and activity in the room slowed and then stopped as people turned to look. Oh, man, this had better work, or I'd have to run like the wind to avoid a ton of awkward questions.

"There are ghosts in the museum today!" I called, waving my arms, the wings on my hat waggling. "Woooo!" A little kid examining a display of fossilized mammoth poop began crying and clung to a teenage goth boy, who patted him on the head. "The exhibit of Princess Natalia's haunted bedroom is now open three galleries over." I gestured in a helpful but hopefully spooky way. "I was the first ghost to emerge, but there are others! Three more ghosts will be appearing in the next fifteen minutes. Don't miss this once-in-a-lifetime opportunity! Oooo!"

Man, I was overdoing this. Maggie would have done it better. I was getting all sorts of reactions from the crowd, from confused smiles to head shaking and open laughter, but none of them were moving. A bead of sweat trickled down the back of my neck.

"But that's ... that's not all!" I yelled. "Any visitors present at the haunted bedroom exhibit when the last ghost appears will win a one-year membership to the museum, absolutely free!" There were whoops, and a happy chattering filled the room. Yes! It was working! All the big groups and families left, but there were stragglers. Come on—I needed this place empty. "And one lucky visitor will receive . . ." *Think, Abby, think!* "An . . . um . . . a lifetime supply of candy from the gift shop! Woooo!"

That did it. There were more cheers, and screams of joy from a few younger kids. The little boy who had cried laughed excitedly from the goth teenager's shoulders as they hurried into the next room. Within half a minute I had the place to myself.

I ran straight for the woolly mammoth. I felt a tiny bit sorry for all those people waiting around for ghosts that would never arrive, and for whoever at the museum would eventually have to deal with it, but I couldn't worry about that now. I had to escape.

The mammoth's tusks were sturdy, but it was still a struggle to get enough of a foothold to reach the creature's open mouth. Especially given my fancy outfit. After an embarrassing amount of flailing, I finally managed it, tumbling headfirst into the squashy pile of pillows inside the mammoth's belly.

I flopped back in the gloom, panting. Victory! I was through the worst part. I was back on track. I was safe.

When I had my breath back, I pulled the single wall pillow free, and yes, thank the ghost moose forever, there was Bobby's blue-star fort, just like Maggie had described it.

I started forward, then scrambled back as something dark loomed into view on the other side of the link. Before I could raise my hands, before I could even blink, it leaped, a slinking shadow with glinting eyes, and landed, heavy as a dire wolf, right on top of me.

THIRTY-FIVE
Maggie

Cat tracking was tough work in the underwater mushroom colony gloom of the Hub, but I managed to piece together Samson's sudsy trail.

I ran from clue to clue with my head down, completely losing track of where I was until I pushed past a foam-flecked tapestry and found myself standing in the Hall of Records. The golden light from the long line of chandeliers smacked me hard in both eyes.

"Saaamsonnn!" I called, squinting around my tears. *Oh, great plan, Maggie.* Like any cat in history ever came running when it was called.

But there *was* something moving down at the end of the hall.

I jogged after it, waving at the pillows of famous former NAFAFA members I recognized along the way: Aretha

Franklin, Yo-Yo Ma, and my old buddy Alex Trebek.

I reached the end and stopped, looking around. Where was Samson? He should have been right here, cornered. There was nowhere else for him to go, except . . .

The pillow set into the wall at ground level was standing crooked. The extra-special velvet pillow that led to le Petit Salon.

Oh. No.

Imagine Samson in that room, his snagglepaw getting into *those* pillows. Forget foam fiascos—if Samson tugged enough pillows down, he could break the links connecting all the global networks. Plus he'd be trapped in that room forever.

Praying I wasn't too late, I crouched down and pushed through the link.

It was as cramped as ever under the sofa, especially since I was one year bigger. I reached around carefully, feeling for a purring ball of fur, but Samson wasn't there.

I crawled out into the room. The curtains were partly open, filling the room with dusty sunlight. And there, stretched out like a prince on the First Sofa's patched and faded seat, was Samson.

"Buddy!" I said, rushing over and burying my face in his still kinda sudsy fur. Samson bumped his forehead against mine, purring. "You," I said, sitting up and wagging a finger at him, "have really done it this time. But I'm just glad you're safe."

He looked so regal it was a shame to shift him, but I had to get him away from the First Sofa and all its easily snagged pillow links. I slid a hand under him and pulled. Samson gave me a disappointed look and stretched out even more, closing his eyes. "Oh, come on, don't be like that," I said. "I promise you'll be happier back at Kelly's."

A short struggle followed, which mostly involved Samson staying fixed to the sofa by his snagglepaw and me trying everything I could to coax him up.

"Seriously, buddy," I said as I finally got the snagglepaw free and he casually relatched himself onto the sofa with the others. "I'm done playing games. We have to get back to—"

"Ouch!"

I released Samson and scrambled to my feet. The cry of pain had come from directly under the First Sofa. And it was not a kid's voice.

A grown-up was crawling into le Petit Salon.

Oh, cantaloupes. There was nowhere to run! There wasn't even time to hide behind the curtains.

"What the—ow!" the grown-up cried, and the sofa gave a jerk. Samson, who had begun washing his ears, raised his head, sniffed, and started purring again. Huh.

A foot appeared from under the sofa. Then a leg, another leg, a torso, and finally the rest of the someone. He climbed to his feet and spotted me. We shared one second of absolute shock, then . . .

"MAGGIE!"

"UNCLE JOE!"

I threw my arms around him, and we hug-danced in a circle. "How . . . where are . . . what . . . ?" he said, half laughing.

We broke apart. He was wearing the most ridiculous outfit I had ever seen: a pink-and-black-striped smock decorated wih silver moons, a poofy sort of jacket with lace at the cuffs and collar, dark blue tights leading to a pair of extra-poofy shorts, floppy black boots, and a pirate-style hat with a giant feather in it. He looked like an extra from a Three Musketeers movie.

"How did you get here?" I asked, whapping him on the shoulder. "And why are you all dressed up?"

Uncle Joe looked completely overwhelmed, like he might put his fingers in his ears and start la-la-ing again.

"Where . . . you . . . Where's Abby?" he said, scanning the room like he expected her to be there.

"That's what everybody's trying to find out. Wait a minute, why? Have *you* seen her?"

Uncle Joe nodded.

"When? Where?!"

"Oh, wow," said Uncle Joe. He sat down on the First Sofa and ran a hand along Samson's shoulders. Samson went back to cleaning his ears. "I feel like someone put everything on shuffle. I don't know if this will make any sense, Maggie, but here goes . . ."

And he launched into what I can honestly say was the most ridiculous story I'd ever heard in my entire life. He talked for ten whole minutes, and in the end I felt about as tangled and disoriented as one of Ms. Sabine's splatter-dance paintings.

"So Abby was with you this whole time?" I said, trying to sort out the pieces. "On this island place?"

Uncle Joe nodded. "She got there a little after I did."

"And then she went through one of these Palace Doors all on her own, and you found out and followed?"

He nodded again. "That's why I'm dressed like this. I'm supposed to be an Italian ambassador, or something. Helene and Antonia came through the Deer Door too, but they stayed behind to distract the security guards while I took the link after Abby."

"But how can you be sure she even found the link?"

"She must have. The guards said Abby had been right next to that little room one minute, and then she was gone. They had all the exits covered by that point. The only way out was through the pillow fort. She was incredibly lucky she found it."

"So if she got here," I said, trying to get everything to settle into place in my brain, "what happened next? She's gone now, obviously. It was just Samson when I came in."

"Yeah." Uncle Joe's face suddenly brightened. "So, hey, maybe everything worked out! Maybe Abby found the key and went straight back to the island with it! Maybe that's why she's not around!"

I shook my head. "Sorry, but Ben from NAFAFA has the Oak Key. He found it under the sofa yesterday, and he's been wearing it around his neck ever since."

Uncle Joe groaned. "Whale poop! Why couldn't things just go the way we wanted for once?" I waved my hands overhead in enthusiastic agreement. "My guess is Abby's still searching for it, then," he said. "I think she really wanted to get that key back to make things up to Helene and Antonia. Any ideas where she would go from here . . . ?"

But any ideas I had were cut off by a fresh outburst of scuffling under the First Sofa. Samson looked up and sniffed again, but there was no purring this time as Ben himself crawled into the room, his silver sunglasses gleaming, the Oak Key swinging on its slightly sudsy shoelace, and a look of borderline panic in his eyes.

He did a perfect double take between us, then gave Uncle Joe's outfit one openmouthed look from head to toe.

"You," he yelled at him, "are a grown-up and not supposed to be here! And you"—he rounded on me—"are supposed to be back at camp! What do you possibly think you're doing?" His voice was going all squeaky.

"Easy, easy," I said. "Everything's fine. Look, I found Samson."

Ben looked and screamed. "Cat on the sofa! Cat! On the

sofa!" He swooped down and frantically tried to pull Samson free, but he had even less success than I had. He tugged and tugged, but finally something seemed to collapse inside him, and he gave up, dropping onto the sofa and throwing an arm over his face.

An awkward silence filled le Petit Salon.

Uncle Joe and I exchanged a few thoughts through eyebrow wiggles.

"So, hey, did you get the foam party under control then, Ben?" I asked, after it became clear no one else was going to restart the conversation.

Ben lowered his arm, staring at the ceiling. He nodded. "Every one of my clipboards was ruined in the process, but yes, we did. I was coming here to reach out to the European Council—"

"To apologize, like Miesha ordered you to," I interrupted with a smile.

"—like I was supposed to for the plan," Ben finished heavily. He looked so overwhelmed and upset that I actually almost felt sorry for him. The loss of those clipboards must have been a real blow.

"Well, don't let us being here get in the way of the plan," I said. "Although I don't think—"

But it was Uncle Joe's turn to interrupt as he held up a hand and said, "Shh! I hear something!"

We stopped and listened. A gaggle of grown-up voices

rose in the hall outside, headed our way. Uncle Joe's eyes went wide. I flapped a hand at him.

"Oh! Oh!" I whispered. "This is awesome!"

Ben got to his feet, groaning dramatically. "I've heard this speech a hundred times."

"Well shhh," I hissed. "This is Uncle Joe's first." I put a finger to my lips, and Uncle Joe nodded.

The voices stopped outside the door, and one rose above the others—the tour guide, in her rapid-fire French. The murmuring died away as the unseen group listened. I grinned, knowing what was coming. Whatever Ben said, it was fun being here for this again.

"So," the woman said, as she switched to English in her gorgeous accent. "As before, I will repeat for our guests who do not have the French. This room here is one of the favorite mysteries of the Palace of Versailles. It is called le Petit Salon, or the Little Room, and it was shut and locked during the reign of King Louis the Fifteenth, which is nearly three hundred years ago, and has never been opened since."

The crowd murmured. Ben raised his hands in a neener-neener gesture and stuck his tongue out at the door.

I smiled even wider at the soft clunk as the tour guide grasped the handle, wiggling it to show her rapt audience that it was good and locked.

But the handle . . . moved.

The door creaked . . .

. . . open.

The lights of the hall flooded in, and the dust-filled sunlight streamed out.

There's probably never been a silence like that in the entire history of the world.

Everyone stood, frozen as tree trunks, staring. Ben still had his tongue sticking out and his hands in waggling position beside his ears. Uncle Joe, in his ridiculous movie costume, gaped from the sofa. I was caught in a sort of horrified grimace, one hand stretched toward the door as though I could will it not to open.

Even Samson stopped washing to look up, his back leg sticking straight up in the air.

It was Ben who broke the silence. With a sob that sounded pulled from the bottom of his soul, he turned his back on the open door of le Petit Salon and dove under the sofa. There was a moment of scuffling, and he was gone.

The tour guide, who was round and elegant and dressed all in black, from her shoes to the head scarf framing her face, took a hesitant step toward us. "I . . . I don't—" she began, but the crowd behind her shifted as another woman stepped forward.

"Maggie . . . ?" The woman's voice was faint. "Joe?"

I took a deep, slow breath. The marble floor felt like water beneath me.

"Hi, Mom," I said.

THIRTY-SIX
Abby

Hot breath hit my face. Four paws pressed into my stomach and ribs.

"Gah!" I yelled, as the whatever it was began licking my ears. I pushed an arm up, holding it back enough to get a look at my attacker.

It was a dog. A sweet-faced, floppy-eared, honey-colored dog wearing a rainbow collar with a tag shaped like a dolphin. I squinted at the tag.

"Sprinkles?" I said. The dog's tail waved frantically, smacking against the wall of the woolly mammoth fort. Ha! This was Miesha's dog, the one Ben fell in love with last year when it was a puppy. "Sprinkles! Are they letting you wander around the forts on your own now? Or were you lost like me?" I scratched his ears, and he pushed happily into my fingers, his tongue lolling. "Let's go find our friends, buddy."

Sprinkles got in one more slurp on my face as I sat up, then bounded through the pillow link. I followed.

Bobby's fort was exactly as Maggie had described it in her endless planning sessions, where we went over every detail from the summer before. It was neat and comfortable, with blue sheet walls and ceiling, rows of books, a corner stacked with lounging pillows, and twinkle lights strung overhead.

And, okay, I was in Bobby's fort. Excellent. Beyond that entrance sheet was the Hub, and that meant pillow fort kids who could help me find a way home. Or, more important, a way back to camp. I was done chasing Ben and his key. There was too much at stake. I'd just gotten the luckiest break ever escaping from Montreal, and I wasn't about to risk it all again. It was time for me to get back to camp, and Maggie, and the real world, before terrible things happened.

An image of Antonia and Helene's disappointed faces swam across my brain, but I pushed them away. That would have to wait until I'd set things right. When I knew there was no danger of my dad's honeymoon getting ruined, or Camp Cantaloupe getting in trouble because I was missing, then I could worry about my pirate friends on the island.

Until then, I'd just have to live with the fact that I'd let them down. Even if it hurt.

I opened the entrance sheet a crack, surveying the view as Sprinkles flopped happily over my feet, making himself comfortable.

Whoa! The Hub had really changed. It was dark, and empty, and a whole lot tidier than I remembered. What happened to this place? What happened to the chandelier? And where were all the kids?

The sounds of a commotion were coming from somewhere out of sight. I pushed my shoulders out and craned around to look.

Hmm. Okay, well, I'd found the kids. The entire far side of the Hub was covered in foam, like a massive washing machine had exploded, and an army of kids with buckets, mops, and towels was attacking it. Foam was flying, kids were shouting, headlamps were flashing; basically, it looked like fun.

I was halfway out of the fort to join them when golden light suddenly poured into the Hub from along the wall. Someone was hurrying in through the nearest tapestry door. Someone short, and wearing overalls, and ... crying.

I'd never actually met him in person, but thanks to the sunglasses and overalls, I knew exactly who this someone must be.

"Ben?" I yelled, as he ran down the aisle. My heart leaped. "Ben!" He didn't look up.

Before I could think twice, I scrambled after him, barely aware that Sprinkles was joining me. He was right there! I could still pull this off! I had one last chance for victory!

Ben ran straight across the dark Hub, and I managed

to keep up, weaving through the gloom after him toward another tapestry door. He yanked the fabric aside and disappeared.

Sprinkles and I followed.

The tapestry led into a long hallway made of bare concrete. Ben was already at the far end when we entered, tugging open a heavy metal door and squeezing into the darkness behind it.

I sped up, panting from running in my ridiculous outfit. Sprinkles was panting too as we pushed past the heavy door and looked around. Now we were at the bottom of a stairwell, with metal steps leading up and up and up. Cold white lights sputtered on the walls, one for each level. I could hear Ben's clanging footsteps.

Stairs? Ugh. Thanks for nothing, Ben. Where on earth were we going? And who wants to run when they're crying? I hitched up my dress and started up, Helene's complete ring of keys dancing at my side.

I'd slowed to a walk, panting and clutching a stitch in my ribs, by the time the stairs finally stopped at a landing. There was another metal door. I pushed, and the door screeched open, revealing a dark doorway full of graffiti and cigarette butts and an oily, drying puddle.

The door slid shut behind us as Sprinkles and I stepped out of the doorway . . .

And into the heart of a city.

It looked like midafternoon here, with a high sun and thin clouds streaking the blue sky. I shook my head. I wasn't even going to try to keep track of all these time zone jumps. That was more Maggie's territory.

There were people all around me, singing, laughing, and talking. The air smelled like mouthwatering grilled food, and car exhaust, and perfume, and warm concrete. A billboard across the street was advertising dishwasher detergent. In Spanish. Huh.

I glanced behind me at the door, making sure it was still there, then craned my neck back, and back, and back, until I realized what I was looking at. Sprinkles and I were standing in the shadow of a massive stadium. The huge walls curving away to either side were hung with glossy banners of soccer players. A neon sign flashed ads for rallies and concerts and sports games. And from the look of the crowd pouring onto the street farther down the wall, one of those games had just ended.

Whoa. The whole tangled beehive of the Hub was down there, under this soccer stadium, under the city's feet, and no one knew it.

I turned back to the street, my eyes traveling over the crowds of people obliviously walking over the heart of the North American pillow fort kingdom. The sports fans, the food trucks, the bikes and the cars and lights . . . and Ben, sitting alone on a lumpy modern art sculpture, his arms wrapped around his knees, still crying.

I wove through the crowd and sat down on a sculptural swoop of stone beside him.

"Ben?"

He looked up. He'd taken off his silver sunglasses, and his pale face was all blotchy. He sniffed.

"Who are you?" he said. "How do you know my name?"

Oh, right. We'd never met. Plus I was wearing a pretty unusual outfit. "It's me, Abby," I said. "Abby Hernandez. I followed you up here from the Hub."

Ben's blotchy pink face went through a hilarious parade of emotions. "Of course you are!" he said when he was able to speak again. He barked out a shaky laugh. "Of course. Why wouldn't you be here, after everything else? Why would any of the rules and regulations apply anymore? It's a free-for-all! Every pillow fort for themselves!"

People passing by were looking over as Ben had his little meltdown. He seemed about ready to run away again when Sprinkles, who'd been carefully peeing on every piece of modern art, barked happily and jumped into his lap.

Ben screamed—hey, like a peacock, just like Europe Girl said—but then Sprinkles was licking his ears, and Ben was burying his face in the dog's fur and, from the sound of things, crying again. I watched the crowd, waiting politely for him to finish. Finally, he resurfaced.

"You really shouldn't be here," he said, sniffing.

A knot of people in soccer jerseys passed by, their arms linked, all singing at the top of their lungs. "Really?" I said. "Why? Where are we?"

"Mexico City," said Ben. "And you really, *really* shouldn't know that, since you're not in NAFAFA, but obviously it's too late now."

Whoa. Mexico City! I looked around again, paying more attention to the beautiful people and voices and smells, and smiled.

"Why did you follow me?" Ben asked. Sprinkles was biting at the shoelace dangling around his neck. Something flashed at the end. The Oak Key.

"Because of that," I said, pointing. "I need it."

"The key?" Ben looked down. "What? Why? You already had it, didn't you? And then you lost it again. We had a whole meeting about it. Anyway, it's—it's worthless now. You used it in that treehouse, and someone else unlocked the door of le Petit Salon, and there's nothing left." His face crumpled, tears running down his cheeks.

Whoa. Was that why he was so upset? Because someone beat him to his dream?

But . . . wait.

"How, um, how do you know someone unlocked that door?" I asked.

With a whole lot of sniffling, Ben told me about meeting Maggie in le Petit Salon—*Mags was running around the networks looking for me!*—along with Samson—*My baby!*—and Joe—*How the heck had he gotten there?*—and being interrupted by the tour guide when the door just ... swung open.

And oh, my head. I did that. I unlocked the door to look outside, but then Europe Girl turned up and I got all distracted. And totally forgot to relock it. And now, because of me, Maggie and Samson and Joe were all cornered in le Petit Salon by an army of grown-ups. Man, that was really gonna make Europe Girl mad when she found out.

I shivered as the seriousness of the situation hit me: le Petit Salon, the Little Room, home of the First Sofa and center of the Pillow Fort universe, was open to the public after three hundred years.

Seriously, when it came to wrecking things this summer, I was on a roll. I fell through the trapdoor of the Shipwreck Treehouse, messed things up in Buckingham Palace, stole Captain Emily's ring of keys, *really* messed things up in that German place, got stuck in a museum and sent all the visitors there scrambling after freebies, and now this.

"So everything's ruined forever," Ben concluded, rubbing Sprinkles behind the ears. "And the worst part is I'll never even find out who actually unlocked that door. With all these people running around, there's no way to tell!"

I coughed. "Um, actually, it was me."

Ben's face went through its parade of emotions again as I told him about the Iron Key and my long, winding journey through trapdoors and island palaces and various pieces of furniture, all to end up here, trying to get back the same key I'd lost in the first place.

"So there's a key that truly goes to the le Petit Salon door?" said Ben. "And you've got it? You've got it here?"

I pulled the Iron Key from the pocket of my dress and held it up. Ben's eyes locked on it, shining with the same worshipful glow Samson got whenever I offered him a piece of salmon.

"Hey, you know what," I said, struck with a sudden idea. Why on earth didn't I think of this before? "I'll trade you."

Ben looked at me, his expression going from Samson-in-love to Samson-being-offered-spinach. He looked wary. I couldn't blame him. He'd only just gotten his beloved Oak Key back. It must have been hard to try and transfer that love to a new one.

"Come on," I said. "You said yourself the Oak Key is useless now. And with this one, no matter what happens with those grown-ups getting into le Petit Salon, you'll know that you, Ben, are the only person in the entire world who's got a key to that door."

That did it. Ben's eyes lost their uncertainty, and the

corners of his mouth perked up. He pulled the shoelace over his head, whispered something to the Oak Key, and held it out.

We made the trade.

I could have run around screaming like a peacock, right there in Mexico City in my old-timey dress and swoopy-winged hat. I had the Oak Key! My mission was achieved! Well, once I got the key ring back to Helene, that is. Which would be next to impossible, now, since le Petit Salon was crawling with grown-ups.

Ugh, it was always something.

"Hey, so we should probably go on a rescue mission to le Petit Salon, now, huh?" I said. "Since Maggie and Joe are trapped and cornered?"

Ben was examining every millimeter of his new key, Sprinkles panting in his face. "No point," he said without looking up. "I told you, Abby Hernandez. Everything is ruined. Mainly because of you."

I glared at him. "Fine, but I've still got work to do. I need to return these keys to the island, and get Joe and Samson home safe, and get Maggie and me back to camp before everything goes wrong there too. And that means getting into that little room. This mission isn't over yet."

"So what's your plan?" Ben asked, finally looking around. "Do you have some wild, Hetzger-Hernandez scheme ready?

Some complicated way to get all those grown-ups to just leave, and close the door, and forget everything?" He shoved the Iron Key into the pocket of his overalls. "Trust me, it's over. That is never going to happen."

I hopped up and stretched. Modern art was super uncomfortable. "You can believe whatever you want, Ben," I said. "But I've got friends who need me, and I'm going to go try and save them. Besides"—I looked out at the people and families and crowds around us, all living their tangled, complicated lives one on top of the other, with a secret pillow fort kingdom under their feet—"I think when it comes down to it, we can only control a tiny bit of what happens anyway, and the universe or life or whatever will always find a way to—" I stopped dead, staring with my mouth hanging open.

"To what?" Ben said.

"—to surprise us." I took two steps forward. Ben and Sprinkles both looked where I was looking.

Two men holding hands, one short and muscly, the other tall and slender, were walking past us in the crowd. They were wearing matching jerseys from the game at the stadium.

And I knew both of them very, very well.

THIRTY-SEVEN
Maggie

"So, how's the conference going?" I asked.

The tour had been canceled, and all the tourists whisked away as first the security guards, then a pack of palace historians, then the media crowded in. After being asked dozens of questions none of us knew how to answer, Uncle Joe, my mom, Samson, and I were sitting on a bench in the hallway while the historians—whose boss, it turned out, was the tour guide lady—examined every inch of le Petit Salon. We weren't officially under arrest or anything, as far as we knew, but they weren't letting us go, either.

"How's the conference going?" repeated my mom. She laughed, a bit hysterically. "The conference is going fine, Maggie. Thank you for asking. There's lots of interesting medical research being discussed. And we had a free

morning today, so I thought, 'Hey, why not go on a tour of Versailles? That will be wonderfully relaxing!'"

I adjusted my lapful of Samson. "Sorry it's not."

"I'll survive. But now my turn." My mom faced me. "So, how's Camp Cantaloupe going, Maggie?"

Uncle Joe and I grinned.

"It's going okay, thanks," I said. "The art teacher likes me, and I met this girl who was sort of my biggest enemy, but now I think we might be friends. We're doing a scene together for drama class, and we're supposed to start doing this big letter-writing project with some younger kids when I get back."

"When you get back," said my mom, fixing me with a very parental look. "Which will be soon, right? You've been counting the minutes to that camp all year. I can't imagine Abby is glad you're gone like this."

"Oh, well," I said, and Uncle Joe shifted on the bench beside me. "Abby still has to, um, sort of . . . get back to camp, too."

My mom put her face in her hands.

"I wonder what they're all looking for in there," said Uncle Joe, peering over at the historians in le Petit Salon taking photos and measuring and elbowing each other for spots. "It's not that big a room."

We could see right into the room from where we sat. The

historians were definitely being thorough, and they seemed to be focusing on the walls and windows. They probably thought we'd snuck in through some secret panel or hidden door and were racing to find it. They all seemed scared to go near the sofa, like they were worried it might collapse into dust if they even breathed on it.

My mom looked up. "Joe," she said, "I love you, but I think the real question here is how we're going to get Maggie—and Abigail, wherever she is—back to summer camp. Not to mention there's this cat to deal with. And if I remember last summer correctly, the way to do that has something to do with that sofa over there. And ... well ..." She gestured at the packed little room, and the hallway full of palace officials, police, security guards, and reporters, all clutching cameras, phones, and notepads.

Getting back into le Petit Salon and slipping discreetly under the sofa was looking less and less possible.

"We either need a really, really, really good distraction," I said, remembering the last time I had to get grown-ups out of my way, "or a plan to make all these people do what we say." I did a quick mental search through my inventory of secret-agent plots and schemes, but nothing came to mind that would help in this situation. Well, not without me finally having my own helicopter.

It looked like we were well and truly stuck.

But as I slumped back on the bench, something inside le Petit Salon snagged my attention. A flash of silver . . . under the sofa.

I sat up, staring. There it was again. Then a face, for the briefest of seconds, and a hand, only visible from where we were sitting, beckoning me over.

"Wait here," I said, getting to my feet.

My mom looked up. "Maggie, they said to stay. Please don't make it worse."

I ignored her and headed for the room. Head Historian lady blocked me in the doorway.

"No, mademoiselle," she said firmly. "It is our turn to explore the room, yes? You have had yours, I think."

"But I—I lost my necklace!" I said, improvising. Ooh, actually that worked! The necklace Abby had made me was hidden under my shirt. I put on my best sad-little-kid face. "It's my very favorite. I've had it since forever. I think it fell off near the sofa."

"Then we will find it. And return it to you when we have completed our survey of the room."

I looked up at her, thinking hard about all the awful things that would happen if we didn't find a way out of this mess. The trouble I would be in. The trouble Camp Cantaloupe would be in. The trouble my mom and Uncle Joe would be in. The trouble Abby and Samson would be in. I felt my eyes fill with tears. Success!

"Ah, no! Oh, no, okay," Head Historian lady said. "No tears, please. Yes, you may go find your necklace. But quickly, and be *very* careful around that sofa!"

I gave her a watery smile and ducked past before she could change her mind. Some of the other historians in the room rounded on me, but she held up a hand and stared them down. I crossed to the sofa, made a big show of patting around the edges of the seat, then peered underneath.

And there were Miesha, wearing Kelly's space helmet over her silver Council sunglasses, and Bobby, wearing his usual massive smile.

"Maggie!" Bobby whispered. "Hi! How are you? Are you having fun?"

"I guess so," I breathed back. "Why are you wearing that, Miesha?"

"It was Kelly's idea," she said, her voice slightly muffled. "To let me leave the Archives without having an allergy attack. So far it's working, although don't ask me how."

"Awesome!" I said. "Hey, so you're probably wondering why I didn't go back to camp." For some reason the sight of them cramped under the sofa filled me with a deep need to explain myself. "Everyone was just so busy with the foam fountain thing, and then I spotted Samson's trail and followed him here. He's out in the hall with my mom and uncle now. Oh, wait, you don't know, my uncle showed up too, and—"

"That's not important, Maggie Hetzger," Miesha interrupted. "What's important is that there are grown-ups inside le Petit Salon! How exactly did you unlock that door?"

"I didn't!" I protested, going flat on my belly, pretending to dig around under the sofa. "We were listening to the tour guide and the handle just turned! Like it wasn't locked at all!"

Miesha looked over her sunglasses at me for a long moment. "Hmm. Well. Maybe it's a good thing you were here, then. If the door was already compromised, we might have shown up and found the room full of grown-ups with no warning. But whatever. Bobby and I are here to rescue you."

"Yay!" said Bobby.

"Thanks!" I said.

"Thank Carolina," Miesha said. "She's the one who saw Ben run out of here crying and came to see what had happened."

"Carolina's here, too?" I said. "Where?"

"Over there." Miesha pointed past my shoulder. I glanced back and saw Carolina sitting on the bench in the hall beside my mom and Uncle Joe, chatting away. She was wearing a silver baseball hat that matched her sunglasses.

"But—how did she get out there?!" I whisper-yelled.

"Secret-agent stuff," Miesha said. "We were getting

cramped, and she wanted to stretch her legs. She's good, isn't she?"

That was the understatement of the entire summer.

"Okay, so what's your rescue plan?" I said. I'd been pretending to search the sofa for a while now. I wouldn't have long before the Head Historian lady kicked me out.

"We're going to take back control of le Petit Salon and this sofa," said Miesha.

I blinked. "How are you planning on doing that?"

"With this." Miesha turned to Bobby, who handed me an ancient-looking piece of paper covered in old-fashioned writing. I had trouble making out the letters, but it looked to be in French.

"This is our secret weapon," Miesha said. "It's that lead I found while I was stuck in the Archives. Bobby just finished the translation. It's pretty perfect."

"What's it say?" I asked. They looked at each other. Bobby suppressed a giggle.

"It'll be more fun if we don't tell you," said Miesha. "Just give it to that lady in charge. The rest will take care of itself."

I looked back down at the paper. "Just give it to her? That's all?"

"Yup," said Bobby. "You can say you found it under here."

"And it will get us out of this?"

"It should," Miesha said. "If you don't get carried away

trying to control everything. Just let the document do its work, smooth out any little bumps with those improv skills of yours, and we'll be fine."

"You'll do great, Maggie!" said Bobby, giving me two thumbs-ups.

Well. Okay. I guess this was what we were doing. I got back to my feet and approached Head Historian lady, pulling the necklace out from under my shirt.

"Well," she said, not looking at me. "Did you find your necklace?"

"Yes," I said, patting it. "Thank you. But I found this, too, sticking out of the bottom of the sofa. I thought it might be important." I held out the paper. She glanced at it briefly, then did a double take and turned her full attention on me.

"Oh," she breathed. "An artifact!" She took the paper, holding it by the edges. I watched as her eyes flashed across it, apparently having no problem with the old-fashioned writing. Her beautiful, framed face shifted wildly as her expression went from reverence, to confusion, to blank shock. She stopped at the bottom of the paper, then went back to the top and read the whole thing over again.

"Excuse me a moment, please." She stepped to one side and spoke in French to the rest of the historians. They gathered around her, all reading the document together in a clump.

Out in the hall, Uncle Joe and Carolina had swapped hats and were chatting happily. My mom was watching me, frowning. She tilted her head in a question, and I gestured to the knot of historians and shrugged.

Suddenly the knot broke apart, all talking at once. Some of the historians pointed angry fingers at me; others pulled out cell phones and began shouting into them; and a couple went straight to the gaggle of media types waiting with their cameras in the hall. If I'd thought things were confusing before, everything seemed a hundred times worse now.

What had Miesha and Bobby gotten us into?

The storm of yelling grew. People were running in every direction. Reporters were hurling questions at the historians, security guards were practically spitting into their walkie-talkies, and the piece of paper was getting passed from hand to hand and shouted at too.

And then the Head Historian, who had her phone pressed to her ear, hollered at the top of her lungs over the din. Everything went quiet. She beckoned me with an impatient gesture, still speaking into the phone. I walked over, glancing behind me at my backup. My mom and Uncle Joe looked worried. Carolina was smiling.

Samson was playing with his tail.

Head Historian lady was listening and nodding, nodding and listening. She shook her head. She nodded again, her eyes on the far wall. I stood beside her, shifting from foot to foot, aware that every freaked-out grown-up in the vicinity was watching the two of us. Waiting.

The lady spoke two words. There was a pause, then, "Oui." She pressed her thumb to the side of the phone and lowered it. She looked at me. She looked around at the crowd.

"This, ehm, document," she said, so everyone could hear. "This document is an early historical draft of legal language that Louis the Fifteenth had placed in the constitution of the nation of France as he ruled it."

There was dead silence in the room, and in the hallway outside.

"It details certain . . . conditions, for the achieving of a certain . . . position within the government of France." She paused. Whatever she was getting at, it was clear she didn't want to say it. "These conditions center on this room, le Petit Salon, and by tradition have been included in every version of the French constitution for the past three centuries as a nostalgic nod to the history."

More silence. "So?" someone burst out. "What does it say?"

"It says," the lady said, raising the paper, "and I have here spoken personally with the president as well as experts in the historical archives and received full, legal confirmation . . . ahem. 'If, by some condition, the door to le Petit Salon should be opened from without, and persons are discovered to be within, let the first person to have entered therein, even should they appear unusual in dress and appearance, be recognized legally and royally as the sole and rightful head of state of the nation of France, and be treated as such, with all due rights and privileges therein pertaining.'"

There was a pause like a bubble filling up, and then absolute chaos erupted. The media was going wild, and the historians were jockeying for position in front of the cameras. Head Historian lady was suddenly being interviewed by five different journalists at once, and camera operators were running laps inside le Petit Salon, gathering background footage.

"Do you want to hear the rest?" said a voice in my ear. I jumped. It was Carolina, wearing Uncle Joe's feathery pirate hat.

I nodded, and we slipped back to the bench.

"Miesha found that document in one of Louis's old journals. Apparently there was only ever one key to this room, and Louis was constantly almost losing it. He made them put that bit in the constitution so if he ever came back through the pillow fort links and realized it was gone, and someone seized the throne in his absence, he could pound on the door until the guards broke it down, the statute would go into effect, and he'd be king again."

"He thought someone might take the throne while he was stuck in here?" I said. "That doesn't sound like a super likely problem to have."

Carolina shrugged. "Louis was a king; he was paranoid. Plus he spent a lot of time in disguise, running around with his friends. He thought maybe one of them would try to take his place by pretending to be him someday. This was his backup plan."

"Attention! Attention everyone, please!" Head Historian lady was clapping her hands again. Cameras swiveled and voices faded as everyone focused on her. "Many people are asking me, 'Who is now the head of state for France?' and I am sorry to say I am not yet able to tell you."

"But you said you were the one who opened the room!" shouted one of the reporters. "Are you changing your story on us? Are you trying to suppress the facts with a cover-up?"

The lady fixed the man with a look, and he shrank back.

"It is true," she said, "that I was the one to turn the handle, as I have many times tried to do before, and this time I succeeded. But the document refers not to the opener, but to who is found *inside* the room, and inside the room I found not one person, but two."

She looked at me, then at Uncle Joe, who definitely fit the *unusual in dress and appearance* description, especially since Carolina's silver baseball hat was way too small on him. All the faces and cameras looked with her.

"So the answer to the first question," she finished, "lies in a second one: Who was first to arrive in le Petit Salon?"

Uncle Joe and I locked eyes. I could almost hear him thinking the same thing I was. He had arrived in le Petit Salon after me, but I hadn't been first in the room. Not technically.

Wordlessly, moving as one, Uncle Joe and I raised our arms . . . and pointed straight at Samson.

THIRTY-EIGHT
Abby

"Ben, shhh! They'll hear you!" I hissed, peering out from behind the plastic tablecloth at the two men we'd so expertly followed.

Maggie would have been proud of the way we'd secret-agent-trailed them for three blocks, ducking behind cars and fading into the crowd. But sitting crammed together under the table of an ice cream stand was turning out to be a lot more challenging.

"You be careful!" Ben whispered back. "I wouldn't have to keep saying *ow* if you'd quit jabbing me in the eye with your hat. Hey, ow!"

"Shhh!" I whapped him on the arm. "Put your Council sunglasses on if it's a problem."

"I had them on! You keep knocking them off! Sprinkles, no!"

Sprinkles had already sniffed out every ice-cream-cone crumb within reach and was making it very clear he wanted to go out and search for more. Ben latched his arms around him, trapping him in cuddle prison.

We looked back out at our targets. Oof. I'd been through some weird stuff the last couple of days, but this was the most unbelievably wild thing of all.

Because the man on the left was my dad, Alex. And the man on the right was my new stepdad, Tamal.

And oh my goodness, they were so freaking cute, sitting with their elbows touching, talking and laughing over their ice cream.

I would have given all of Antonia's tiaras to hear what they were saying. But the radio on the ice-cream truck was blasting music, and there was no way we wouldn't be spotted if we tried to get closer. It was just gonna have to be enough for me to sit here, miraculously somehow on the same street of the same city at the same time, and watch a piece of their honeymoon.

I snorted. Good thing it was me here and not my brothers. They would have snuck up on Dad and Tamal from behind and hug-tackled them, probably singing wedding songs at the top of their lungs and throwing rainbow sprinkles around like confetti.

Hey, knowing them, they probably had something exactly like that planned for our first day in the new house.

The new house. It still didn't feel real, even with all the packing I'd done before camp and the SOLD sign swinging by the curb as I drove away. But it was, and when camp ended, and I went back home . . . new family, new house, new bedroom, new view, new kitchen, new address, new yard, new route to school. New everything.

Only that thought wasn't making me as nervous as it had before. Maybe because I'd gotten some moving practice under my belt these last few days. I'd seen more bedrooms and hallways and living rooms and lounges than I bet most people saw in a year. Palace after palace after palace, some of the fanciest homes in the world. And my new place was going to be better than all of them.

Because my dad would be there, and my brothers and Samson, and Tamal, and Maggie coming over every day because there was no way she wouldn't. And sure it was cheesy, but so long as they were around, I could deal with anything. The location of home didn't really matter; only the people in it.

Although a big aquarium wall like in the Island Underneath would be nice.

And an elevator.

And a private beach.

And a throne room.

Over at the table, Tamal said something and held up his ice-cream-free hand, and my dad did the same. They clinked wedding rings.

"Aww," Ben and I said together. Sprinkles, who had given up the fight and was lolling in Ben's lap, wagged his tail.

My dad finished his cone and got to his feet. Tamal did the same, putting his arm around my dad's waist. My dad's arm went around Tamal's shoulders, and he kissed him on the cheek, and they headed off again into the crowd.

We waited a full minute before we climbed out from under our table.

"That was kind of fun," said Ben, stooping to keep one hand looped through Sprinkles' collar. "So were you still gonna go try and salvage whatever disaster is happening in le Petit Salon? 'Cause I know it's all your fault, and that's why you want to fix it, but I wouldn't mind helping, if you want. I mean, that could be fun, too."

I stretched my arms over my head, taking in all the sounds and smells and lights of the city, and the world beyond all my pillow fort mess-ups and palace catastrophes, which by the look of things was going along just fine. I dropped my arms and smiled.

"It sure could," I said. "Let's go."

THIRTY-NINE
Abby

Ben and I could hear the ominous clamor of voices as soon as we got past the tapestry. The pillow leading to le Petit Salon was lying open, and the noise echoed down the Hall of Records.

Sprinkles sniffed the air, his tail wagging, and shot off past the columns. "Hey, wait!" called Ben, but Sprinkles slipped through the link and vanished.

"No, no, no!" Ben said. "A surprise dog visit is the last thing they'll need in there. I mean, they're already in big trouble, right? If they could have gotten themselves out by now, they would have."

I nodded. Ben had said only Samson and Maggie and Joe had definitely been caught inside le Petit Salon when the door opened, and by the sound of things, they'd gotten a whole lot of company. This was bad.

We reached the link, and I crawled through first, pausing under the sofa. The voices overhead were talking excitedly, and I could see feet moving around the room, and Sprinkles's dancing paws, and the door leading to the hallway, which was . . . closed. Huh.

Deciding this was just one of those all-or-nothing moments, I took a deep breath, pushed out into the room, jumped to my feet . . .

. . . and got three seconds to register the sea of familiar faces around me before someone shrieked like a third grader presented with pie, and suddenly everything was arms and elbows and bushy hair as Maggie, my own dear Maggie, was hug-tackling me.

We danced in a circle for a long time. We stepped back.

Maggie looked great. She had glitter paint on her pajama pants, dust bunnies in her hair, dark circles under her eyes, and holes in her Camp Cantaloupe T-shirt. I glanced down at myself and my sweaty, wrinkled silk dress, my fancy ring of keys, and my old-timey slippers, almost disintegrating after their trip through Mexico City. Ha! I felt like we'd been separated for a hundred years, and we totally looked like it, too. We made such a good pair.

The rest of the group crowded around, resolving itself into Maggie's mom, Joe, Carolina, Bobby, Miesha—who was wearing some sort of homemade space helmet and holding a very happy Sprinkles over one shoulder—and my own perfect, wonderful Samson, watching regally from the sofa.

Maggie and I were both talking at once as Ben crawled in behind me.

"How are you even—"

"—will *not* believe—"

"—fell through that door—"

"—earth are you *wearing*?"

"—never find my way back to—"

"—so many people saw—"

"—think we might be on the TV!"

We stopped, grinning, and Maggie pulled me into another hug.

"I'm so, *so* sorry," she said. "I've been worrying nonstop about you this whole time. I'm sorry I didn't manage to rescue you."

"Aw, Abby didn't need any rescuing," said Joe. "She did awesome!" We high-fived.

"What happened with that navy ship and Florence?" I asked him, as Maggie's mom grabbed me for a hug, too. "Is the island safe? Are Antonia and Helene mad at me for ruining their loops to all those palaces?"

Joe waved his hands. "It's all okay. Helene repaired the dolphin remotely in the nick of time. And the palace situation might be a little sticky, but I think those two can fix anything they put their minds to."

"When you say 'repaired the dolphin' . . ." began Bobby, but Ben, who'd been staring around red-faced with shock, interrupted.

"Will someone please tell me what has been going on here?" he said, his voice all squeaky. "That door was open when I left. And a wall of grown-ups was staring in. How in the world did you get them to go away?"

The others all exchanged grins.

"The super-quick version," said Miesha, her voice slightly muffled through her space helmet, "is that I found a piece of paper in the NAFAFA Archives, and now Maggie is the Queen of France."

"I thought we decided on president," said Maggie. "And anyway, it's really Samson who's in charge of France, since he was first in the room. But the Head Historian lady said she thinks that law doesn't apply to cats, so it passed to me as the first human."

"How does your cat keep being elected leader of things?" Carolina asked me.

"Fine, so Maggie Hetzger was declared President of France," said Ben loudly. "Of course she was. Then what happened?"

"Well, after she addressed the nation—" Murray began.

"Addressed the nation?" I said.

"The TV cameras were right there," said Maggie. "It would have been rude not to." Her mom smiled proudly and patted her on the back.

"After that, Maggie Hetzger ordered all the police and reporters and historians and everyone to leave the room," said Carolina. "And as head of state, she gets to do that, so then we had the place to ourselves."

"It was ah-may-zing!" said Bobby.

Ben was staring at Maggie, clearly very impressed. "And all those police and historians and reporters and everyone just went home?" he said.

"Oh, no," said Miesha. "They're still out there." She waved a hand at the door. "We were debating what to do next when you and Abby arrived."

"And Sprinkles," said Ben.

"And Sprinkles," agreed Miesha. "And speaking of, it's so good to have you back, buddy." She squeezed him, and Sprinkles licked her space helmet. "But we've got some big decisions to make here, and it would be easier without you around. Any volunteers to take my baby back to the Hub?"

"Sure, I will," said Bobby from the sofa. Samson was sprawled comfortably across his lap. "Should I bring this handsome lion with me, too? Seems like he and Sprinkles have gotten used to each other, and I know Kelly will be excited to see him!"

"Is that okay, Abby Hernandez?" said Miesha. "Can Bobby take your cat back to Kelly?"

I agreed, and after a round of hugs and air kisses for everyone, Bobby headed off to the Hub with Samson purring around his shoulders and Sprinkles on a leash made from Ben's old shoelace.

"So what now?" I asked, as the energy in the room became more businesslike. "What are these big decisions you were talking about?"

"We're trying to decide our next move," said Maggie. "I ordered all the grown-ups to stay out, but we all think that'll only hold them for a while."

Carolina nodded. "Even with direct orders from President Maggie, the temptation to look in here is probably going to be too much. Especially if that Head Historian lady walks by it every single time she leads a tour."

"I just wish we had a way to lock it again," said Miesha. "But we don't even know how it got unlocked to start with."

"Actually, that was me," I said, raising a hand. "I had the key with me and wanted to take a look out in the hall, but then I got distracted. Sorry."

There was a pause, then an explosion of shouting.

"You seriously found the real key to that door, Abby Hernandez?" Miesha said over the others. "Do you have it with you right now?"

"Nope, I do," said Ben, and he pulled the Iron Key out of his pocket.

Everyone goggled, their heads turning.

"Helene gave that key to you, Abby," said Joe. "Why does this kid have it?"

"Because we did a swap," I said, and I pulled out the Oak Key.

Everyone swiveled back to me. This was getting fun.

"You got it!" Joe yelped. He leaned in for another high five. "Go, Abby! Mission accomplished!"

"So does this mean Ben can lock the door again?" Murray said as the two keys got passed around and examined. "We can keep the grown-ups out! Le Petit Salon is saved!"

"Speaking as the only grown-up here not wearing a Three Musketeers costume," said Ms. Hetzger, "I'm afraid not. Even with the door locked, kids, I don't think you'll be able to keep everyone out of here forever. This place is only going to get more famous, judging by the amount of press we saw out there, and historians from all over the world are going to demand a look. Maggie's orders might stand for a little while, but if people aren't getting the access they want, it's only a matter of time before they take it for themselves."

The excitement over the keys popped like a soap bubble. Ms. Hetzger was right. The historians would never let le Petit Salon stay shut forever. The room had been opened, and the mystery was known. There was no going back.

"Well, I think what we need, then," said Ben into the worried silence, "is a whole new le Petit Salon." Everyone looked at him in shock. "Think about it. We don't have to meet *here*. We can set up another global meeting place like this anywhere, so long as the Continental Councils all have links to it. We can bypass the First Sofa completely. Only this time, we should make the secret base somewhere really out of the way, somewhere absolutely no one can find us. Somewhere safe."

Joe and I looked up at the same moment, smiling in unison.

"We might know the perfect place," I said. "How do you all feel about islands?"

It took a lot of explaining, and some complicated finger drawing in the dust, but eventually Joe and I got everyone up to speed on the basics of the island and how its looped furniture system worked.

Miesha and Carolina insisted we all swing by right then, bringing a piece of the sofa seat cushion so we could build a fort linked back to le Petit Salon for easy back-and-forth access before making our proposals to Antonia and the crew.

"Well, if everyone's going off to this magical island," said Ms. Hetzger, "I should get back to what's left of my medical conference."

"Sorry you got caught up in all this again, Mom," Maggie said.

Ms. Hetzger smiled. "Honestly, Maggie, I'm proud. All parents have to deal with some trouble from their kids, and I'm just happy you've made all these nice friends to help get you through your adventures. And hey, at least the trouble you get into is interesting!"

"Do you want my help getting past all the media and officials and stuff out in the hall?" Carolina asked.

Ms. Hetzger shook her head. "I'm sure you'd be amazing," she said. "But no, thank you. I am a doctor. I can handle a crowd of curious grown-ups."

She turned and hugged Joe, then me, and finally Maggie, whispering something in her ear. When they broke apart, Maggie was beaming, and her eyes looked a little bright.

"See you at the end of camp," Maggie said as her mom waved goodbye to everyone else and headed for the door.

"And no sooner!" I added.

Ms. Hetzger laughed. "Oh, Abby. I hope that turns out to be true." She opened the door just wide enough to slip through, walked out into a massive wall of sound, and pulled it shut behind her.

"I think you're up, Ben," said Carolina.

We all watched as Ben crossed slowly to the door. He took a deep breath, held it, fit the Iron Key into the lock, paused for a long count of ten, and turned it. The lock clicked shut. Ben pushed on the handle. It held, and he let out his breath in a sigh of complete contentment.

Miesha led a slightly sarcastic but friendly round of applause. Ben gave a bow. Given his years-long obsession with that door, getting to lock it himself must have been like solving a really hard riddle, or scratching an itch you could never quite reach.

"Ready to go through the secret panel to the island, then, folks?" Joe asked, clapping his hands. Everyone nodded.

I couldn't wait to show everyone the island, especially Mags, and present the finally finished ring of keys to Helene. But as I ducked my head awkwardly to crawl under the sofa, I realized I was almost as excited about getting to change back into my regular clothes.

The dress had been okay, and the shoes had just about made it, but if I ever got a chance to head off on a day of adventuring again, I was definitely going to choose a more sensible hat.

FORTY
Abby

It was evening on the island when we arrived, and Ariadne was waiting for us.

"Hi again, buddy!" I said, bending down to pat her floofy feather head as Maggie, Joe, Ben, Miesha, Carolina, and finally Murray appeared one by one on the stump behind me.

"That was so cool!" said Murray, turning circles on the spot. "It's like I just grew here!"

"Who's this?" Maggie asked me as Joe greeted the chicken, too.

"This is Ariadne. Ariadne, meet my best friend, Maggie."

"Ariadne? Like the lady with the string from the old Greek legends?" Maggie said. I stared at her. She shrugged. "I'll tell you the story back at camp. Anyway, Abs"—she stretched out her arms—"this place is amazing!"

It was a perfectly beautiful evening. The rain was gone, leaving everything smelling lush and green, and a golden sky arced over the sea. Miesha had dumped her space helmet in the grass, and the members of the Council of NAFAFA were running around the grove of Flappy Trees and sprinting down to the Beachy Beach like a pack of third graders, whooping.

"Hey, you four," I called. "Come on, we've got work to do here."

"Please, young people," Maggie added. "Remember your better selves!"

I snorted.

The plan had been for Joe and me to lead the others to the Palace, where hopefully we'd either find Antonia or be able to call the elevator to the Island Underneath. But there was no need, as a shout rang out from the direc—ton of the Little Lagoon, and Helene and her mother came striding over the Island toward us. The Council members ran back to the grove.

"What in the name of Captain Emily's cutlass," said Antonia, her blue silk scarf rippling in the wind as she came to a halt, staring around at all of us, "is going on here?"

I remembered what Helene had said in the command center about me and Joe counting as an invasion. Having this pack of kids in silver sunglasses and Maggie in her pajama pants appearing on the island must have been off the charts.

"And you, Abigail," Helene said, rounding on me. "Do you have any idea what you've put us through? What do you have to say for yourself?"

"First that I'm so, so sorry," I said, handing over the ring of keys. Helene seized them, clutching them to her chest. Then, figuring there was no point in wasting time, I dug into my pocket and pulled out the Oak Key, its silver leaves and sun gleaming in my fingers as I held it out. "And second, I hope this makes up for it."

Helene and Antonia's reaction was everything I could have hoped for.

When the yelling and dancing were over, and I'd been hugged at least a dozen times by each of them, I made the formal introductions between the leaders of the island and the Council of NAFAFA. Names were swapped, titles were exchanged, and hands were shaken. Ariadne made a point of introducing herself to everyone, too, and received so many pats on the head she began to look like she was wearing Kelly's space helmet.

"So," said Antonia, finally, "I assume there is some reason beyond the return of the Oak Key for Abby bringing you all here?"

"There is," Miesha said. "But it's going to take some explaining."

"Really long explaining," said Carolina.

"Well begin, then," said Helene.

I raised a hand, glancing over at Maggie. "Well, the thing is, some of us really, really should be getting back to camp," I said. "So maybe we should build the fort back to le Petit Salon first so we can head home before all the talking starts." The Council was here to ask permission to start a new global pillow fort Hub somewhere on the island, and much as I hated to miss out, Maggie and I didn't strictly need to be here for that.

"No one is leaving this island until I have a thorough and satisfactory explanation of what has been going on," Antonia declared. "You will just have to wait while we throw a party."

"I don't know if Maggie and Abby really have time for that . . . ," Joe said.

"Nonsense!" said Antonia. "There is always time for an efficient party. Things should be done properly. Dignity and tradition are the most important things, remember."

"I like this lady!" Ben whispered to Murray.

"Now," Antonia called, "does anyone here need to borrow a floaty?"

Joe and I had to explain the floaty situation to the others. Miesha frowned. "I don't know if floaties are really going to help us with this one," she said. "But, hey, do you all have a whiteboard? I think the main thing we need for this party is a whiteboard. A big one."

Antonia looked to her daughter.

"I don't think we have one of those," said Helene, thinking. "But maybe . . . hmmm . . ."

Twenty minutes later Joe and I had changed back into our normal clothes and rejoined our friends and the crew in front of the great glass wall in the Island Underneath. The members of our group who hadn't seen it before had settled down, and Ben had stopped his peacock screaming at all the whales and sea turtles and fish, and everyone listened as Helene explained the plan for the meeting. The finished ring of keys glinted at her belt, and she looked very happy.

"Remember, this is not a routine party," she said, speaking to the crew gathered cross-legged on the floor. "A routine party involves singing and shouting and floating. And that won't be helpful right now. What this party involves is pens." She held up a bucket of dry-erase markers. "And respectful listening, and neat handwriting."

"Woo! Handwriting!" shouted one of the crew, and the others cheered.

"Thank you," said Helene. She passed the bucket around to the Council, Maggie, Joe, Antonia, and me. "Now let's get started. Does everybody who's presenting have a pen?"

Joe, Antonia, and I cheered. The others held up their markers and looked confused.

"Does everybody know what they're going to tell us?"

We cheered again, with Maggie and Miesha catching on and joining in.

"And does everybody feel okay drawing charts and pictures and maps on the wall while they speak?"

Everyone cheered that time. The crew gave a round of applause.

"Then let's begin!" said Helene.

And so we did.

At Antonia's insistence, I went first, explaining what had happened to me after I disappeared with the ring of keys through the Deer Door. It took plenty of diagram drawing along the glass to explain the tangled path of loops and links I'd taken, but eventually Antonia nodded, and it was Miesha's turn.

Maggie went after her, then Carolina, then Ben, then Murray, then Joe. Piece by piece we sorted out what had happened over the last few days, who had had which keys when, and how the two ridiculously complicated magic doorway systems that had made it all possible worked.

Helene was just rubbing her temples and suggesting it might be time for a tea break when something happened on the other side of the glass that made everyone in the room gasp, even the crew.

The golden sunset had been dancing down through the

water for a while, but now it shifted ever so slightly, angling off the curve of the glass, sending little rainbows twirling through the air just as an entire pod of dolphins swam into sight on the other side of our charts and drawings.

"For real?" Miesha said, taking off her silver sunglasses to watch.

"Okay, deep breath," Maggie said to her in a calm, soothing voice. "You are swimming through ancient seas. You are bathed in rainbows and sunlight. Everything is beautiful. The midnight blue deeps—"

Miesha threw her pen at her. Maggie grinned and threw it back.

"Hey," I said. "That one dolphin looks different. Is that ...?"

"Florence!" said Helene. "She has her own sensor for when dolphins are near. She likes the chance to play."

Outside the glass, Florence the mechanical dolphin—who turned out to look totally lifelike, apart from her glowing green eyes and black racing stripe—pranced and danced and swam with the visiting pod, all of them dappled in sunlight and rainbows.

It was hard to get the meeting back on track after that, but Antonia managed it. I was beginning to feel antsy. All this logistical talk and diagram drawing and loop-link analysis was interesting, but the Camp Cantaloupe clock was ticking.

There were still some big moments to get through, though. The first came when the crew voted unanimously to allow the Council to construct a pillow fort back to le Petit Salon, and eventually a whole new global Hub in the Island Underneath.

"We've got plenty of room," Helene said, waving a hand at the rock wall. "And you won't find a more secure location anywhere on the planet."

"Oh, I disagree, dear," said Antonia, who had been standing back, thoughtful and silent. "I can think of one place better." She clapped her hands. "Everyone, I have an announcement to make. I have been thinking, and I have decided I am not going to live in the Palace anymore."

The reaction to that statement from the crew and Helene was so loud, even the dolphins looked around in surprise.

"I've realized there's no need anymore," Antonia went on. "The final order of Captain Emily has been fulfilled by these children, who have gone back to Versailles and most definitely got everyone's attention. And you, dear"—Antonia turned to her daughter—"you have the ring of keys, complete at last. Things are being pulled together that have been apart for a long time, and I'm not going to keep swimming against that tide. I will come below and live with you."

Helene looked like she was caught between crying and laughing.

"But . . . but . . . what about Captain Emily's other final wishes?" she said, finding her voice. "The order to look after the Palace? You're not just going to abandon it after all this time, are you, Mama?"

"Of course not!" said Antonia. "The Palace will go to these children, and their international friends, for their new base. It is self-contained, with easy access to the beach, and plenty of space, not to mention plenty of pillow fort provisions. It should be ideal. If they are interested, that is?"

Miesha and the other Council members accepted so eagerly their sunglasses almost fell off.

"Understand, of course," Antonia said, giving them a stern look, "that we are placing a great deal of trust in you. And in your ability to be responsible for your own behavior in this shared space, as well as the behavior of the members of your networks. And there will be conditions. You will have to keep the Palace clean, and change the flowers on Captain Emily's portrait, and make the food for the chickens. Ariadne is very particular, you know."

"What kind of food do you make for her?" asked Murray. Antonia described the necessary chicken feed. Miesha raised her eyebrows.

"Wait, you mean Cheerios?" she said. "Seriously, you have no idea how much we've got that covered."

Antonia seemed a little skeptical, but with the whole

Council plus Maggie and me agreeing with Miesha, she let the matter go.

"If I understand everything that I've heard," Helene said, eyeing the mess of scribbles on the great glass wall again, "getting a new global Hub set up is going to be very complicated. It will have to be built and made secure. The other Continental networks will have to be successfully linked in. There will have to be a clear schedule, with rules and rotations and record keeping. It'll be a big job. Is there anyone in your organization who's up to it?"

Miesha, Abby, Carolina, Murray, and I all turned to look at Ben. His pink face went bright red. He smiled, suddenly looking a lot more like the ten-year-old he was.

"Excellent," Antonia said. "And can you do all that and still perform your own duties as . . ." She consulted the bit of wall where Ben had printed out his titles. "As a Council member and network head?"

To my surprise, Ben paused, considering. "Before, I would have said yes," he answered. "But with the west coast, things have been getting super stressful. There's *so* much training that has to be done, and explaining the rules and systems to new kids over and over. You might not have noticed, but it's been getting to me." Maggie snorted. Ben looked around. "Please don't be shocked, everyone, but I don't think my network should control the west coast anymore."

Everyone was shocked anyway. After all that time fighting and scheming to get it, after everything we went through last summer, Ben was willing to just let the west coast go?

"I want to do a good job on this island-coordinating position," he explained as we all spluttered. "A really good job. And the west coast needs someone who can give it more attention than I can right now."

Miesha recovered first. "Okay, fine," she said. "Anyone object to Ben's network going back to being just the Great Plains Sofa Circle?"

No one raised their hand.

"Motion passed. Next item: who should take over the west coast? There are already new forts that will need guidance and direction." She looked to me and Maggie. "Any interest in restarting Camp Sofa Fort, you two?"

Maggie's mouth fell open, her eyes shining, but I whapped her on the arm. She was my best friend in the whole world, but honestly, that was the last thing this summer needed.

"We'd love to," I said. "But Maggie and I are going to be at Camp Cantaloupe for the next five weeks, and we can't really restart a network from there. Plus we're aging out soon when we turn thirteen. It's not really worth getting super involved like that just for a few months, is it?"

Maggie shut her mouth with a snap, looking seriously disappointed. But she nodded. "Abby's right. The west coast should have someone who'll be around for a while to lead it."

"Any ideas?" said Murray.

Maggie and I locked eyes.

"Kelly," we said together.

"Isn't she a little young?" asked Ben.

"Same age as you," I pointed out.

"Perfect!" Miesha looked really pleased. "Done. So, if she wants, Kelly can join the Council as head of a fifth network representing the west coast. We'll need to order another chair for the Council table. And she'll have to get started designing an official banner."

I caught Maggie's eye again and grinned. There was a one hundred percent chance that banner would revolve around a picture of a cat floating through space.

With all the major party business checked off, the party broke up. Helene led the crew in the traditional closing sea chantey; while Joe went to fetch my supply pack from the Palace; Miesha and Murray built a temporary fort to le Petit Salon over a pair of armchairs; and the rest of us cleaned off the great glass wall.

"One thing we never did figure out," said Carolina, watching me wipe away my brilliantly simple diagram of the links in the Montreal museum, "was that prophecy about the door in le Petit Salon."

"Oh, yeah!" I said. "Hey, Mags, wasn't that step seven? The prophecy dealy?"

Maggie looked over. "Totally! Whoever opens the door will be the chosen one who will uncover the secrets of the origins of linking—"

"—and bring about a new golden age for the world of pillow forts," finished Ben.

"Right," I said.

"So, did all that happen?"

"Seriously?" Ben said. He was turning bright pink again. He pointed at Maggie. "You used the Oak Key in its proper door." He pointed at me. "And you discovered the secrets of the origins of the pillow forts and unlocked the door in le Petit Salon. After all this I cannot *believe* you fulfilled that prophecy between you and didn't even know it!"

"So who's the chosen one, then?" said Carolina. "Abby or Maggie?"

Everyone looked at each other, eyebrows raised, mouths quirked. No one spoke.

"Oh, come on," said a passing member of the crew. I recognized my friend the T. rex. "I listened to every word the lot of you said, and the chosen one is obviously Samson."

Soon the glass was clear, the negotiations and planning were put on hold for now, and we were all saying goodbye.

Joe was going back with Murray, whose network could

get him close enough to his Alaska research station that he could make it the rest of the way himself. He gave me and Maggie big hugs outside the new fort.

"Don't forget to send me postcards!" he called, still waving as he crawled out of sight. "I might have built a new Fort Orpheus in my cabin this year—just saying!"

Antonia and Helene didn't ask for postcards, but they thanked Maggie and me over and over for the return of the Oak Key. I gave Antonia my worst curtsy ever in return, and she laughed and pulled me into a hug.

Finally, with one last wave to the crew and Ariadne, and one last look around the Island Underneath—for now—I slung my supply pack over my shoulders and followed my best friend in the whole world back through the links, to find out what had become of our camp.

FORTY-ONE
Maggie

There was a happy surprise waiting for me in my art cabin fort at Camp Cantaloupe: my patchwork scarf, neatly folded on top of my gear pack.

"Hey, keep it moving," called Abby as I scooped up the scarf and hugged it. I moved aside, crawling out into the cabin, and Abby followed.

The cabin was deserted, and, weirdly, it looked exactly the same as when I'd left.

"It's so bizarre being back!" said Abby. "And, whoa . . ." She took in the easels and drizzle paintings chaos of Ms. Sabine's art explosion. "What happened here?"

"Ms. Sabine got a little carried away last night," I said. Had it seriously been only last night? "But I don't get why it hasn't been cleared up by now. What did they do for class?"

Abby picked her way over to the window. I saw her freeze.

"Um, Mags," she said. "You might want to come see this."

The whole camp was gathered on the field. All the kids were on one side, and the counselors and staff on the other, and in between was an army of search and rescue officers, their uniforms and badges visible from here. I spotted the barefoot drama teacher, spinning his whistle nervously while a strange man in a trench coat addressed the crowd through a megaphone.

"Do you think they're talking about us being missing?" Abby asked.

"They have to be." I checked the clock on the wall. "We're definitely past the deadline for camp being shut down if you weren't back." I threw the patchwork scarf across both our necks. "Whatever happens, no matter how much trouble we're in, we are *not* getting separated again, no matter what. Agreed?"

"Agreed," said Abby, putting her shoulders back and wrapping her end of the scarf around her hand. We shared a solemn nod, then marched out of the cabin with our heads held high.

Outside we could hear what the man with the megaphone was saying.

"... important that you all feel safe in this extremely serious situation," he said, his amplified voice all crackly. "We are doing everything possible to recover the missing . . . the missing . . ."

He stopped, staring, and there was a buzzing murmur, then a clamor, then a roar, as the sea of Cantaloupers spotted us striding toward them over the field.

Of all people, it was our cabin counselor who reached us first.

"Ohmygoodness, ohmygoodness," she kept saying over and over, hugging us tight.

Kids were pressing forward, asking what happened, where we'd been. I heard the man in the trench coat shouting for order.

"But where did you come from?" our counselor asked, looking back toward the art cabin. "And where's Charlene, and Director Haggis, and Ms. Sabine?"

"Huh?" Abby said. "Wait, are they missing too?"

"Oh, no," I said, remembering. But before I could fill Abby in, there was another roar from the far side of the crowd, and everyone turned to look.

The megaphone crackled and hummed as Trench-Coat Man raised it to his mouth, took a deep breath, and completey lost track of what he was doing as . . .

. . . a moose cantered out of the woods.

It was a giant moose. A huge moose. A high-crowned moose of mammoth proportions, with the biggest antlers, the biggest eyes, and the biggest nostrils the world had ever seen.

And riding on its back was Charlene, in her pajamas and Safety Monitor sash. And behind her was Director Haggis, in his rumpled suit and mustache. And behind him was Ms. Sabine, in her crown and paper chain necklace.

The moose trotted right across the field, towering over the officers and the counselors and the man with the megaphone, and stopped, snuffling in a friendly sort of way, in front of me and Abby.

There's no silence in the world quite like the silence of two hundred–plus campers and officers waiting for a girl on a moose to speak.

"You will not believe," Charlene shouted, looking down at us with the world's biggest smile, "where we have been!"

Later that night, after an unspeakably long day of dealing with too many grown-ups asking too many unanswerable questions, Abby and I found ourselves back in our bunks, staring up at the splintery wood ceiling of our cabin, together again at camp.

After the police and search teams and reporters had finally left, Ms. Sabine and Charlene had cornered me, gushing about all the fabulous new ideas their trip into the woods had given them for our art mentoring project. Abby seemed very impressed when I explained the situation. I got the feeling that of everything that had already happened this summer, me teaming up with Charlene Thieson to help homesick little kids might have been the biggest surprise.

Charlene was now the most popular person in the entire camp, and her triumphant entrance on the back of the moose was guaranteed to carve her a spot in Camp Cantaloupe legend forever. Everyone seemed to decide all the other disappearances must have been part of the same story—even Abby's, since she and I returned just before Charlene—so we got to share some of the glory without having to answer too many more questions.

"Maybe that was your mysterious step eight," Abby said, as we watched Charlene tell her new friends about her adventures with the moose. "Helping Charlene's dreams come true."

"Ooh, right!" I said. "I completely lost track of those steps in all the running around, but we can definitely check that off! That makes it all totally worth it."

We'd barely gotten any time to ourselves to catch up, just the two of us, but we'd swapped the letters and cards we'd written, and we had the whole rest of the summer together to go over the details.

I reached up and picked at a splinter in Abby's bunk. There was whispering all through the cabin, and I could hear the counselor joining in. It sounded like waves hitting the shore, and I smiled to myself, thinking of the island. What was happening there right now?

It was nice lying in bed at camp, knowing that somewhere out in the middle of the Atlantic was a secret island run by a mother-daughter team, guarded by a mechanical dolphin named Florence, and home to a brand-new pillow fort base where kids from around the world were forging new links. Looping together a whole new chapter.

And just getting started.

EPILOGUE
Abby

One Week Later

"Shh! Mags, not so loud!" I hissed.

Maggie was busy chiseling a piece of driftwood, and getting a little too carried away for where we were: sitting among the ruins of the Shipwreck Treehouse, ten minutes after midnight.

"Almost finished!" she said, blowing wood shavings off whatever she was making.

"Can I finally see it then?"

"No!"

I tsk-sighed and adjusted my headlamp. "Well, just keep it down. We really don't want to get caught."

I got to my feet, wiping pine needles off my pants, and looked up into the tree. Last time Maggie and I snuck out here, we'd been alone. Now the tree was packed with the best carpenters and knot tiers from the crew of the island, crawling silently from branch to branch, rigging the fallen treehouse back together. The floor was already set, and the driftwood wall was curving into life, wilder and more seaweed-curvy than before.

"Hey, Maggie Hetzger!" came a whisper-shout from above.

Maggie looked around. "Crescent!" she called back. I snorted.

The whisper-shouting crew member dropped a rope between us and slid down.

"What exactly did you say you wanted this thing to look like, again?" he asked.

"Like an octopus sea god temple that wandered up out of the ocean and decided to try being a bird's nest for a while," said Maggie.

"Oh. Okay. Fun." He climbed back up the rope.

"I'm still not sure about this whole silent building technique," I said, watching him go. "I mean, I know the planks-and-ropes thing works on ships, and on the Island Underneath, but do you really think Director Haggis is going to let anyone near it? There's no way this is up to any sort of code."

"Don't worry about Director Haggis," said Charlene, appearing out of the night pulling a rolly bin full of driftwood. "He's a lot less worried about that sort of thing since he met the ghost moose."

"Woo! Ghost moose club!" said Maggie.

"Anyway," she went on, "when all the kids wake up tomorrow and see the treehouse was magically rebuilt overnight, I don't think keeping them away from it is going to be an option. Especially our little letter writers, Maggie." She turned to my best friend. "They're keeping their eyes peeled for magic everywhere."

"And now they're getting it!" Maggie said, still chipping away at her mysterious driftwood.

Maggie and Charlene's letter-writing, fort-building, anti-homesickness art project had been a huge success. Ms. Sabine kept pulling them from their regular activities to come give crash courses to every eight-year-old in camp. And the funny thing was, Maggie was thriving. She loved working with the little kids, and she was turning out to be really good at it, too. She and Charlene even had this whole odd-couple comedy thing going, and the kids ate it up. It was weird to say, but it was making me a tiny bit jealous.

"Yes, they are," said Charlene. "And now I need to get these supplies up to the builders. Carry on, Cantaloupers." She saluted and headed off, pulling the rolly cart over to the platform elevator the crew had rigged up with counterweights and pulleys.

"Hey, is this the party? Sorry we're so late!"

Maggie yelped and dropped her driftwood as Matt and Mark appeared in the light from our headlamps, led by Kelly, her brand-new silver sunglasses perched on top of her head.

"What are you doing here?" I asked my brothers, after all the hugging and excited whispered greetings were over. "How did you two even get here?"

"Kelly!" said Mark. "She called to see if we had any spare pillows we were getting rid of in the move."

"I was running out," Kelly said. "I'm remaking my fort as a space station so I can run the west coast better. And your brothers were so nice, Abby! They gave me all these old floor pillows from their room. But I still need more."

"Ugh!" I held up my hands. "One more reason we shouldn't have gotten rid of that orange plaid sofa I totally loved. It would have been perfect for your space station, and we just gave it away."

Matt and Mark grinned.

"What?" I said.

"Should we tell her?" said Mark.

"It was supposed to be a surprise," said Matt.

"Tell me what?"

Mark shrugged. "I won't tell Dad if you don't."

"Deal."

"Will one of you please tell me what you're not telling me before I scream?" I said.

Matt smiled. "The thing about that old sofa is we all knew how much it meant to you."

"So we only pretended to donate it," said Mark. "We actually put it in storage."

"And Dad and Tamal are going to convert it into this sort of bunkbed-loft thing for you for your new room."

"And have it finished before you get back from camp."

"As a surprise."

"Which we just ruined."

"Surprise!"

Oh. My. Mammoth. I had the best family in the whole entire world. Ever ever.

"But that still doesn't explain how you got here," I said when I finished hugging them again. "I mean, which fort did you use to get in the networks?"

"Our own," said Mark. "We made one after Maggie's first call about how you were missing. Just in case. And when Kelly's parents drove her over to pick up the pillows, she saw it."

"And I got a token to them right away," jumped in Kelly. "Then when I told them I was going to this treehouse-fixing party tonight, they wanted to help."

"And she came and got us special permission from

NAFAFA," Mark said, "and we went from our place to Kelly's space station, to the Hub, to your fort in the art cabin, Maggie, and now here we are!" He raised both hands over his head.

"And if you'll excuse us," said Matt, "we are totally going up in that completely awesome treehouse to help do some fixing right now."

They turned, raced each other to the ladder, and scampered out of sight.

Maggie's face had gone red. "Hey, so, what else has been going on, Kelly?" she asked, trying to pretend she wasn't all flustered and smiley after seeing Matt.

Kelly turned out to be full of news. She still hadn't picked out a name for her network, but her banner—cats in space, as predicted—was coming along well. The dimmer switch on the Hub chandelier had been properly installed. Samson was doing great, and was staying out of the networks for now like the good little King of France he was.

"And how are things on the island?" I asked. "How's Antonia? And Helene? And the crew?"

"So good! Antonia comes up to the surface every day to make sure Ben and the other Continental reps are feeding the chickens enough Cheerios.

"She and Helene keep talking about how cool it is that the pillow fort networks happened by accident because of Captain Emily's loops, and now after hundreds of years they're both on the island. Helene says it's the magic of the trees slowly pulling things back together, no matter how far apart they got."

"Aw, just like us," Maggie said, tipping her head back and giving me the world's cheesiest grin.

"Only because I can't get away from you, you menace," I said. "And are you finally done with whatever that is, or not?"

"Yup!" Maggie hopped up, hiding her project behind her back. "Presenting my gift to the kids of Camp Cantaloupe's future ... the new trapdoor!"

She held out her hands. She was holding a tiny door the size of a paperback book, with one old hinge and a little hook latch holding it in its frame.

"What?" I said. "Is that a trapdoor for, like, squirrels?"

"It's symbolic!" said Maggie. "I scrounged up the pieces of the old Oak Door. This was all that was usable."

"Oooh! So does it still link to the First Sofa?" asked Kelly.

Maggie shook her head. "Sadly, no. But look—I carved our names on the frame." She ran her finger along the edge, where *From Maggie and Abby, Best Friends* and the date were carved in choppy letters on one side, and *Sorry we broke the old one* on the other.

"Aww," said Kelly as Maggie grinned again and I bopped her on the arm.

"What now?" I asked.

"Now we go up and install it!"

We took the elevator, since Kelly hadn't had the chance yet, and she laughed and laughed as the platform creaked us up into the tree.

"Um," came a voice from the tangled construction zone overhead. "Anyone know whose chicken this is?"

The elevator stopped, and our headlamps found Matt, his arms full of driftwood and a floofy white chicken with a sort of white floofy hat perched on his shoulder.

"Oh, that's Ariadne!" I told him. "She's from the island. She kind of goes wherever she wants."

Matt angled his neck to look at his new friend.

"Huh," he said. "Okay." And he and Ariadne went back to work.

The three of us stepped off the elevator. "Yay, Abs, it's looking so good up here!" Maggie said, bopping me on the shoulder. "Kelly, I don't want to see you anywhere near the edge."

I looked away and grinned. Maggie was sounding more like her mom every day.

The treehouse was bustling. Mark was hoisting in the surviving half of the old ship's wheel on a rope on the far side; Charlene was attaching a new telescope donated by Antonia to a finished section of wall; and the crew danced all over, securing lines, tying the treehouse together, and balancing on the branches like they were solid ground.

"I think the new trapdoor should go here," Maggie said,

pointing to a gap near the trunk. "So kids won't step in it or trip if the lock gets broken or something. Anyone want to give me a hand?"

A couple of the crew were swinging down to help when there was a loud bang. The remains of the old wooden steering wheel had slipped through Mark's hands to the floor.

"Sorry!" he said as the entire treehouse shushed him. "This thing isn't as solid as it looks. One of the handles just snapped right off!"

"Hey, what's that, though?" said Charlene. She was pointing to the gap in the wheel where the handle had been. We all looked, and something metallic glinted back at our headlamps.

"Oooh!" Mark pulled his rope out of the way and Charlene crouched down to tug at the metal. It pulled free, and she held up a thin, foot-long tube. "There's, uh, there's a cap here," she whispered, her eyes as big as the ghost moose's.

"Open it, open it!" said Matt.

Charlene had to dig her fingernails in and scrunch up her face like Samson that time he ate a soap bubble, but she did it. The cap opened with a pop, and a long coil of paper slid out into the light.

Matt and Kelly stepped forward to help unroll it, and we all crowded around to see.

"Cantaloupe, cantaloupe . . ." I whispered.

"Moose, moose, moose," finished Maggie.

It was a map. A perfect map, with a scale and a key and everything, showing a collection of islands off the end of an unmarked chunk of land. There was even a dotted line leading to an X. Right at the top, stretching from corner to corner, was a drawing of an enormous, gray-tentacled octopus. I glanced over at Maggie. Her mouth was hanging open. She looked like she'd been struck by lightning.

"How old was that ship's wheel?" one of the crew asked, breaking the collective awed silence. "And where did it come from?"

"It was an original part of the treehouse," said Charlene. "It washed up during the same big storm as the moose."

Matt shook his head. "And it was hiding this for all these years. It looks like you've got a real treasure map here."

"Woo! Treasure!" called one of the crew.

"Pity they spelled *margins* wrong, though," said Maggie, suddenly.

I blinked at her. "What?"

"There, on the edge where it should say *Here There Be Margins*. The last word's spelled wrong. That's definitely not an *M* at the beginning."

"Mags, it never usually says *margins*. That was the joke with our map last summer. Old maps like this say something else."

Maggie squinted at the page in the clustered glow of our

headlamps. "Well, I can't read it. Anybody want to take a guess?"

Kelly leaned in, her nose right above the ancient paper. "Dragons," she said, quietly. "It says *Here There Be Dragons*."

There was a cool, dark, starry silence. The branches swayed around us in the saltwater-scented breeze. Charlene was clutching the steering wheel. Matt and Kelly held the map. Mark shifted his coil of rope, and Maggie hugged the trapdoor with our names carved into it to her chest.

I felt a sudden lurch in my stomach, like the Shipwreck Treehouse had caught the wind and set sail, and something heavy locked behind my ribs eased, floating up into the warm, glimmering summer night.

Ariadne burped softly, and as though we'd been waiting for the signal, everyone turned to look through the gap in the branches, out west over the sea. I couldn't be sure, but I thought I saw something huge and sleek and dark curve up into the starlight and roll away again under the waves.

"Well," I said, looking around at my friends, my family, my crew. "We should probably go find them, then."

Maggie shifted beside me, pressing her shoulder against mine. "Definitely," she said. "Absolutely. No matter what. But hey, Abs? Let's get through summer camp first."

ACKNOWLEDGMENTS

They say second books are harder to write than the first, and holy cantaloupe they were right! That means the person to thank first and foremost is the best editor in the world: Elizabeth Lynch. Thank you for your unbelievable support, encouragement, and patience. Thank you for slogging through those terrible early drafts, deciphering my convoluted linking and looping charts, and giving me the time I needed to stitch it all together. Thank you for believing in Maggie and Abby in all their silliness, and for believing in me. This book would never have happened without you.

Neverending thanks as always to Emily Keyes, for pulling Maggie and Abby out of the slush pile and getting this cast of characters a home on a bookshelf.

Thank you to my family, for always cheering me on.